Sacred Lies

The Avenging Series: Book Two

KEYLEE HARGIS

The Avenging Series: Book Two

SACRED LIES

ISBN: 978-1-7359207-8-8

First Edition: 2022

Printed in the United States.

Cover character art by Witchlingsart

To the people who see the best in everyone: I guess our favorite color is red because damn…we sure like to ignore those flags.

Sacred Lies Playlist

Chapter One: Pacify Her—Melanie Martinez

Chapter Two: Where's My Love—SYML

Chapter Three: Little Lion Man—Mumford & Sons

Chapter Four: Monsters—Ruelle (Acoustic Version)

Chapter Five: Grace—Lewis Capaldi

Chapter Six: I'll Be Good—Jaymes Young

Chapter Seven: I Would've—Jessie Murph

Chapter Eight: Demise of a Nation—Secession Studios

Chapter Nine: Fantasy—Bazzi

Chapter Ten: Control—Halsey

Chapter Eleven: Welcome to the Jungle—Tommee Profitt, Fleurie

Chapter Twelve: Deep End—Ruelle

Chapter Thirteen: The Beginning of the End—Klergy, Valerie Broussard

Chapter Fourteen: Man or a Monster—Sam Tinnesz, Zayde Wolf

Chapter Fifteen: Butterflies—Kacey Musgraves

Chapter Sixteen: Arsonist's Lullabye—Hozier

Chapter Seventeen: Human—Rag'n'Bone Man

Chapter Eighteen: Do I Wanna Know?—Arctic Monkeys

Chapter Nineteen: Hayloft—Mother Mother

Chapter Twenty: She—Harry Styles

Chapter Twenty-One: You Don't Own Me (feat. G-Eazy)—SAYGRACE, G-Eazy

Chapter Twenty-Two: Dancing After Death–Stripped—Matt Maeson

Chapter Twenty-Three: Doom Days—Bastille

Chapter Twenty-Four: Black Sea—Natasha Blume

Chapter Twenty-Five: Sea Shanty Medley—Home Free

Chapter Twenty-Six: Soldier—Fleurie, Tommee Profitt

Chapter Twenty-Seven: Hurts Like Hell—Fleurie, Tommee Profitt

Chapter Twenty-Eight: Bloody Mary—Lady Gaga

Chapter Twenty-Nine: Raise Hell—Dorothy

Chapter Thirty: Is This Love?—James Arthur

Chapter Thirty-One: Sweet Creature—Harry Styles

Chapter Thirty-Two: Wait—M83

Chapter Thirty-Three: Man Eater (slowed)

Chapter Thirty-Four: Howlin' for You—The Black Keys

Chapter Thirty-Five: All of Me—John Legend

Chapter Thirty-Six: Born For This—The Score

Chapter Thirty-Seven: Warriors—League of Legends

THIS STORY CONTAINS content that may be troubling for some readers. This may include, but not limited to, sexual assault, references to death, acts of self-harm, vivid and graphic violent scenes, suicide, manipulation, sexual scenes, abuse, and strong language. Please be advised before you continue reading. If you seek assistance or know of a loved one experiencing any of these things, please don't be afraid to ask for help by calling one of the following numbers:

National Sexual Assault Hotline: 1-800-656-4673
National Suicide Prevention Lifeline: 1-800-273-8255
National Domestic Violence Hotline: 1-800-799-7233

PROLOGUE

The clock ticked, making the silence in the room nearly deafening. The room was dark with just an ounce of the sun trying to pour out from behind the curtains. Cigar smoke filtered through the air and there was one small lamp that lit a portion of an old, mahogany desk near the windows. Behind the desk sat a man who nervously puffed his cigar, glancing at the ticking clock every so often as if it were a time bomb—his black suit wrinkled and his tie undone, unlike most days.

Well… before he experienced what happened in that disgusting warehouse that Addison had brought him to—what Addison had offered him. Instead, he was still sitting in the office feeling like he had a target on his back rather than having a merciful assassin that had once been promised to him—an assassin that knew how to kill without blinking. An assassin that held so much power but didn't even know it. An assassin that could speak to the dead and command them.

A Holden.

His hand shook as he placed the cigar down when nausea washed over him. It had been days waiting in his safe house—days that he waited to hear the news that determined the outcome of his life. Nothing came. Not yet.

A subtle knock on the door brought him from his thoughts and he cleared his throat. "Enter."

The door creaked open to reveal one of his men wearing the familiar navy colors of his organization he created so long ago. "We have received word about the MOT," the man said, piquing his interest.

He sat up straight, gulping at the comment. "Well, out with it then!"

The man standing at the door suddenly smiled. "There was a funeral within The Messengers of Truth, sir."

Relief like no other flooded through his body. But before one of his own men could see how frightened he had truly been, he waved them off and when the door was shut, he finally slouched within his chair.

Rubbing a hand over his face, he let out a curse at how foolish he had been the past week while hiding away like a coward. He had nothing to worry about at all. The curse of the MOTs was true—the curse would relinquish its wrath on those who abused it or killed anyone other than the MOT's target.

He couldn't sleep without seeing his men being slaughtered and dismembered. That woman cut through his numbers like a vengeful Goddess. It was nothing he had ever witnessed—the power and strength one small, fragile woman contained. But he didn't forget those eyes with hues of blues and greens staring at him numbly when he peered back over his shoulder. He watched as she raised a bloody sword at him and he knew exactly what she meant.

You're next.

So he ran and fled the states the quickest he could and hopped on his jet to get as far away before she could come for him. It was a cowardly act, but even he knew that he or his men didn't stand a chance against a woman that had been burned too many times. *A Holden*, he corrected himself.

But alas, his worrying was for nothing. He could return back to the states and pick up where he left off—he just needed to figure out how to take down The Messengers of Truth for good now that he knew where he stood.

Haven McKinley was dead.

CHAPTER ONE

Jay

I tried to keep my chin held high as Nikita clung to me and wept into my neck. I held her against my side tightly, trying to stay strong for the both of us. This wasn't something I ever suspected to happen so soon. We were too young, barely even twenty-five, dealing with the loss of someone we cared for so deeply. We had no one to aid us, no one to lead us, and we had no guidance on what we were supposed to do.

Knox was dead, Saul and Everette were gone, and Clarrisa and Dexter were nowhere to be found.

And Haven…

I shook my head at the thought, trying to fight back the tears as we walked up to the casket next as Nikita's sobs grew louder. Her tears leaked down my neck as I stared down at the familiar face, my heart aching with sorrow.

She left us too soon.

"Nikita," I croaked. "Do you—"

"No!" she sobbed. "I-I can't look."

I nodded, walking her away from the casket as we headed back to our seats while other MOTs came behind us. "I got you, you're okay."

I helped her sit down, taking in the sad faces and wet cheeks of our organization. There were a few MIRs in the back, their heads cast down. We were all a wreck. Neither of our organizations had our leaders and we were completely clueless.

It made me so fucking angry.

The minute other organizations heard what had happened, they came for us. Suddenly girls that were out on missions were being taken and delivered to us with their throats slit and their eyes wide in horror. I couldn't count on one hand how many times I've thrown up in the last week alone.

Two weeks.

That's how long it took for people to realize The Messengers of Truth were unguarded without the fearful Everette and vengeful Knox. That we no longer had someone running this place and were cracking with each passing second. It took two damn weeks for our whole worlds to burn to the ground and there was nothing we could do about it.

And Nikita? She just had to witness her sister die in her arms.

We were out on a mission two days ago when we were attacked. Our numbers grew slim ever since we got the other women from the manor and brought them here. We thought we were doing the right thing, but the only thing that we did was bring them to their deaths. We had no idea other organizations would strike so fast, yet there they were destroying us one at a time. On that mission, we decided to group together to prevent any more deaths. Clearly, things didn't go as planned.

Commander Addison was beneath the school, chained up in a cell but you couldn't even recognize her after what Haven…

I couldn't even say her name.

Three days.

It took Haven three days to rip the commander apart before she put her back together and did it all over again. Each hour I stood outside of that cell door, I grew a little weaker with each blood-curdling scream that left my previous commander. The woman in that room causing all that pain was not Haven McKinley. I… I don't know who it was, but it wasn't my best friend I had known all these years.

I would watch her leave covered in blood, no emotions present on her face as she spit another piece of information she got out of Addison to me before sauntering off. Then she would return hours later to do it all over again. Each day, Haven's body grew weaker. And weaker.

And then… she was nothing.

I dragged my eyes across the room as I looked towards the back doors. A thin, pale body stood there. Bags rested underneath the woman's eyes like she hadn't slept in days and no emotion was present while she stared ahead at the open casket, but her fists were clenched. She didn't speak. She didn't smile. She didn't… live. She just…

Existed.

Every morning we woke, she was gone. We don't know where she ran off to or what she was doing, but she returned each night looking the same: covered in blood and even weaker than before. She had been lied to, just like the rest of us.

Not even a curse could kill that woman, and at this moment in time, I felt the only way she could be killed was by her own hand and doing.

Suddenly, she straightened her posture and turned to walk out of the room and The Men in Red snapped up, following after her like an army of soldiers.

"We're never getting Haven back are we?" a soft voice asked.

I looked over to the fiery redhead as Sam stared at the doors I had just been gazing at. Looking back, I shook my head. "I don't think Haven McKinley exists anymore, love."

Because that wasn't Haven McKinley… that was McKenzie Holden.

CHAPTER TWO

Haven

I marched down the hall, hearing the footsteps of The Men in Red trailing after me and my fists clenched at the sound. I don't know why everyone suddenly turned to me when Knox and Everette were gone. I was no leader. I was anything but a damn leader. Maybe the old me would have loved to be such a thing. But now? I didn't want to lead. I didn't want to follow. I wanted pain and suffering. I wanted to see bloodshed from the people who dared to ever fucking cross me.

Maybe I was the villain after all.

God knows I wasn't the hero.

Step by step, I made my way down to the basement of the school. My adrenaline kicked in and that dark, scary beast inside me started to rear her ugly head at the thought of making the commander scream until her throat was so dry that nothing came out.

I enjoyed her tears.

I enjoyed teetering on the line between life and death. Just when she was about to cross to the point of no return, I yanked her back on that thin string she used to have me on. It was ironic. Now she was my puppet—my toy. And I wasn't going to stop making her dance until I got everything I needed from her. Then… then I would drive a dagger into her stomach over and *over* again just as she *him*.

"Open the door," I commanded.

The MOT who had been monitoring the cell quickly scrambled with the keys to the door. She was tense in my presence, and I couldn't help but enjoy the odd pleasure that brought me. When the cell door creaked open, I heard her sobs start.

"Please! Please… don't. I can't… I can't take anymore!" the commander wept.

I grinned maniacally as I sauntered in, seeing her cower away in the corner of the prison she was confined to. "Oh, commander, begging does not look good on you."

"Haven, please…" she breathed out, utterly tired. "I've told you everything I know."

I cocked my head to the side. "Have you? If that was the case Everette and Saul would be here instead of me and yet," I looked around mockingly. "Oh! They're not."

"I told you that the man I worked with has control over that. He was to bid them off and I would get a profit! I don't know. I really don't…"

I freed my dagger, making her pale at the sight. "A name, Addison. I need a name."

She held up a bruised and bloodied hand, one that was full of ripped-out fingernails, and she began to shake. "I told you he goes by Ghost! I don't know his real name. Have mercy on me, please."

I froze, my jaw ticking at the word.

Step by step, my slow pace made her cry out before I snatched her hair and thrust her head back. "Have *mercy*?! Where was your mercy when I was begging you to spare Knox? Huh? Where was your mercy when you were selling *innocent* women, Addison? Where was your mercy when you were poisoning MOTs to make them think they were *dying* because they killed outside of their target? Huh?!"

She howled, shielding her face as I raised my hand. My hand held the dagger in the air, shaking as I stared down at her battered form. Angry tears filled my eyes as I let my hand stay there, not being able to deliver the final blow just yet. I wanted to end her *so* damn bad. I wanted her dead, yet I knew I couldn't until this was all over and my family was back where they were supposed to be. Slowly, I lowered it.

"You better get to thinking of every girl you sold. I want numbers and names by nightfall. If I don't have them, I'll chain you to that fucking chair and I'll take a finger for each minute that passes after. You better hope it's not past ten… because then I'll move on to other appendages." I shoved her back forcefully, letting her head smack into the concrete wall.

Turning around, I saw MIRs gulp as I faced them. Reese stepped up, lowering his eyes. "What do you need from us?"

I placed my dagger back in its sheath and sighed. "I want my swords. She gave me a name yesterday about a man that may have the answers I need. We can go after him at dusk."

"I'll have them brought to you."

I didn't reply as I marched past them.

Eventually, I found myself sitting behind my mother's desk as I dug through more files like I had been the past week. I had no idea if my parents had been tracking Addison's movements long enough to know the girls she sold off or not, but I was determined to do all I could to figure it out.

I let out a huff as I set another useless file aside. Placing my hands against my face, I fought back the tears that so desperately wanted to leak out.

I felt useless.

Looking up at the ceiling, I blinked furiously to try and clear them out. Being weak would get me nowhere. I had people counting on me.

Mom, Dad, Saul… Everette. I couldn't let them down, not after all they did for me and the women of my organization.

It took two weeks for everything to fall apart. Whoever had ambushed Knox and me in that warehouse must have sent word that the MOTs and MIRs had lost their leaders. It took no time for other organizations to seek the rest of us out. The girls fought bravely, but that didn't matter when they were delivered back to us with their throats cut.

And I hid away like a coward.

I couldn't face them. I thought when I sliced through those men and cut their heads from their bodies that I wouldn't last but a few days before I died—before the curse took its wrath out on me. Instead, the third day came around and I was still breathing. One couldn't understand the pain I felt when the commander told me that she and prior commanders had been poisoning the girls who dared to kill outside their targets. It was some sick game of control they cooked up knowing the girls would fear for their lives and walk a straight line—never stepping out of order once.

I had been one of them.

I had been a fool.

A puppet.

Sitting back, I bit my trembling lip. How could I face those women? They looked up to me and expected me to have the answers to get them through this. I didn't. I didn't have a fucking clue how we were supposed to overcome this. And Jay and Nikita? They couldn't even look at me.

When I heard of Nikita's sister, my heart broke all over again. I knew right then that I had failed them—all of them. So I stayed away. I went out to find out what I could, I let my anger out on those who most deserved it, and I came back covered in the blood of my enemies. I wouldn't face them again until I had the answers I needed. Until I knew what to do. Until… until I didn't feel like a damn failure.

That night replayed on repeat in my mind. The commander finding us, telling us her plans and what she was going to do, her… killing the man I had grown to care about.

And he died thinking I didn't yearn for him. That I had only been confused and never really wanted anything with him. Yet when my mind realized what was happening right in front of me, I knew that ache, that… gut-wrenching pain was not for a man I had *only* been fond of.

It was so much more.

And he lied to protect me—to try and keep me at arm's length so I would change my mind and let go of whatever hope I had been clinging on for whatever was happening between us. I was so blind to see the truth and I could do nothing but watch like a damn coward.

Some leader I was.

Sighing, I pushed myself from my seat and strode across the room. Just as I reached the door, it opened and revealed Reese holding two shining swords of steel. Warily, he let himself in and held them out to me.

"You weren't in your room so… I thought I'd bring them here and see if you were ready."

Gently, I took them from him. I hadn't worn them since the night I learned the truth about Knox. I tried, but each time I went to leave the school these past two weeks, I ended up tossing them aside and grabbing Everette's dagger.

When I first got them back, I noticed the saying engraved into each hilt—the same one that was on Everette's dagger, and just like that, my chest ached even more.

"We're going to find them, Haven," Reese nearly whispered. "I just know it."

I managed a small nod. "I sure hope so… will you?" I motioned to the swords.

"Of course, but… the girls wanted me to give something to you first, but only if you will take it."

I raised a brow. "And what's that?"

He stepped back out into the hall, leaning down to get something he had left outside. When he stepped back in the room, I took an unsteady step away from him at the sight of the material he clenched.

"I believe Sam made it, but all the girls wanted you to have it."

I shook my head, looking away so he couldn't see the tears that resurfaced. "I can't accept that."

"You can and you will, Haven. You are all they have left. You're the last Holden—the rightful born leader of this organization after your father. Just do *something* for them. If you keep running around and doing nothing, they're all going to fall apart more than they already have. I'm trying my best to keep the MIRs standing, so you need to do the same with your own group."

It was the first time he spoke with that familiar, threatening tone all The Men in Red carried. Everette and Saul would have been proud.

"I'm no leader."

He stuck out the material once more, holding it close to me. "Nor am I, but I stepped up until we can get the right ones back where they belong. You want to find your parents and the men we lost? Well, this is a start. You have to step into their shoes, Haven. Think like them. Act like them. *Be* like them. Then maybe… just maybe we can find them."

A moment passed before I reached a shaky hand towards the material. It was the real MOT uniform, but instead of a black hood, one of the MIRs' hoods had been stitched to it, no doubt symbolizing the people they wished for me to get back and symbolizing two organizations coming together as one.

"Okay…" I croaked out.

"I'll wait outside while you change. Just call out when you're ready for me to help you get your sword holster adjusted."

Once the door was shut, I turned away as I held the uniform close to my chest. Taking in a deep breath, I slowly stripped off my clothes and pulled on the uniform before shrugging on the familiar cloak I once was jealous of. Before I turned to call out to Reese, I caught my reflection in one of the windows and gulped at the sight of me.

This was the least I could do.

"Reese," I called out. "I'm ready."

CHAPTER THREE

Haven

As I darted across rooftops, the feeling of adrenaline pumping through my veins, it was as if my vision turned red and my sorrow morphed into a fit of blazing hot anger that was ready to be released.

Reese ran next to me, not leaving my side as we led the other MIRs, and I could feel the tension in the air that surrounded us all. We knew that this was the last lead we had with someone who may have known where Everette and Saul were taken to.

Knowing that we could potentially head back home tonight without the answers we needed was something I wasn't ready to face. It was something that I knew would break me all over again. Ever since the commander spit out a name she thought might know, I had been clinging to some small sliver of hope.

Hope so small it could easily be squashed within seconds.

"We're nearing the last building!" Reese called out.

Seeing a small jump ahead, I prepared myself for the launch. Reese jumped, nearly diving headfirst to make such a leap and I repeated his movements without fear seeping through me.

Weeks ago, I had prepared myself for a death that never came, and now? Now I was just waiting until death himself reared his ugly head. It was only a matter of time for people like us. We never knew what the next day would bring and that should scare me more than it did.

Once I made it safely across, diving headfirst into a roll, I didn't miss a beat as I rolled right back up and came to the edge of the building. One after the other, we scaled down the sides of a warehouse—one that was supposed to contain the last intel we had.

I took in a deep breath as our feet touched the ground and Reese neared the back door. It wasn't long until we were all standing there impatiently. Reese stuck his hand out, giving a familiar signal that Everette used to and at the sight of it, my heart clenched a little.

Everette would be so damn proud—I just know it.

I repeated the motion and gave him a sharp nod. My hands lifted to grab the hilts of my two swords and before I knew it, two MIRs kicked in the door. I flew through it after Reese and quickly did a three-sixty to check my surroundings, as did the others.

The building seemed to be a place that hoarded different shipping crates and as I looked around, something caught my eye.

"There!" I shouted at the sight of a man running down a far hall.

We took off, sprinting after the man who wore a navy hood. Commander Addison had mentioned a man that worked for Ghost, whom she met in this very warehouse, to start the connection of getting to the apparently unreachable, unnamed man—looks like for once in her life she didn't lie. The man that was running far away from us may just be the key if he's the one people come to in order to get in touch with Ghost.

Some of the MIRs pushed themselves harder, flying past Reese and me as we closed in behind the hooded figure. He glanced back, worry flashing across his face from our close proximity, and before he could reach the back door, one of our men sprung forward and tackled him. They rolled to a stop as we reached them and I was quick to stalk over to him, ripping him up by the collar.

"Where are they?" I snarled, my grip tightening as the man went pale.

"W-who are you talking about? I don't—I..."

"You damn well know these cloaks, so I will ask again, where are Everette and Saul? If you're not spitting out answers in the next few seconds, you won't get the chance to speak ever again, do you hear me?" I unsheathed my dagger, sticking the point underneath his chin. "I will carve out your fucking tongue."

He gulped, trying to push his head away, but I only pushed the dagger deeper into his chin, causing a droplet of blood to slide down the blade and the sight fueled the beast within me that was clawing to get out.

Kill him, it chanted.

"We don't know!"

I arched my brow. "Is that so? Your people—dressed in this same sickening color—jumped them. They also raided a warehouse with a horrible woman and killed one of our own. You know where they are, and you *will* tell me."

He shook his head, trying his best to not let the point of my dagger dig into his skin any further. "We had them on t-the ship. T-they were going to be shipped off, but... *he* came."

I glanced at Reese who leaned in. "Who?" he gritted out.

"The man that even Ghost has never been able to catch or see in person. He's known to run around with the real MOTs. The hitman that everyone fears. Axton. Axton Rivers. At least, we think it was h-him. The leather jacket is his signature. Before the ship could leave its port, it was in flames and a man dressed in all black was seen helping two red-cloaked men off the boat."

My heart dropped.

But I knew it wasn't the man I had known for all these past few weeks—the one I watched die right in front of me. He had simply stolen a name to keep a fake identity.

It was my cousin. Was he truly back? Did he really come to see us that night? Because he had vanished and no one could reach him after the... *incident.*

I cut my eyes to Reese who looked just as shocked as I was. Looking back at the man beneath me, I threw him to the ground. "Were there any other sights of where they went to?"

He shook his head. "Not a trace. It's what Axton is known for. If he wants to stay hidden, you won't find him."

Slowly nodding my head, I gritted my teeth together. I had looked up Axton with all the information my parents had about him, but I could never find anything that gave me the answers I needed. I knew what he looked like, but who knows if the pictures the commander had shown me were up to date or not.

"He thinks you're dead," the man blurted, his eyes still wide with fear.

I glanced back down at him with curious eyes. "What do you mean?"

"Ghost. He thinks you're dead. He fled the states and waited until the curse took its wrath on you, but... you're still alive. How?"

Slowly, a cruel smile crept onto my face. "Not even this damn curse could kill me, and I showed him a promise that day. He will get what is coming to him." I squatted beside him. "How did he hear word that I was dead?"

"Our organization had been keeping tabs on the MOTs. We saw a funeral and reported back to him. Then the numbers kept adding up, so we assumed it truly was you and others were dying because they had no leader to guide them."

What a stupid mistake on his part.

"And what? Everyone thinks I'm dead now?"

The man nodded. "It was broadcasted that the MOTs had truly fallen and there were no MIRs to protect them. Clearly, we were wrong."

The men around me chuckled.

"Clearly," Reese said, a wicked grin on his face. "But we can't have anyone knowing you're still alive, can we, Haven?"

I hummed, tilting my head. "We can't."

The man paled once more. "Please! I won't say anything. I've willingly told you everything I know. P-please don't kill me."

I clicked my tongue. "You're right, but I'm not done getting answers out of you." I looked over at Reese. "Take him back to the interrogation rooms. Get everything you possibly can out of him."

"Done." Reese nodded as two MIRs gripped the man by his arms and jerked him up.

"Oh, God," the man cried out, thrashing in their hold. "Please don't do this!"

I stood up, putting my dagger back in its place. "Those are the same words I screamed as your boss watched one of my men get slaughtered in front of me. He didn't show mercy, so why should I extend you any amount of my own?"

He gulped. "We're all different. We joined his cause for different reasons. It wasn't supposed to be like this. Not all of us are bad people. Ghost… he turned our original organization into some… nightmare!"

I nodded. "If there is one thing I have learned… it's that this is what happens when you follow people blindly instead of doing something about it." I turned but cast one last look over my shoulder to him. "It's only a nightmare until you wake up. Maybe you can see that with your time spent with the MIRs. We'll see where your alliance stands after they've ripped you of everything you used to be."

"We'll see you later?" Reese called out.

"Yeah… I have a hitman to find."

With that, I took off.

***

Staring up at the familiar apartment building in front of me, my heart clenched at the sight. In my hand was the spare keycard Knox had given me so long ago—one where I could access Axton's penthouse at any time. I had no idea if Axton would be stupid enough to come back to this place, but I had to hope it had some type of answer that I needed.

My hands shook slightly with each step closer to the front doors. I went back to my apartment in search of this card, which had been tucked away in my sock drawer with the old burner phone Knox had given me, and I nearly wept at the sight of them both.

I could almost smell the cinnamon whiskey scent that seemed to follow me around everywhere I went.

I tried to look as calm as I could manage when I entered the building. I was back in normal clothes, no MOT attire in sight. I walked past the front desk with ease and made it to the elevator as my heart lurched in my chest when memories of Knox and I entering and leaving this elevator together flooded my mind.

Once inside, I prayed it would still work, and as the elevator started moving after I swiped the card and pressed the PH button, tears flooded my vision. I knew I wasn't ready to enter the home Knox had stayed at for so long, but a small part of me thinks I needed to.

I had to do this.

For Everette.

For Saul.

For Knox, *who had given his life for me.*

When the doors opened and I stepped out into the familiar penthouse, my bottom lip trembled at the sight. My head whipped back and forth as I assessed what laid out in front of me, and just like that… that small sliver of hope I had started to seep out of me.

It was empty.

"No!" I sobbed, stumbling forward.

Looking around, there was nothing. Not one damn thing.

My hands found their way into my hair as I struggled to breathe. This was my last bit of hope of finding Axton or anything that could give me some answers to where he had gone. Why would he just leave? He knew my parents had this organization. He may not know where it was, but he damn well knew what had gone down if he saved Saul and Everette.

What is he planning?

I managed to venture further into the apartment and down to where Knox's room was. The door was already open and as I went to take a step into it, something cold was pressed against the back of my head.

"Take one more step, and I'll blow your fucking brains out," a gruff voice spoke.

Eyes wide, I froze.

Slowly, I raised both my hands as if I was surrendering, and the minute I felt even the slightest bit of pressure let up from the gun pressed to my head, I spun, grabbing the gun with one hand and delivering a punch with the other. The man grunted, doubling over as I sent a knee into his stomach right after.

Just as I wrapped my arms around his neck, he effortlessly maneuvered out of it and slung me against the wall before he placed the gun back into my face. "Who are you?!" he snarled.

Blonde hair.

Blue eyes.

The picture.

"Axton?" I breathed out.

His brows furrowed. "How do you know that name?"

"It's me… It's Haven, Clarrisa's daughter."

Recognition flooded his features and he reluctantly put down the gun, his eyes dragging over me. "You… they said you were dead."

I let out a sound between a laugh and a sob. "Well, they were wrong."

Axton moved back a step and ran a hand through his short, blonde hair. "How did you know about this place?"

"I… I stayed here with Knox at one point. It's a long story, but he gave me a keycard when I was living here so I could come and go as I pleased. That's how I got in. I was hoping there was something here that could give me any answers on how to find you, but I never expected you to actually be here."

He sighed. "I got a security alert someone had entered here. You're lucky this place hasn't been sold yet. Is Knox okay, too? Have you found your parents yet? I haven't been able to find where they went after they were separated from the ship that Everette and Saul were on, and I didn't realize until I had gotten them off it. I was waiting for Saul and Everette to show up. Your father said they would be retrieving me to take me to the warehouse, but before I could make my presence known, the commander showed and—"

"Axton, please slow down," I mumbled, pushing myself off the wall as my head started to pound. "You mean my parents weren't with Saul and Everette?"

He shook his head. "No, when the commander ambushed Saul and Everette, she had gotten to your parents beforehand."

I closed my eyes in defeat. "And how did you escape?"

"I always stay out of sight until I know the right people show up. I trust your father with my life, but I am a hitman with many targets on my back and I have never met Saul or Everette before. I had to make sure it was really them before I made myself known. I'm glad I stayed back, though, because the commander had no idea I was already there. I was able to follow them to the ship they were taken to and got them off, but I searched every bit of that place before I put it up in flames. Your parents weren't on it."

"Do you think the commander knows where they are?"

He shrugged. "No idea but a man was with her… he may know."

I nodded. "Ghost is what he goes by, apparently, but I haven't been able to get anything on him."

He cursed at the name. "I hate that fucker with every fiber of my being. I've never seen him in person—well, until then—but I know the stories."

"You're not alone there."

He suddenly frowned. "So… Where is Knox then?"

I gulped. "He… I… he's dead. The commander killed him. Right in front of me."

His features dropped, and a look of sorrow crossed his face. "Haven, I'm so sorry. Your father mentioned you had grown close with him."

I shrugged. "It doesn't matter, but what does matter is getting our people back and getting Knox the justice he deserves. He gave his life for my father and me. We owe him that much."

"He was a good man, Haven."

I sniffled, wiping away a stray tear. "And Everette and Saul? Are they okay?"

"They were beaten up pretty badly, but they're managing. They've been bedridden until just yesterday, but… they're going to be glad to see you. We all thought you and the MOTs and MIRs were done for after the news broke out you were dead. They've been upset lately."

"You have no idea the relief that went through me when I heard you saved them. Thank you, Axton."

He gave me a sharp nod. "Of course. Your parents thought highly of them and if they helped my family… I had to return the favor."

"Can you take me to them? Please… I can't wait any longer."

"Sure thing, but there is something I think you should see first. It didn't make sense to me until now…"

He brushed past me into the room Knox had been staying in and I was quick to follow after him. Aside from the bed being gone, there were a few small boxes in the corner of the room labeled 'Knox'.

"As you know, Knox was staying here to watch the place for me while I completed a mission. After all of this, I came to move and I had messaged Knox a few times telling him I had a few of his things, but I now see why he hadn't replied in time. I think I already knew after hearing the rumors about you all… but I didn't want to believe it. I had known Knox for a long time. It's why he was the only person I trusted here. Anyways, these are a few of his things that he left behind. I don't want them to go to waste, so you should have them."

My bottom lip trembled once more as I walked toward them, dropping to my knees as I raised a shaky hand and opened the box's flaps. "Thank you…"

The first thing my hands felt was leather, which caused a weak sob to leave my body as I pulled out one of his leather jackets. Immediately, the smell of cinnamon and spice entered my senses, and I couldn't help but bring it close to my chest as silent sobs wracked my body.

"I'll give you a few minutes," Axton mumbled, giving my shoulder a small squeeze.

It wasn't long before I forced myself to get it together and I angrily wiped my eyes with the sleeve of my shirt and placed the jacket on my lap as I dug through the boxes more. It was a few of his clothes and other small trinkets, but when I opened the last box, I placed a hand against my chest.

Now I see why Axton had been confused.

Letting out a small, crying laugh, I pulled out the napkin from where Knox and I had grabbed pizza. Despite the horrible night it had turned into, a smile pulled at my lips as my finger trailed across the date scribbled in chicken-scratch handwriting. I placed it down, looking back into the box at another note. At the top, it was scribbled 'Haven's taco soup recipe' with ingredients my father had blurted out that night.

"Oh, Knox," I choked out.

There were a few other small things he had kept, even the damn receipt of the takeout food he had once stolen after our first encounter.

I knew he had kept tabs on me before we had officially met, but most of this was after… And the thought of Knox keeping these things as a reminder of the moments we shared together was like a punch in the gut.

All the things he said about not wanting to be anything more than friends were a lie in order to try and protect me because he knew how it ended for him, yet like the coward I was, I made myself think I was clinging to some false hope of accompaniment from him and he died thinking I didn't feel for him like he once had thought.

A coward indeed.

Just as I went to put everything back, one last thing caught my eye.

A flash drive.

"You ready?" Axton called out.

Slowly, I pulled on Knox's jacket and tucked the flash drive into the pocket. "Yeah, can you get these boxes to me later?"

"Of course."

CHAPTER FOUR

Haven

My heart was beating furiously within my chest as Axton drove us to wherever Everette and Saul were staying at. It wasn't surprising when we pulled up to yet another expensive apartment building.

"You have a taste for luxurious things, don't you?"

Axton cracked a grin as he put the car into park. "Something like that. I'm always on the move, so I don't stay in these places long, but I can't lie when I say I like to pamper myself. I never had it as a kid, so… this is my way of making up for it, I guess."

"How many people did you—" I immediately stopped the joke as it nearly rolled off my tongue.

"What was that?"

I shook my head. "Nothing. I'm glad you finally have gotten what you wanted since you were a kid."

As we walked side by side, he explained the extent of Everette and Saul's injuries but said they were quicker to recover than he previously thought. The only thing they had left was a few cuts and bruises. Saul was still getting over a dislocated shoulder.

Not shortly after, we hopped on the elevator and headed up as my palms started to sweat. I was more than eager to see these men, but I was also nervous to share the devastating news of what had happened these past few weeks.

When the doors opened, Axton was the first to step out. The place was similar to his old penthouse, and it had the same beautiful skyline with ceiling-to-floor windows but also the same untouched feeling of a man who was always on the run.

Soft music played throughout the penthouse, and I didn't miss the empty chip bags scattered across the living room's coffee table.

"Saul can never clean up after himself," Axton grumbled, swiping the empty bags off the table.

"Are they here?" I quietly asked, looking around the room.

"Yeah. Everette stays to himself mostly, but Saul is usually running about somewhere—despite me yelling at him to get back in bed. The man was stabbed. Twice. Yet he didn't care. I feel like I'm watching a toddler most of the time."

I couldn't help but grin at the sound of that. Saul and his golden retriever energy were something I desperately missed recently. "Sounds just like him."

"Saul! Everette! Come out here, there's someone who would like a word with you," Axton called out, and a small grin tugged at the corner of his lips.

I heard footsteps come down the hall and Saul was the first to round the corner, his hand in another chip bag as he looked down at it. "Axton, we're going to need some more…" Saul trailed off as his eyes raised and landed on me, causing Everette, who had been following behind him while reading some papers, to crash into his back.

"Shit, Saul, watch where you're going," Everette grumbled, stepping around the side of him, his eyes not leaving the papers he was reading.

"Haven..." Saul whispered.

Everette's eyes snapped up at the sound of my name and before he could react, Saul took off. His muscular body collided with mine, and I let out a yelp as he picked me up, spinning me around. Despite the shoulder I knew he was still nursing back to health, he didn't care to hold me tight as if I'd disappear at any second.

"We thought you were dead, Haven," he breathed out, placing me back onto my feet.

I smiled up at him, tears building in my eyes. "I'm right here, big guy. Takes a lot more to get me to stay down."

I've never seen Saul cry before, but the tears that were welling up in his eyes made my heart clench within my chest as he pulled me back into another tight hug. "Does this mean we get to do more karaoke nights?" he joked.

I let out a sniffle, giving him a small squeeze. "We'll have one every fucking night if we have to, Saul."

He let out a soft laugh, releasing me. Next to us, Everette stood and looked just as shocked. "You're okay..."

I nodded. "For the most part."

"Come here," he breathed out, and for the first time, Everette pulled me into a backbreaking hug.

His hand was against the back of my head, his other around my waist while my arms were around his neck, my tears no doubt leaking down his neck as I buried my face there. "I'm so damn glad you all are okay."

"Same," Everette replied as we moved apart. I noticed the faint bruises scattered across his face, but he didn't mention them as he looked me over. Shaking his head, he said, "When was the last time you slept? Or ate? You look like shit."

I belted out a laugh that I'm sure made me look insane. "God, you have no idea how nice it feels for someone to insult me. Never in my life would I have thought I wanted to hear such words."

He didn't crack a smile. "I'm serious, Haven."

Looking away, my smile faded. "I don't know. I have been too determined to find you all… and with Knox—"

"What happened with Knox? Where is he?" Saul was quick to ask.

I gulped. "He's… gone."

"What?" Everette frowned, taking a step closer. "Was it the commander?"

I nodded. "She made him choose. He was supposed to bring my father and me to her or she would kill him. Guess which option he went with."

Everette cursed, pulling me back into another hug as a tear escaped down my cheek. "I'm so sorry, Haven."

"We're going to get revenge," Saul declared. "We're going to make this right."

Leaving Everette's grasp, I nodded. "We're going to make them pay. The commander has given me all the information that I think she honestly knows, but I'm sure she can be of more use to us than just rotting away in a cell."

Everette's brow raised. "She's still alive after what she did to Knox?"

"I told her if she laid a finger on him that I'd rip her apart and put her back together again until she was begging for a death I would not grant her."

"And I'm assuming she's begging for it, then?" Everette asked, folding his arms, anger sketched across his face.

I let out a humorless laugh. "Oh, she's not begging for it… she's *screaming*."

And she wouldn't be stopping any time soon.

CHAPTER FIVE

Haven

Axton drove silently as the four of us made our way back to the school. I could tell Saul and Everette were eager to see the group they considered their family, and I selfishly was glad that someone else would now be at the school for everyone to look to instead of me.

"Can I ask you all something?" I blurted out.

"Sure," Saul replied.

"Why didn't you come to look for us? I mean, after everything."

"Oh, they tried," Axton replied humorously. "But I wouldn't let them. Saul was beaten up gruesomely and so was Everette. Both had more than one stab wound and Saul dislocated his shoulder slamming into some guy that got Everette pinned. I had a friend come to stitch them up, but if they were running around… it wouldn't have been pretty. They're lucky that they are still breathing."

"Flesh wound," Everette grumbled from next to me as we sat in the back of the car.

Saul turned around from the passenger seat and reached out, placing his hand on my knee. "Haven, we didn't want to believe it when we heard the news. After a few days, I came to and was back on my feet. I was ready to find you all—find our men. At least, I was ready to see it for myself. I ripped my stitches that day, got bitched out by Axton, and was forced to get back in bed. Everette was still out cold but when he did wake, he tried the same. Our bodies just fought against us."

I nodded. "I see..."

"I tried looking, too, you know. When Everette and Saul told me where the school was, I went there, but I couldn't find anyone. It was empty."

I sighed and glanced down at my hands. "We've lost a lot of people over the past couple of weeks. The girls started to go out in groups to do their missions—the dead never stopped showing, not that we'd expect them to for our benefit. And I went out with the MIRs most nights in search of you all."

Everette averted his eyes. "How are my men?"

I looked out the window at the streetlights passing by. "They're doing their best. You'd be proud of Reese, though. He has stepped up a lot."

Saul let out a small laugh. "That's why he's our third in command. I'm glad he's doing well. We thought... we thought that either the MIRs left or were dead. It's insane the type of rumors that were circulating. How do we even come back from this?"

"We use it to our advantage," I mumbled. "We strike back ten times harder and they won't even see it coming."

Everette leaned forward, and I didn't miss the wince he gave. "What's our first plan?"

"I am trying my best to find my parents, but I haven't gotten any leads. When I get back to the school, I told Addison that she better have the names of the MOTs she sold. Maybe we can start there and see where they went off to. Maybe my parents went to similar places."

"I just don't get it. What would anyone want with your parents? Your mother doesn't have the curse," Axton asked.

I finally met his eyes through his rearview mirror. "I asked myself that continuously for the last two weeks. I think they're just using them as a bargaining chip. Like blackmail. In case the MOTs were to come after them—they have something to use against them."

"We'll get them back," Axton replied, his hand gripping the steering wheel even tighter.

I gulped. "I sure hope so."

We all fell silent as the school came into view and I was itching to get out of the car to run back to the comforts of my room. I knew everyone would be excited, but a huge part of me just didn't think it would feel the same without Knox with us—without all the others we have lost.

We weren't whole anymore.

When Axton parked, I glanced over at Everette who eagerly unbuckled. Saul ran after him as they exited the car, nearly sprinting to the front doors. Axton and I followed them and before we all even reached the doors, they opened.

Reese grinned as he darted out, tackling Saul and Everette in a big hug. "I saw the car on the cameras and I knew… I just knew," he nearly whispered.

Everette gave him a slap on the back. "Good to see you, brother."

"We heard you've been doing well with keeping the MIRs sane," Saul mused.

Reese rubbed the back of his neck awkwardly. "I tried." Looking away from the two men in front of him, his eyes trailed to meet mine. "Thank you, Haven."

I nodded, motioning to Axton. "The hitman the guy mentioned. This is my cousin, Axton Rivers—the *real* Axton Rivers."

"It's nice to meet you," Reese replied to which Axton dipped his head in acknowledgment. "Everyone is going to be happy to see you all. We were doing a last minute training session when I got the alert on my phone someone was pulling up. The girls have a mission tomorrow."

I looked down at my feet when I felt Saul and Everette's eyes on me.

"Well, let's go inside before I freeze my balls off," Saul replied, pushing past Reese.

Numbly, I went inside with them and watched as they all quickly hurried down the hall, but I slipped away before they noticed I was gone. My feet led me upstairs and to the roof—my safe haven for the past few weeks.

I leaned against the ledge, looking out over the city at the blinking city lights and buzzing of cars. The smell of New York invaded my senses and despite the cool air nipping at my skin, I basked in the breeze of the night.

Winter would soon be here in a few months, which was something I wasn't ready for in the slightest—I hoped it wouldn't be a problem for our missions. I always hated going on missions when it was snowing. It was pure hell.

As I stared out into space, I jumped slightly when something was laid over my shoulders. A thin blanket. I looked over at Axton who leaned up next to me. "Not in for the welcoming party?" he mused.

I sighed. "I don't think most of the girls want to speak to me right now."

His brows furrowed. "Why is that?"

"I was a shitty friend these past few weeks. But can you blame me, though? Someone I deeply cared about was murdered right in front of me and everyone was looking to me for answers at the same time. Nothing made sense to me and I didn't want to lead an organization, I wanted to find my family. I know I have a duty to this organization, but I also felt I had the responsibility of getting Saul and Everette back."

"I know these past few weeks haven't been easy for you, but you can't just cut everyone out of your life, Haven. Healing isn't ignoring what lies ahead of you that makes you sad or upset, healing is going through it headfirst and knowing you made it out and that you *can* continue on."

I scoffed. "No one knows how to heal from something like this. There's no handbook on it, so how can you say that? It's not that easy, Axton. It is still fresh, and it still hurts."

"It will always hurt."

I rolled my eyes. "Thanks for stating the obvious."

Axton shook his head. "What I'm trying to say is… you're never going to fill that hole in your chest, but you can learn to grow with it. That hole? That ache? It will shrink, but it will never go away. Instead, you have to push through. You have to look at what you can do going forward—you can't keep looking back at the past wishing you could have changed it."

However true his words may have been, the stubborn part of me didn't want to hear them. I don't know Axton's story, but everyone handles grief in their own way. How can he say how one is supposed to handle such a thing?

"Tell me about him," Axton mumbled, leaning forward as I was.

"What?"

"Tell me about Knox. Sometimes, talking about it can help."

I opened my mouth but no words wanted to come out. It was as if my body wanted to reject any thought of the man who had stolen my attention for the weeks prior to his demise. "I don't think I can."

"How did you meet?"

I let out a snort. "He tried to kill me—well, he acted as if he was. Apparently, it was all some plan in order for him to gain my trust. My father started all of this to eventually get me back and Knox was his helping hand for God knows how long."

"Sounds like an idiotic way to try and gain someone's trust."

The corner of my lips tugged up. "He wasn't always the smartest, but this time it did work. He went about things in the shittiest of ways, but somehow… I learned to trust him."

"He was a good man. He was such an asshole—and arrogant—but there was just something about him that everyone loved."

I nodded, a ghost of a smile on my lips as I hugged the blanket closely to me. "He was. He was loyal and he would take a bullet for those closest to him. I only got to know a few things about him from his past, but for the most part… I know he was a genuine guy."

"Did you love him?"

I sighed. "No? I don't know. I don't think I had enough time to fall in love with him. We had only known each other for a small amount of time, but I do know I cared deeply for him. I was head over heels not shortly after before I realized it. Then when we got close, he pushed me away. I didn't understand at first and I convinced myself I didn't really care about him romantically—intimately. Little did I know he did that on purpose because he knew he was going to hand himself over to the commander instead of turning me in to her."

"Is that what hurts you the most? You think he died thinking you didn't care about him?"

I nodded. "That and the fact I was responsible for his death."

I don't know why I was confiding in this man I barely knew. A small part of me screamed to put my guards back up and to turn away from him right now, but with him knowing Knox… I almost needed this.

"That's not possible. From the look I just saw on your face as you talked about him, he knew you cared for him. He knew. And you're not responsible for all that, Haven, the commander is."

My bottom lip trembled. "You think so?"

"I know so."

I looked back out in front of me, a thought pegging my mind. "Do you think he's out there? Do you think he's stuck here in our miserable world just like an informer would be? Because someone took his life?"

Axton shook his head. "No. I don't think he is. To me, Haven, it seems like he made peace with his decision before the commander took him from you."

"Why do you say that?"

Axton glanced at me, pushing off the wall. "Because he was doing something for the woman he loved. I know I would." With that, Axton gave my shoulder a small squeeze, causing me to stiffen, and walked away.

My nails dug into the soft skin of my palms as I fought the urge to let out a scream. How could I be so blind? How could I be so… *weak*? For years I followed the commander like a lost puppy, and now I sit here after she nearly took everything from me—without even lifting a finger. If I could barely stop her then, how could I stop something she already did? How could I find my parents or those women she sold off?

"Didn't want to join all the fun?" a familiar voice asked.

I glanced to my right, seeing Jay had walked up. "Not really."

She sighed, relaxing next to me as Axton did. "When are you going to come back to us, Haven?"

I raised a brow. "I've never left."

"Oh, but you did. You ran at the first sight of something that scared you. Why? Why would you leave the minute you needed us the most?"

I pushed myself off the ledge I was leaning against and shook my head. "I'm not doing this right now."

Jay gripped my arm, refusing to let me leave. "No. We're doing this now."

Ripping my arm from her grasp, I stared up at her with angry eyes. "I said I don't want to talk about this."

"Boo fucking hoo. Grow the hell up, Haven. No one else is going to tell you, but I don't give a damn to. Get your shit together! What happened to the 'I run the show' energy you had when you stopped the commander? What happened to the woman who used to put her life on the line for days at a time to save our organization? Because all I see is a damn coward."

I flinched from her words. "Jay, I'm begging you, please just–"

"No! You lost my respect the day you knew Nikita's sister was dead and you didn't even blink! You left. You left her to grieve when she needed us the most."

"Because I was ready to die, Jay!" I shouted, my hands flying out beside me. "I accepted *death*. I did run the show—I fucking did for what I thought was my last few days. I got all I could from the commander and did my part. Then I waited. And guess what? On that fourth day, *I woke up*. I wasn't dead. I had been lied to yet again by someone I used to trust, which hurt so much more knowing she willingly killed people I grew up with. You act as if I didn't care that Nikita's sister died, but I did! I went out and I found those men responsible, and I cut their heads clean from their bodies. *I slaughtered them*!"

She shook her head. "Still doesn't explain why you left, Haven."

I scoffed. "I couldn't get a break. She wasn't the only one grieving, Jay. I lost so many people in the span of one damn night! And then everyone turned to me—they turned to the one person who had no idea who the hell she was or what the hell she was doing. So, yes… I fled. I would much rather you all hate me than for me to give you false hope. The commander had done that for way too long."

Jay tilted her head, letting out a humorless laugh. "That's what this is. You're afraid you're going to turn out like the commander."

I rolled my eyes. "Don't be ridiculous."

"No, it's true and you know it. You feel as if you're going to fuck everything up just like the commander did. Guess what, Haven? You're not her! You stopped her, freed us, and gave us an opportunity to grow. Yet instead of us working together to find your parents and Everette and Saul, you shut us out—abandoned us. So what did I do when you left? I stepped up as you should have, and I did what I had to in order to give these women hope. We have a chance to win here, especially with Everette and Saul back, but you refuse to see that. I know what you were thinking about bringing them here… I'm not stupid. You thought you could dump them on us and that everything would be fixed. We're not the same without *you*, Haven. We needed you—we still do, dammit! You got us this far, so own up to that and help us *win*."

I fought down the tears brimming my eyes. "I… I can't. I'm just… I'm just so…" my voice trailed off as a sob crept its way up my throat.

Jay's features softened as she stepped closer. "Let it *out*, Haven."

Meeting her eyes and seeing the hurt in them made my chest clench. "I'm… lost. I'm angry. I'm heartbroken. I'm… *scared*. Why would you all even want my help? I caused *all* of this."

Jay shook her head. "You didn't. That woman downstairs did. Use that anger and heartbreak to fuel your mission to succeed. We can do this. We can get the women she sold back. We can get your parents back. We can get them all back if you just work with us and let us help you. You don't have to go at this alone anymore. Stop shutting us out. Please…"

I looked back over the bright lights of the city, my eyes settling on the familiar pizza place that brought back many memories. The sign above the restaurant randomly flickered, causing goosebumps to trail up my arms as if Knox did it, telling me to listen to her.

I gulped, taking in a deep breath. "Okay…"

Letting out a sigh of relief, Jay tugged on my arm. "Come on, everyone wants to see you."

CHAPTER SIX

Everette

I watched as my men brought up the security footage of where the commander was being held. When the screen popped up, showing the woman inside, my eyes widened. She didn't even look the same. She was caked in dried blood, her fingernails were missing, and she was bruised all over. I leaned forward, nearly second-guessing myself at the woman who used to never have even one hair out of place.

"Did you all do that?" I asked, glancing down at Reese who was controlling the computers.

Reese shook his head, biting his lip as he looked at the commander. "That was all Haven."

I sighed in defeat, my eyes closing as the mental picture of Haven's small form doing so much damage. "I didn't want to believe it."

"Believe what?" he asked.

I opened my eyes, looking away from him to the commander. "That Haven went off the deep end there for a while."

"Everette, I don't think she's come back from it. Do you know the curse of the MOTs? That day she slaughtered those men that killed Knox… she came back covered in blood and mentally was not here. She accepted death and defied the curse knowing that she was going to die. Yet she didn't. It was all a lie—the wrath of the curse. Do you realize what she has done these past few weeks? Whoever has been running around in her place is not Haven McKinley. No… She sacrificed Haven McKinley so she could find you all again."

Why did that statement make my chest ache?

"I guess that's why she ran off once we got here? She's in a downward spiral?"

Reese nodded. "I've tried my best to do what I can to help her. I've made our men go with her. I stayed by her side, but she didn't care. I don't know who could get through to her at this point."

"I'm hoping Jay will. I saw her marching up towards the roof a few minutes ago. Hopefully, she can bring Haven back to her senses."

"I don't know, man, but I feel like Haven is the key piece to this whole shit show, and without her… I don't know if we'll ever find the people we're looking for."

I turned to head back to the doors. "I know. I don't plan to let her get too far from us. If there is one thing about Haven that I've learned these past few months, it's that she's a warrior. She's a fighter. I know she'll come around and do the right thing. I just know it."

I left the security room just in time to catch Haven and Jay talking with a few other MOTs. The urge to walk towards her beckoned me near, but I fought to stay back. She needed that—needed them.

When Sam jumped up to hug Haven, a small thread of hope laced through me. The other MOTs joined in and before I knew it, I saw Saul emerge from out of nowhere, throwing himself into the group of hugging girls as they all laughed with one another, letting him join in. Grinning, I turned and headed up the stairs to the familiar room I used to stay in when I was here on long nights.

However, when I opened the door, I saw it was already in use. Books and papers were laying around and clothes were strewn everywhere, but what caught my eye was the black cloak with a red hood sewn into it laying across the end of the bed.

"Need something?" a soft voice asked from behind me.

I turned, seeing Haven there staring at me with tired eyes. God, I wish I knew how to make her look and feel alive again. This wasn't the stubborn, feisty woman I was used to seeing.

"I used to use this room when I stayed some nights, but I see that you're occupying it now. Sorry, I'll leave you to it."

As I moved aside to let her in, her arm struck out and grabbed onto mine. "Don't go. I mean... I think we need to talk."

Without even questioning her, I nodded and walked into the room. Haven shut the door as I walked further into the mess of a place. Nearing the cloak, I grabbed it as a grin spread across my face. "This is new, Red."

Haven let out a small laugh. "The girls made it for me. I guess to show the ties our organizations now have."

Placing it gently back onto the bed, I shot her a small smile. "I like it."

She shot me a nervous glance before making her way over to her desk, sitting in the chair. "I know Axton was making Saul's and your injuries seem minor. I damn well know that you two would have been here the minute you woke—if not for us then for your men. I've seen you wince multiple times today… so what the hell happened, Everette? Two weeks. You were gone for two weeks. I thought I really lost you two."

I gulped, knowing this talk was coming, and took a seat on the edge of the bed, leaning forward to rest my forearms on my knees. "We almost died and it was no easy recovery—we haven't recovered, really. We are still mentally and physically fucked. That day the commander took us, we did fight to the best of our abilities but there were, what? Fifteen of those men? And two of us? I had a sword plunged through my stomach—a wound that Axton said I should have died from."

I finally took a glance at Haven whose bottom lip quivered. At the sight of it, a small part of me urged me to move to her and comfort her, but I knew I couldn't. That wasn't my place and it never was.

It never will be.

Looking away before I acted on that impulse, I continued. "Saul did dislocate his shoulder but that wasn't the brunt of it. When he saw that sword go through me, the man went feral. He ripped through the people around him to try and get to me. In doing so, his abdomen was torn to pieces and when he did reach me, that's when he slammed into the guy. He had been through so much that he passed out shortly after and when I saw him go down, I blacked out."

"God, Everette, why didn't you all tell me this from the beginning? Should you even be up?"

"Probably not, but two days ago I was growing restless. I told Axton if he didn't let us at least start moving around the penthouse, I'd find a way to leave. I was in and out for about a week after Axton got us off that ship. When he found us, that's when I woke up for a bit, but when he had his doctor friends working on us, I blacked out again. The pain was… the worst I've ever experienced. So I woke up a week later finally coherent and I was up that instant. I didn't wait for anyone and Saul tried to convince me to stay put and went to search for Axton. I snuck out, made it maybe halfway to the school and once again… I collapsed, ripped my stitches, and didn't know I had a nasty infection—one I'm still fighting off. Axton found me nearly dead in some alleyway."

"Why didn't you go to the hospital?!" Haven nearly shouted and I looked at her as if she had lost her mind.

"So they could have the police question me? Hell no. Tell me you're not that stupid, Haven."

"It's better than you being dead."

I scoffed. "It would have been. I would have been thrown in a jail cell. God knows what they could have tried to link me to. God knows that the system isn't exactly perfect. Plus, I couldn't risk anyone finding out about what really goes on in this school, which is something you need to be considering if someone realizes your parents are missing."

Haven slouched in her chair. "I just can't fathom losing anyone else I care about."

Trying to lighten the mood, I asked, "Worrying about me, Red?"

The corner of her lips tugged a little. "It's weird, I know, but I've never really had a family. I mean, the MOTs were there when I needed them, but we were all forced together. Over these past few months, I realized I had started to view Knox, you, Saul, Jay, and Nikita as my safe place—a small little family that I pieced together. I know you all don't see it that way, but I do. Then it all seemed like it was slipping from my fingers before it really began and that wrecked me more than I thought it would."

I frowned, wanting to curse the pained look that was etched across her face. "Family is not always through blood," I mumbled. "Sometimes it's with those you've gone through hell and back with. Sometimes those people are your home."

Haven's eyes drifted to meet my own and she gave me a small nod. "Yeah… I'm starting to see that."

Rubbing the material of my pants nervously, I asked, "So, what's our first move?"

She shrugged a shoulder in response. "I have no idea, but I think we all need to sit down and conjure up a plan before discussing it with the others in our organization. With you being hurt and—"

"I'm fine, Haven."

Her brow arched. "No, you're not, Everette. You just admitted you're still fighting off an infection and I'll be damned if you get even worse because you're pushing yourself too much. You are taking it easy and that's final."

I had to admit, her protective demeanor was one of the things that drove me crazy.

"Fine. Just… don't look at me like I'm some damsel in distress."

"I don't. I still think you have a black heart and soul, though. I know you can take care of yourself."

I couldn't help but grin at the genuine, humorous look in her eyes. It was the first time I had seen that look with my own eyes since being back and just the thought of that poured more hope into me that maybe we haven't lost the real Haven completely.

"Well, let's get to making some plans then, shall we?" I stood up from the bed and started to make my way to the door, trying my best not to wince at the aching throb in my side. I was beginning to wonder if this damn wound would ever heal at this rate.

"Wait… first, I want you to look into Axton."

I halted at her words, my hand resting on the doorknob. "You don't trust him?"

"I do, but I learned the hard way that sometimes everyone is not what they seem. I just want to do it right this time and make no mistakes."

I sighed, nodding my head. "That's fair. I can have Reese look into him, but he's not known for being some recluse hitman for just any reason, Haven. He's pretty much nonexistent—he made it that way for solely *this* reason. He doesn't want to be known."

She bit her lip nervously, the sight of it zapping me into an odd, electric feeling that I knew I had to stop letting happen. "That's what I'm afraid of…"

"Then we'll look into it."

I opened the doors, passing through the threshold just as she called out my name once more. "Yeah?"

"I'm glad you're back," she whispered.

I smiled, trying to mash down that pesky warmth wanting to spread throughout my chest. "Yeah… me too."

CHAPTER SEVEN

Haven

I faced my computer with shaky hands. Next to it, I held the thumb drive that I had found in one of Knox's boxes. I didn't know what it contained, but I had to try and see why Knox would keep this with things that were about me.

Slipping the drive into the computer, I waited until a small file popped up. I clicked on it and when it opened the file to contain multiple documents, that wasn't what caught my eye. It was the video at the end of it all. I nearly closed the computer at the sight of the small frame on the video.

It was a video of Knox himself.

Taking in a deep breath, I knew I had to push through my heartache. I clicked the video, my bottom lip quivering as Knox's face came into view. He was sitting at his desk with red eyes, showing that he had been crying before making this.

"Where do I even begin…" he mumbled and at the sound of his voice, a sob finally broke through me. "Haven, I really hope you find this, and if you're not Haven… kindly fuck off."

I laughed.

Maybe sobbed. I don't even know what my mind was trying to comprehend at this point.

"Haven, if you're watching this… I'm gone," he let out a shaky breath, wiping his hands along his pants, "And I'm sorry. I'm sorry that I lied to you for so long and I'm sorry that I pushed you away the past few times we had been together. I never wanted to hurt you, but recently I got a letter from the commander, which you probably know about now. I want you to know that I made this choice and I'm at peace with it, so don't beat yourself up over it. I know you stubbornly are, so just quit."

I blinked rapidly, trying to unblur my vision from the tears continuously welling up in my eyes. Without realizing it, my hand had reached out to trail a finger across the screen. God, I missed him so much.

"Fuck. I don't know what to say. I… I fought alongside your father for years to bring this organization up and to help him get you back. For once in my life, being a part of this place… I felt like I had a purpose. Little did I know it would lead me to be infatuated with this woman who drove me absolutely crazy every chance she got," he let out a small laugh, "and I think you knew that. Haven, I was madly head over heels for you… I still am and I will take that to the grave with me. You have to know that. And I know that you spewed bullshit that night in your kitchen, but I know you care about me, whether you want to admit that or not. I can only wonder what we'd be like if we met under different circumstances…"

I did too.

"But it doesn't matter, because I know how this ends for me. I just hope you find someone that will love and protect you just as fiercely as I always tried to. But just know that I'm leaving this world in peace… *please*. Haven, you must know that. I did my part. I did what I promised your father all those years ago. I got you back and I got you back into his arms and knowing that I achieved that—that I got you free of that hell hole—it's the most amazing feeling. But the commander is going to come for me, and I don't know how much longer we have together. It's been eating at me for a while knowing that… but I'm going to be okay. And you are, too. At least, I hope so. If you don't make it out of this, just know that I will haunt you in the afterlife completely pissed off."

Despite the sobs that had been wracking my body, another laugh broke through the mess of feelings I was experiencing. Knox went quiet for a few seconds, looking as if he was trying to get his words together.

"There are documents, papers, witnesses, and more on this drive to help you in taking down the commander and people she has worked with in the past. I hope that it helps in some way." He blew out a puff of air. "So I guess this is where I say my goodbye? No… Not a goodbye. How about a… see you later?" Knox grinned and leaned forward as if he was about to stop the recording but froze and glanced back at the camera. "And Haven?"

I almost replied, leaning forward eagerly as I awaited his last words.

"Is this where you say make me?" he asked, a grin crossing his features.

I bit my lip, watching the recording stop, then quietly whispered, "Because I can make you do a lot of things, *darlin'*."

CHAPTER EIGHT

Everette

Haven didn't come back down last night. Not that I expected her to. Even after the commander coughed up the whereabouts of some of the MOTs she sold, Haven didn't make an appearance and I didn't know if that should have worried me or not. That woman was losing her mind a little bit each day, according to Jay.

We were all in the gym-like area where the MOTs sparred and trained. I didn't realize how true Haven's words were when she said they lost a lot of people until I saw it with my own eyes. They had to have lost at least a dozen women these past few weeks—including Nikita's sister. My eyes drifted across the room to her and Jay. Nikita looked… numb. She tried to smile as she talked to Jay, but I could see how much she was still grieving.

I would be the same if I would have lost my sister.

The thought of my own sister made my mind drift to Knox. He had once mentioned to me that he had a family outside of this organization and that he still tried to remain close with his sister, Fallon. When would she realize her brother isn't replying to her?

How long until she comes looking for answers we can't give her?

"Can we start this already?" Anastasia huffed. "Obviously Haven isn't coming down, but we all knew that already, didn't we?"

I never liked that woman. The sight of her made my skin crawl and her anger towards Haven was only fueled more after she heard about Knox. It was clear that Anastasia was in love with Knox, even though he hadn't shared the same feelings. Her jealousy spiked when Haven came back, with the notorious title of being the missing daughter and a skilled fighter, and then she found out Knox was getting close with Haven.

"I'm not in the mood for it today, Ana, so could you just not?" Jay spit out, stretching her arms behind her head.

"I don't understand why we are still trying to have hope for her. She got Knox killed! And then she practically vanished when we were at our lowest."

I gritted my teeth together.

"We all heal in different ways," Nikita spoke up, finally looking over to Anastasia.

"Bullshit. She left us. Left you after June died! How is that a friend? How is—"

"Enough!" My voice boomed across the gym, causing the women to stiffen. "She lost just as much as you did that night. You weren't there when she was up countless hours of the night grieving and pushing herself to try and find us. You act as if she didn't care but she did. As Nikita said, we all grieve in different ways. She lost her parents, Knox, and us… and she thought she was going to lose her own life, too. One of which she was willing to give up to stop Ghost's men and take down the commander to get the answers *you* all needed. Another word about her and you're dealing with me. Got it?"

But when I finally glanced around at the women, their eyes weren't on me but on whoever was behind me. Slowly, I craned my neck to see Haven standing there looking as apathetic as ever.

She glanced over at Anastasia whose back straightened when she noticed. "Please, don't stop talking on my account."

Anastasia rolled her eyes, looking away as Haven walked up to me. Despite the morning that felt strained, I managed a small smile. "Morning, Red."

Haven lowered her voice, shooting me a worried look. "Should you be training?"

"What did I say about looking at me like a damsel in distress? Plus, I'm taking it easy. Just instructing today. If we plan to hatch some big idea to stop all of this, our training can't end. We need to be prepared."

She rubbed her arms subconsciously. "I get that, but I just don't want you to hurt yourself. Where's Saul?" she looked around, and my chest ached at the look on her face.

It was as if she was worried we'd vanish all over again.

"He went back to your old manor."

"What? Why?"

"The commander coughed up some answers last night about the MOTs she sold, but apparently most of the information we needed was in her office there."

Haven's eyes slightly widened. "And you let him go alone? What if it's a setup? What if—"

I placed my hands on her shoulders, cutting her off. "Haven, calm down. He's with some of our men. Reese is with him. It's fine. They are to retrieve the files and get out of there."

She noticeably gulped. "What is going to happen to that place?"

I shrugged. "We checked this morning and since bills haven't been getting paid… it looks like foreclosure is on its way. That's why they are trying to get everything out, including those files the commander mentioned. Anything that could give you all away, that is. The bringers that the commander was close with fled after they heard what happened. The place was completely abandoned after the MOTs here got the rest of the girls out of there."

Haven's face twisted. "Good. Fuckers can go to hell."

I let out a small laugh, dropping my arms. "I'm sure they will."

Reluctantly, Haven reached out and touched the fabric of my uniform that I surprisingly had missed. "Is it weird that I'm glad to see this on you again? You look so strange without it," she joked.

I folded my arms, grinning. "Well, you're going to be seeing a lot of us more often. We're not going to always be in our MIR attire, so you might as well get used to it."

"Yeah, yeah… What do I need to do?"

I glanced at the women who went back to stretching and chatting with one another. "Grab a partner and get ready to spar."

Her face dropped as she whispered, "Do I have to?"

"Yes." I gave her a gentle shove. "So go."

It was almost cute how nervous she looked walking into the center of the crowd, but that feeling was quick to leave as I remembered how tense the women still were with her. However, as I saw the fiery redhead skipping towards her, that heavy feeling let up some.

Sam smiled at Haven, no doubt asking her to be her partner, and I couldn't help but smile at the sight of it. Maybe Sam would be the one to bring Haven back to her senses. She seemed like a stubborn little woman, and for some reason… I loved that for Haven.

Despite the dull look on Haven's face, I knew that the old her was still somewhere in there with the protective stance she took by Sam's side as if she was ready to shield her from any negative comments from the other women. I don't know why Haven was always protective over the redhead, but I knew Sam would forever have a protector here with how Haven handled the last comments that the older women tried to throw at her.

Clearing my head, I placed my hands behind my back. "Listen up!" The women immediately stopped what they were doing, focusing their attention on me. "Most of you have trained with us before. I want you to go through the motions we all taught you in our recent lessons. Hand-to-hand combat first, then we'll move on to practicing with your weapons of choice. Your objective is to get your partner pinned more than three times. Fail to do so and you'll be running until you're throwing your guts up, is that clear?"

It was almost disturbing how much I enjoyed watching these women's eyes widen, dread seeping through them at not meeting today's goal. The women had been through hell and back, yet the thought of having to run for continuous hours made them go pale.

My eyes drifted over to Haven who stood emotionless yet again. Our eyes met and she didn't even flinch. Not even her usual snarky looks or eye rolls were present.

I hated it.

Clapping my hands together, I yelled for them to get to work as I started to make my rounds. My stomach ached with a dreading pain as I tried to remain unphased by the wound that was clearly working against me. I knew I needed to be in bed, letting this thing heal… but with the threats so prevalent, I couldn't bear the thought of not getting these women into shape for what was to come.

To me, it felt like a war was on its way.

I walked by a pair of MOTs, seeing one struggle to keep her partner pinned. My leg struck out, hitting her weak spot (that was a leg not properly planted) and she toppled to the ground. "You're not keeping her pinned because you're not grounding yourself right. Fix that," I mumbled, continuing past them.

Another painful ache passed through me, causing me to inhale a deep breath. My fingers itched to rub the spot in hopes to soothe it, but I clenched my fists, letting them remain behind my back.

"Why are you doing this?" a deep voice growled out from behind me.

I turned my head, seeing Axton waltzing up. "Doing what?"

"For fuck's sake. Standing! Walking around! You need to be in bed, Everette. You're never going to heal at this rate." He lowered his voice as he neared me. "Do you not remember that I found you nearly dead in an alleyway? I was okay with you coming here to see everyone, but I expected you to at least take another week off to rest."

I clenched my jaw, looking past him. "I have a duty here that I swore weeks ago. I plan to uphold that. Stop bitching or get out of my gym."

Axton let out a sound between a sigh and a growl. "You're going to get yourself killed."

"I've survived worse than this, Axton," I lied, "I'll be fine."

"Why keep this up? What did you swear that has you putting yourself in danger? Even I wouldn't do something so stupid."

I cut my eyes to him, a protective feeling washing over me as I stepped closer to him, my six-foot-three figure towering his six-foot figure slightly. "I swore to keep Haven McKinley alive. I looked her parents dead in the eyes and swore my allegiance to her and the women here. I *always* keep my promises."

His features softened slightly. "She wouldn't want you doing this."

"You're her cousin, Axton! Do you not feel the same?"

"Don't throw family bullshit at me. Of course I care to protect her, it's why I'm here and not on my fucking jet ready to complete another hit, but you can't protect her if you're dead. You'd be smart to remember that," Axton growled out, turning to walk away but halted, throwing a look back at me. "If you bring any harm to her because of stupid decisions… that wound won't be what kills you. I will. She's already been through too much."

With that, Axton marched off, causing Haven to look over at us with curious eyes. She raised a brow at me, her eyes glancing to Axton's pissed-off figure, and then back to me. I shook my head, mouthing for her to drop it.

When Haven put her attention back on Sam, I let out a breath of relief and turned to face the pair next to me. It was Anastasia and a woman I didn't know the name of. I'll admit, Anastasia was one damn good fighter, and I had a feeling her partner wasn't going to get her pinned anytime soon.

When Anastasia caught me looking, she smirked, kicking her opponent aside. "Like what you see?"

I arched a brow. "Is there something that's supposed to interest me?" My eyes skimmed her over. "Because… not really."

I had to hold back my own snicker as I heard a gasp leave her just as the women around her broke out into a fit of laughter. Her cheeks were quick to heat as I kept her stare, allowing her partner just enough time to sneak up from behind. She swooped in with a quick maneuver to take her out from behind, pinning her within seconds.

I sighed mockingly. "Rule number one, Anastasia, never let your eyes leave your opponent."

Grinning, I moved on to the next pair, which happened to be Haven and Sam. It was clear Haven was holding back and I wanted to roll my eyes as Sam easily pinned her. Gripping Haven's upper arm, I hauled her up. "Going easy on her won't teach her anything."

Sam huffed. "I knew it! Come on, Haven, I'm not some kid anymore."

Haven feigned innocence. "I am not! She won fair and square. The small thing has a mean right hook." I gave her a stern look in response and Haven rolled her eyes, getting into the stance that I taught her months ago. "Fine. Don't be upset when I don't hold back, though."

Instead of Sam's eyes widening with fear, they lit up with excitement. My head tilted slightly as I took in the redhead. A few more sparring sessions and she would be a dangerous little thing. I can tell just by how quick she was on her feet—quicker than Haven even.

"Everette!"

I looked over, seeing Saul walking in with Reese and a few others. He held up a file, his expression serious. "We need to talk."

Haven glanced over at me, her brows furrowed. "I'm coming with you all."

"You need to train."

"No, I need answers and he's holding them."

She didn't leave any time for me to rebuttal as she darted towards Saul. Looking up at the ceiling, I cursed whoever put me in this situation. Why do I have to deal with all this shit?

"Get with another partner, she'll be back in a few," I grumbled to Sam, following after Haven.

Once I caught up with their marching figures, I noticed some of the other Men in Red members bringing in boxes full of files and other things. "Did you get all of it?" I asked Saul.

"Yeah, we think so. I have some of our men doing one last round, but I don't like just leaving that place for someone to come waltz in and look around. There are too many unexplainable things."

"The commander had created some lie that made people look the other way," Haven blurted. "I'm sure it will be fine. She knew people would ask questions about why so many girls were in that manor, so she lied accordingly. Apparently, she's good at that."

"For everyone's sake… I sure hope so. We cleaned out her office and the bringers' rooms. Then we tried our best to take anything else that would seem off to someone. But these files I'm holding… you're not going to like them."

I could see the uneasy feeling Haven had as she looked to the ground. Again, that urge to comfort her ripped through me and I had to clench my fists to stop from reaching out to touch her.

This had to stop.

"Let's get to Clarrissa's office before we start talking," I replied, an uneasy feeling sinking deep within my gut.

CHAPTER NINE

Haven

Once we reached my mother's office, I stared at the open door in confusion. Pushing past the men walking in front of me, I walked into her office only to find Axton sitting on the edge of her desk, reading a file.

"What are you doing in here?"

It was hard after everything to trust someone I barely knew. I learned the hard way that not everyone was who they seemed and I had no reason to trust him yet. He may have saved my friends, but who knows if that is a part of some bigger plan.

Axton's eyes didn't leave the file as he flipped another paper over. "Reading."

I scoffed. "Clearly."

Finally, he looked up. "Don't trust me?"

I folded my arms. "You may be my cousin, but we don't know anything about you other than that my father liked you. I won't trust someone so easily again. You of all people should understand that."

He snapped the file shut, a small smile on his face as he crossed his ankles and folded his arms as well. "Good. I would expect nothing less. If I would have met you sooner, I would have told you to not trust a soul around you. *I don't.* It's why I typically work alone."

"Yet you trusted my father."

"Sometimes," he nodded, "but we all have our motives for things in life. You can never be so certain about people. It is why I hid when I first went to meet Everette and Saul. Your father told me I could trust them because he did, yet I was still cautious. Better to be cautious than betrayed." He pushed off the desk and held the file out to me.

Curiously, I walked over and took it. "This is everything your parents had on Ghost. They knew about the women he was buying from your commander."

"How come I didn't see this? I went through all the files here."

"Because your father gave it to me as a hit. I came up here to snoop, not going to lie about it. It was odd to me that your parents knew so much but also so little. I figured he was keeping something from me, but apparently not. They did, however, know about the women… I just can't figure out how."

"You were tasked with killing Ghost?" Everette asked, walking up beside me.

Axton nodded. "The first hit I was never able to complete. I couldn't find him and I can find *anyone*. He's good. Better than me, even. The day he showed up with the commander was the first time I ever saw what he looked like and even then I didn't know who he was until Haven told me yesterday. Now that I know what he looks like, that may give me an advantage, but I'm not certain."

"So my parents wanted you to kill him so they could get back the women the commander sold off?"

"That's what they told me, but I feel there is something bigger behind it. Your father wasn't one for violence. That's why he told the women of the real MOTs to try and get their targets to come forward instead of killing them. It worked and the real MOTs never killed again unless absolutely needed. For your father to ask me to go after this dangerous man, I knew it was serious."

I looked through the file feeling just as confused as Axton. "Do you think it involved me? I mean, why would Ghost show up with her the night she stopped Knox and tried to get to me? And the night we were supposed to meet you?"

By the look on Axton's face, I knew what I said was right. He glanced at Everette before saying, "Unfortunately, I think there is something Ghost wants from you. You're the last Holden aside from your father. The last *female* Holden. I've left some books on the desk for you to read that I found in here. They don't look like much on the outside, so you may have missed them, but they are what your father first showed me when he taught me about The Messengers of Truth. I think you really need to read up on this so-called 'curse' if you haven't already."

I peered around him to find two stacks full of books. Once my eyes landed on them, I gasped at the hard throb of my scar, and my hand immediately found it. Everette lurched forward, gently grabbing my arm. "What's wrong?"

"The curse agrees," I gritted out. "It was either warning me to not read them or warning me for what I'm about to learn."

Axton sighed. "It's a lot."

"Before we go down that rabbit hole, this needs to be addressed as well," Saul finally spoke up, shaking his own file.

Nearly forgetting the important news he had, I quickly urged him forward. We all gathered around him as he opened it, showing a file full of photos and papers. "From what I can tell, this contains all the girls she sold. It's a lot. Thirty, I believe. Looks like she sold them in groups, so there are three groups. Ten girls in each. And the worst part? The groups are in different parts of the globe. If we go after them…" Saul trailed off.

"We'd have to travel the country," I mumbled. "And deal with the fact that we still have missions. We can't just up and leave—not all of us. Plus, to cover that much ground…"

Everette's eyes closed in defeat. "We'd have to split up and hope that no more informers come, or they'll have to wait until this is complete."

Saul looked as if a lightbulb went off inside his head. "Or… only six of us go. Two to each location. The three groups are at three different locations, right? Jay, Nikita, and Haven go with one of us to each one. We need them so they can spot the scars, so we can't just go alone. It would be too hard to figure out who does and doesn't have the scar to prove MOT authenticity. Those pictures could have been taken years ago. Who really knows what these women look like now? Ghost is too smart to not try and change their appearance a bit."

Everette nodded. "He's got a point."

"And the women here?" I was quick to ask.

"Well, the other Men in Red will be here, along with Reese who will be here to lead them. They will be protected and they will be there for the women when they go on missions. Plus, we have to have ties here anyway. We aren't just an organization that sits around with the MOTs. We have our own organization to deal with and one that has its own problems," Everette replied.

I nearly forgot that the MIRs truly weren't just here to protect and train us, and I tend to forget they have their own missions and goals for what they believe in—something Beverly once mentioned to me, and yet I still have no idea what really goes on with the MIRs when they're not around us.

"Are you sure you're fit to travel and go through such a thing?" Axton was quick to fire at Everette with angry eyes.

"Stop worrying about me. I'm fine and I am a grown-ass man. So stop fucking bringing it up."

I nervously looked Everette over, noticing how pale he truly was looking lately. I don't know if he's in any shape to be going with us. "Everette, maybe you should stay back he—"

"Absolutely not! I'll be damned if you go out there and I'm not with you all."

"But what if you get hurt? We can't risk that!" I shouted back.

"My God," he groaned, ripping open his cloak and pulling his black shirt up. "See? It's getting better. It's fine. I'm fine."

My hand covered my mouth in shock. The number of stitches Everette had was unbelievable. I walked closer, getting a better look at it before I tilted my head up to stare at him. "Everette… this looks terrible."

"Because it *is* a terrible wound. But one that is now healing just fine." He pulled down his shirt, his eyes not leaving mine. "Please, just believe me," Everette mumbled, and I don't know if it was the gentleness in his voice or the guilt that wracked my body, but I nodded numbly as I took a step back—feeling as if I couldn't properly breathe with his close proximity.

"Fine, but don't call me to come to have someone stitch you back up." Axton rolled his eyes.

I couldn't help but notice how much this truly bothered him. I understand he was responsible for keeping them alive and he doesn't want that effort to be a waste, but there was some other reason he was so keen on being stern with Everette.

"So, who is going with who?" Saul asked, changing the subject before I had the chance to speak up and call Axton out about it.

"I'm with Everette," I was quick to state.

Everette looked a bit shocked by my sudden comment, but he was quick to cover it up. "That was a fast decision."

"Yeah, well, if you're going hurt like this… I'm not letting you leave my sight. I already feel responsible enough."

"Would you stop that?" he asked, agitated. "None of this is your fault."

"Enough. This blame game won't be won," Saul chided. "I'll go with Nikita because..." He cut his eyes to Axton. "Because Jay scares me a bit. Have fun with that one."

Despite how serious our conversation had just been, a laugh bubbled out of me. "Jay scares you?"

Saul shot me a defensive look. "She's crazy, Haven."

Axton groaned. "God, please no... is that the tall blonde one?"

I grinned, nodding. "That's the one."

"Shit," he muttered. "She *is* crazy. I tried to stop her from talking to you last night and she threatened to castrate me."

"See!" Saul threw his hands up. "I am *not* dealing with her."

"Okay, okay." Everette threw his hands up. "Then it's settled. Now we just need to get them in on the plan and decide when we leave. We also need to figure out the other parts... like how we're going to get these women back here should we find them. We also need to make a deadline and choose when we're all meeting back up. There are other things we need to think about as well, like looking for signs of Haven's parents while we're out on these missions."

I nodded my head in agreement. "The sooner we get this figured out, the sooner we can get this over with and be on our way."

"How are we going to get out of the country with our weapons? I've never flown before, surprisingly," Saul states.

"I'll take care of it." Axton waved him off. "I fly private all the time for this reason."

"Rich hitmen and their money," Saul grumbled, earning a glare from Axton whom Saul winked at in response.

I glanced back over at the books Axton laid out, and my scar throbbed once more. Something in those books was going to be life-altering for me.

I just knew it.

Tearing my attention away from them, I clapped my hands together. "Okay. Let's do this."

"I'll go get Nikita and Jay," Saul said, leaving the room.

Axton sighed. "If you would have told me I would be running around the globe with MOTs a few weeks ago, I would have laughed in your face."

I chewed my lower lip at the thought of Jay being alone with Axton. I knew she was one tough woman and could take care of herself, but I still wasn't fond of the idea of just openly trusting Axton.

What if he betrays us?

"What made you come back then?" Everette asked, folding his arms.

Axton shrugged. "Haven's father called me out of the blue—said I needed to get here and we'd meet up. He had information for me. My guess? He wanted to put all our heads together to see if we can find a way to stop this shit. Then the commander caught wind and everything went to hell."

"You could have run…" I mumbled.

Axton glanced at me, a stern look on his face. "I could have, but I'm no coward. No one, and I mean *no one*, fucks with my family. I may not be around a lot, but I was here when your father started all of this. I helped when I could, but I also had my own jobs to do. Your father was the parent I never had. If the commander took out The Men in Red so easily, I worried what would have happened to you. So I stuck around and I'm glad I did."

His words were somewhat comforting. He seemed to be telling the truth, but my gut feelings got me into trouble in the past, so I wasn't sure if they were something I really needed to be listening to.

"When was your last mission?" Axton asked after I didn't respond.

"Couldn't tell you. I haven't had an informer in a long time."

His brows furrowed. "Odd."

"None at all?" Everette frowned.

"Not one single soul has reached out to me. After I… killed those men in the warehouse… even my scar barely acted up. I thought I had lost the curse altogether."

Axton looked in thought for a moment. "Or maybe it knows what's to come. Maybe it's not letting souls connect with you. The curse connects you MOTs with the dead, explained further in the books I pulled out, but it has the ability to block that bond as well. Maybe it knows you were at a weak point and you needed to gather your strength back."

"An interesting thought…" Everette replied, rubbing a hand over his face.

"Axton, I—" I stopped talking for a brief second, the name bringing back memories I didn't need resurfacing right now. "First, I'm not calling you Axton anymore. I just can't… It's weird. Second, I need you to understand that I feel you have good intentions, but I can't just openly trust everything you say."

He let out a small laugh. "I understand both things. I'm not asking you to openly trust me, but at least let me prove to you that I do consider you family and I am here to help. If you don't trust me after a few weeks of us all working together, I can be on my way."

I glanced over at Everette, who gave me a small nod.

Closing my eyes in defeat, I nodded. "Fine. But if you give me even the slightest vibe that I can't trust you… you're gone."

"Deal. Now, what the hell are you going to address me by if you can't say my name?"

Everette laughed at this, cocking his head to the side as he waited to see what spewed from my mouth.

After a minute, I say, "A.R? Simple initials. Kind of sounds badass."

Axton let out a deep laugh. "Fine, McKinley. That'll do."

I didn't reply as Saul walked in with Nikita and Jay hot on his heels. At the look of Nikita, guilt punched me in the gut. She looked almost as bad as I did.

"You needed us?" Jay asked, glancing around the room curiously.

I braced my hands on my hips. "We have a plan—a plan to start the take down of Ghost."

Jay quickly took a step forward. "What do we need to do?"

CHAPTER TEN

Everette

Jay and Nikita took the news surprisingly well. After Jay threw some harsh comments towards Axton—A.R now, apparently—she agreed to go with him for 'the wellbeing of the world'.

If there was one person that could keep A.R in place, it was most definitely Jay.

Now I sat on the edge of Haven's mother's desk as Haven skimmed through the books A.R. left for her. They were old, the edges cut and nicked in certain spots, and the pages were browning. But from the look on Haven's face, I knew that this was something that needed to be done.

"Do you want some privacy?" I asked, a small part of me hoping she denied it.

"No, it's fine. Besides, I need someone else to learn this crap with me. If something happens to me, someone else needs to know."

I rolled my eyes. "Nothing is going to happen to you."

"You don't know that," she mumbled, flipping over another page. Eventually, she tossed the book aside.

"Nothing?" I asked.

"Nothing new, at least. That one was just about the upbringing, which I already know. Katerina Holden started it with Bethany Holden, yada yada yada…"

She picked up another one, clenching the book as she winced. I leaned forward as my curiosity peaked. "Did your scar throb?"

"Yeah," she winced again. "It's throbbing repeatedly."

Running her hands over the book's cover, she gulped. I scooted closer, taking a look for myself. "*The Wrath of The Messengers of Truth.*"

"Promising title, hm?" Haven mused. "Should I read it now? I mean, after that talk today… we need to start preparing for everything. A.R is already heading to get our flights arranged."

"That's up to you. You can read it on the way there? Maybe keep it fresh in your mind?"

She gently sat the book down. "I think that's a good idea." She looked over at me. "Are you ready to head to Mexico?"

After our talk with Jay and Nikita, we discussed where the pairs would go. Haven and I agreed to head to Mexico. Saul and Nikita are going all the way to London, and Jay and A.R are headed to Russia. Apparently, A.R has contacts in Russia, which put Haven on guard even more.

Was I ready? Not really. My wound ached each time I moved and I didn't want to leave everyone behind. I knew Reese could handle the MOTs and the MIRs, but just realizing what they went through without Saul and me here made me more nervous than I would like to admit.

But we had those innocent women counting on us. We didn't know what we would find once we adventured out to find them, but we owe it to them to at least try and save them if they were never able to get out.

"I'm not ready to be stuck in one place with you and no one else to talk to, but I think I'll manage."

Haven scoffed. "I hate you."

"Do you really, though?" I teased.

It was small, but I saw the corner of her lips tug up. For some reason, I wanted nothing more than to make this woman come alive again. I didn't know how to do that or where to start… but it's my new mission.

After she ignored my comment, continuing to look over the books, I asked, "What are you going to do? If you find Ghost?"

Haven paused, a frightening look covering her face. "Isn't it clear? After I take everything from him, just as he did to me, I will shove my dagger through him over and over again. Just as he watched the commander do. Then, I'm going to slit his throat." With that, she pushed the books aside and stood. "I have some things I need to do. I'll see you later."

I sat in my place stunned, watching Haven march out of the room with purpose in her step. With that look in her eyes, I knew exactly what was coursing through her.

Rage.

Horrible rage.

What exactly was she going to do?

I glanced out the window to my right, seeing the sun starting to set. We spent most of the day planning and organizing our trips and I barely realized that night would soon be upon us.

Night—the time of day when Haven likes to sneak off into to release her anger.

Jumping up from my seat, I sped after her.

I was darting through the halls as I looked for her. I went down staircases, to her room, and back downstairs.

She had already vanished.

"Where are you going?" Saul asked as I walked into the foyer of the school, walking bristly towards a hall that led to a room that held all our weapons.

"Haven's gone."

He gave me a confused look while matching my pace. "What do you mean?"

"I mean I said the wrong thing and got her mind working in a different direction than I would have liked it to. She walked out of the office pissed off."

Saul grimaced. "What did you say?"

"I asked her what she planned to do with Ghost. Short answer? She isn't going to let him take another breath. Not that I'm surprised, but I didn't think she'd march out of there with a hunger to sedate just by mentioning him."

I opened the door to the room that contained my swords. Without waiting for Saul to reply, I snatched them up and began to put my holster on.

"Wait a damn minute. You can't go after her, you need to rest. If you plan on going with us on these trips, you have to get better, Everette!"

I growled. "If one more damn person tells me that, I'm going to lose it. Haven isn't in the right mindset, and I caused this, so I need to fix it. Get out of my way."

Saul folded his arms. "No, I'll go. You need to stay here."

"Move, dammit! You're wasting my time!"

He let out a frustrated sound and moved around me to grab his own swords and holster. "Well, you're not going alone. Come on, we'll check the cameras and then head out."

"Is there still a tracker in her sword's hilt?" I mumbled, panic seeping through me at the thought of Haven getting herself into more trouble.

The swords we gave her weeks ago were a gift, but also a precaution. Since Haven wasn't using the dagger I gave her much anymore, I'm glad I was brave enough to put a new tracker in both her swords' hilts. Then… she was a pawn for me—someone that could help me end a problem, but that changed.

It changed so damn quickly.

"Yeah, and if she finds out what you did, she's never going to forgive you for it," he snapped, adjusting his straps, and then motioned to the door. "At least it came in handy this one time."

Refraining from rolling my eyes, I left the room. Just as Saul and I went down the hall, I wanted to curse as Nikita and Jay rounded the corner with A.R following after them.

"Where are you going?" Nikita asked, stopping in her tracks as she took in our appearance and tense bodies.

"After Haven. She left without anyone and we fear she's going to do something stupid."

A.R frowned. "Do we know where?"

"No, but we… have a guess." I lied, catching Jay's eyes who knew I was spitting bullshit.

"We're going with," Nikita stated and Jay nodded her head in agreement.

"That isn't necessary," said Saul.

Nikita scoffed. "Yes it is. Haven's… going through a lot. I know you may think I'm upset with her, but I'm not. I lost someone I cared about, too, and I know what that does to you. I can't lose someone else I care about, so please just let us come with you. Who knows what she's about to get herself into."

Sighing, I waved them off. "Whatever. Just hurry up. We don't have much time, she's already got a head start."

"I'm coming, too," A.R said, a frown on his face. "I'll be damned if she gets hurt again. Meet you all out front in five." With that, he sauntered off.

Jay and Nikita scurried off after him and I turned to Saul. "Pull her tracker up. Let's get this over with."

I walked outside as I waited for them and my skin itched with the need to get moving. I hated sitting around and waiting.

God knows where she's at now.

It was odd how quickly I grew fond of Haven. At first, she was the bane of my existence—like a gnat nagging at me that I wanted to swat away. Her attitude and personality didn't help with that, but soon she grew on me. I started to understand why everyone smiled when she did and why they laughed when her own laughter flooded the room.

She felt like a forbidden fruit to me—one that I wanted to take a bite out of so desperately but knew I couldn't.

And oh, how that eats at me.

"We're ready," a voice called out, snapping me from my trance.

Looking over my shoulder, I saw the group exiting the house. I now see why many people feared A.R. He was wearing a leather jacket and leather gloves as he twisted on a silencer to the end of his gun.

He looked the part of a notorious hitman, that's for sure.

A.R tucked his handgun away, nodding to me. "Let's do this. Where are we going?"

"A warehouse not too far from here," Saul said. "We believe that's where she is."

Well, her tracker does.

"Do we know what to expect?" Jay asked, pulling her hood up.

I shook my head. "No, and that's what worries me the most. I believe she ran off to let out some of her anger, but I don't trust her out alone with all that has been happening. It's too dangerous."

Nikita pulled her hood up as well, a determined look crossing her face. "Into the night we go."

I couldn't help but crack a small grin as I looked at A.R. "Can you keep up, hitman?"

He gave me a mocking smile. "I run across rooftops for a living. You know… hitman and all. I think I'll be fine."

With that, we escaped into the shadows.

We scaled building after building, darting across rooftops. We were like thieves in the night, not waiting for even a second to prevent anyone from seeing us. We didn't stop. We didn't slow.

Not until we dropped back onto the ground, breathing harshly as we stared up at a huge building before us.

It was eerily silent.

"What's the plan?" Nikita whispered, unsheathing her dagger as did Jay.

I raised my hand, grabbing my sword's hilt. "We get in and don't leave until we have Haven. Anyone you see is a threat. Understood?"

The group nodded as A.R pulled out his gun, cocking it. Giving me a small nod, he started moving forward towards a back door.

Saul put his hand on the door's handle, making a motion with his hand to A.R who understood immediately what he meant. A.R raised his gun, wiggling his fingers before tightening his hold on it and moving one finger to the trigger. In a flash, Saul threw open the door and A.R darted through.

There was a slight whistling sound as my sword cut through the air from unsheathing it, darting after A.R.

The group followed shortly after and we all separated, cautiously doing our rounds as we moved about the place. My eyes darted every which way for some sign that Haven was near, but I found nothing.

Where the hell was she? And what was she doing in this rundown place?

A man's battle cry grabbed my attention and my body expertly swung around, my sword slashing across his abdomen. The man let out a choked sound as another whistling sound cut the air, my sword slicing right across his neck.

His own weapon clattered against the ground as he dropped to his knees, eyes wide.

Sighing, I brought my leg up and kicked his chest.

Turning, I saw none of the others, but also no other men, which meant that whoever Haven was after… they were skilled enough to stay unseen.

Looking down at the man who was bleeding out before me, he wore a navy cloak.

One of Ghost's men.

Out of nowhere, a body flew out from a door to my right and slid across the ground. Jay burst out of the same room, her cloak catching wind as she darted to him, sliding to her knees and she raised her dagger to plunge it into the man's stomach.

Over and *over* again.

She looked up, blood splattered across her face as she caught the sight of me. Her jaw clenched, anger coursing through her as she rose to her feet. With one last final look, Jay gave me a sharp nod and darted back off into the darkness.

This was going to be a blood fest.

I gripped my sword tightly and started to make my way through another part of the warehouse. When I rounded a corner, I saw a cloaked figure dart out of another room just as I saw a dagger spinning through the air and embedding itself into the man's back. He groaned, falling to his knees with an ear-piercing scream.

Nikita came into view as she yanked her dagger out of his back before bringing it around to the front of his neck, sliding it across in one, smooth movement. I winced at the sight, noticing how she threw him to the side with ease, her body tense.

These women's rage was a force to be reckoned with.

The sound of swords clashing made my head snap to the side. Saul fought against two navy-cloaked men and the sight had me sprinting across the room. I slid to my knees, my sword slashing across the back of one of the men's legs.

He cried out, giving Saul an opening to plunge his sword through the man's chest. With one sharp movement, he yanked it out before flipping it in his hands and thrusting it out to the side behind him just as the other man ran up from behind.

The weapon met its target.

"Where the hell is she?!" Saul snapped, breathing harshly. I couldn't gather my words as my abdomen ached with each move I made. The pain was becoming almost too excruciating for me. "Everette! Move!" Saul yelled, but I didn't have time to lurch forward before I heard someone's heavy footsteps.

I turned just in time, eyes wide, to see a man about to thrust his sword through me. But just as his sword was a foot away, a woman's battle cry echoed throughout the warehouse.

Out of nowhere, a cloaked figure dropped from above us, and I knew that familiar sword as it came down through the air—it was like the world shifted into slow motion when the sword split right through the man's skull.

Haven let out a frustrated noise as she yanked her sword back and turned to us—she was covered head to toe in blood. "I'm right here, assholes."

CHAPTER ELEVEN

Haven

Nothing annoyed me more than these fools coming after me when all I wanted was a little alone time—well, time to slaughter the people responsible for taking my parents and killing Knox.

Sheathing my sword, I shot daggers at the two men before me. "What the hell are you doing here? And how did you find me?"

Everette sighed, looking like he was having an internal battle within himself. "I followed you."

Liar.

"And the answer to my first question?"

Saul threw his hands up. "Isn't it obvious? We were worried you were doing something reckless and, no surprise, we were right! Are you insane? Going after Ghost's men without any backup?"

"I didn't need any help. I can take care of myself," I countered, pushing past them just as Nikita and Jay walked up with A.R blocking my exit with folded arms.

I turned, looking back at Saul and Everette who held guilty expressions. I knew those fools didn't follow me. Glancing down at the ground, hurt coursed through me. They weren't following me… they were *tracking* me.

"Let me guess… the hilt of my sword?" I mumbled, cutting my eyes up to Everette.

"Yeah…"

Letting out a dry laugh, I pulled my swords out and tossed them at their feet. "Then I don't fucking want them. Some gift, huh?"

"Haven, don't do this. We were just worried about you."

My fists clenched. "Perhaps… but not back then when you gifted them to me. Am I always going to be some pawn to you, Everette? Someone you have to keep alive because I bring too many benefits to your life, so my death would be a hindrance in your plans?"

His face twisted with anger. "That's not true and you know that."

I took a step forward. "Do I?" In one quick movement, I kicked my sword up off the ground and snatched it up effortlessly as I placed the blade on his neck. I heard the girls gasp behind me, causing my grip to tighten. "How do I know that you haven't been a traitor this whole time? Hm? Because God knows I really have trusted the wrong fucking people."

Everette didn't even flinch. He acted as if there wasn't a deadly blade pressed to his throat as he said, "You're upset, I get it. But we both know you're not going to use that sword on me. We can talk about this back at the school, but this is the perfect reason why we are worried about you. The Haven we know would never do such a thing—especially to someone she considers a part of her *small little family*."

His last words were mocking—reminding me of the information I confided in him about just recently.

Tears brimming my eyes, I pulled the blade away. "You don't understand one damn thing about what I'm going through. The old Haven is long dead, she died in that warehouse with Knox. So get over yourself and stop trying to throw me a pity party, because I politely decline the invitation."

"Haven… please just let us help you," said Saul, a pleading tone to his voice.

I gritted my teeth. "I don't want your help! Stop worrying about me and place your worry somewhere else, like those women we have to help. I'm long past saving."

"We won't…" Nikita spoke up. "We care too much."

It was on the tip of my tongue to blurt out some insult, one that would make her feign back in horror and hate me even more, but for some reason… I couldn't do that to her. "Just stop."

"Haven, please…" Jay trailed off and I gripped my sword even tighter.

"I said to stop!"

Everette's voice swarmed me as he gently said, "Just come back with us where it's safe and—"

"I said to fucking stop talking!" I yelled, spinning with my sword in hand towards him. His eyes widened as I spun, the sword swinging right towards his figure.

He jumped back, horror in his eyes just as I felt something prick my neck. I froze, my sword mid-air as I staggered a bit. The sound of my sword clattering against the ground was the last thing I heard as my hand found its way to my neck and yanked out a small dart.

"I'm sorry, dear cousin," A.R mumbled, catching me as I fell.

***

My head was pounding when I woke up. I groaned, rolling over on my side as I took in my room at the school. Memories flooded through my mind the minute the fogginess left, making my eyes widen.

A.R tranquilized me! That *bastard.*

I flew up, going to throw the covers off me but halted when I saw Everette sitting in my desk chair.

"And she finally wakes."

The look on his face made my palms start to sweat. "What are you doing in here?"

"Making sure you decide not to try and kill anyone else here."

I scoffed, pushing the covers off me. "I'm not going to kill anyone."

He cocked his head to the side, leaning forward to rest his forearms on his thighs. "You came at me with your sword, Haven. You were inches away from slicing up my abdomen."

Rolling my eyes, I moved to sit on the edge of the bed. "No I wasn't. You're being dramatic."

"Dramatic…?" he snarled. "You do realize if you even *nicked* my skin, it would have been fatal for me! Opening these stitches on my stomach again would have been it for me."

I cast my eyes down, guilt washing over me. "I wouldn't have hurt you," I mumbled. "I promise."

"No, you don't know that. Haven, that look in your eyes as you turned… I have never seen that from you before. Not directed towards me at least. A.R seems to know more than we do and said you really need to read those books he gave you. Something about your rage and the curse… it's starting to take over. And you need to get it under control before you hurt someone you care about."

I cocked a brow. "And I care about you?"

Hurt flashed across his face. "You'd truly sit there and say that? Acting as if you didn't slaughter a man that came at me just hours ago? You know what… maybe we should go back to despising each other. At least then I could keep you at arm's length. God knows that's what you're best at."

He stood abruptly, my mouth falling open in shock. "You're not some sunshine character either, you know!"

He looked back at me. "I never claimed to be one, but I do care about you. At this point, the worst mistake I have made is trying to understand you! You don't give a damn about anyone that's trying to help. You don't care about what happens to others in the wake of terror you're trying to bring upon Ghost's men. At this rate, I think you're looking for a way to get yourself killed—or any of us killed."

I stood up, marching over to him. Jabbing my finger into his chest, I said, "I never asked for you to come after me. If you wouldn't have been tracking me like some love-sick puppy, you wouldn't have been in any danger. I don't need you!"

Realizing what I just said, I froze. I opened my mouth to take it all back, the look on his face causing my heart to clench in all the wrong ways, but he shoved me away from him.

Pursing his lips, Everette nodded. "I'll remember that. Honestly, Haven? Go fuck yourself. Because I am *done.*"

I jolted forward. "Wait!"

Everette stopped his march towards my bedroom door once more. Sighing, he looked back at me. "What more could you possibly have to say?"

"I was looking for his body," I blurted. "Knox. I went after those men because… I just want to lay him to rest properly. That is why I have been going after them."

Everette averted his eyes. "If you would have told me that yesterday, we would have all gone with you to help. Now? I don't really care. Tonight, you showed us how you really care… *That* you can't take back. I'm sorry for your loss, Haven, I truly am. But it's been weeks and we have bigger problems to worry about now. Get your head back in the game. Start packing, because we're briefing the MOTs and MIRs tonight and then we're leaving."

And then he was gone.

I fisted my hair, starting to pace my room. Stupid, stupid, stupid!

I kicked a nearby trash can, watching it go flying as tears brimmed my eyes.

"Fuck," I whispered.

What is happening to me?

CHAPTER TWELVE

Everette

I was losing my mind. I was sure of it. I never meant to explode at Haven the way I did, but that woman just had ways of getting under my skin that I never imagined. The mouth she had on her… it made me clench my fists and bite my tongue from doing something I would regret. But most of all? Her words were sharp and deadly. Never have I cared what a woman thought about me, but hearing her say she couldn't give a damn about me… that stung.

No. It fucking wrecked me.

Because I've seen the way she looked at me prior to Knox's death. I remember the night in the manor when I gave her dagger back. I relished the way her body reacted to my touch—the way she leaned in wanting me to do more but knew I wouldn't. Then, I had a small infatuation with her. Now? It was so much worse.

I was going to lose my mind.

Perhaps it's already gone.

I shoved some clothes into a bag, trying to get my mind off the woman down the hall. I didn't know what to think. A.R said to think nothing of it, which made me wonder what exactly he knew from those books he gave her. At this rate, I hoped it gave us something about why Haven changed so much lately. I understand Knox's death took a toll on her, but there was something else playing into her rage.

I just knew it.

She didn't even act this upset about her parents being gone, which is what made me worry even more. Something about that night—watching Knox die—shifted something in her. Was it because she killed outside of her curse? Was that it? Or was it something entirely different?

A knock sounded on my door before it opened, revealing Saul. "You good?" I nodded, sticking some more clothes into my bag. "You don't look good."

"Thanks," I muttered. "I feel marvelous."

Saul blew out a puff of air, closing the door behind him. "We're going to get her back."

Letting out a humorless laugh, I zipped my bag up. "I don't care at this point."

"That is such bullshit and you know it."

Yeah, it was. But I hated knowing that everyone around me was seeing just how much Haven affected me. It was screwing with my head, and the part I hated most was that I felt so… hopeless.

Defeated.

"She's too far gone, Saul. We just need to get these missions over with and be on our way."

"You truly believe that?" Saul walked over, snatching the bag away from me and tossing it on the ground. "Look at me."

Sighing, I gave him my attention. "I don't know what I believe, but just trying to talk to her moments ago went to utter shit. She is too far fixed on ending all those men and it makes me wonder how she is going to be on the missions to save those women. She quite literally said she doesn't give a damn about me, so why should I keep trying?"

His features softened. "Because you care about her. Deeply."

"Does it matter anymore? She was ready to kill me today."

"She didn't mean to snap. We pretty much ganged up on her to hold some shitty intervention after she just slaughtered the men responsible for killing someone she could have possibly loved. There is something wrong with her, that much we know, but if we give up on her… who else does she have? She clearly doesn't care what happens to herself."

I turned my back to him so he didn't see the tortured look on my face. It was like I was being pulled every which way and I had no idea which direction to take. Give up? Keep fighting?

"Let's put it this way… would you be okay finding her dead one day? Hm? Because you gave up on trying to save her from herself?"

I flinched. "Of course not."

"So there's your answer. We're not stopping until we see the old Haven again."

I sat on my bed feeling completely drained. "I don't know if I can survive this trip with her. Literally, what if she tries to kill me again?"

Saul snickered. "Don't piss her off then."

I stared at him agape. "That's hard to do when everything she says literally makes me want to…" I trailed off, catching myself before I said something stupid.

Saul belted out a laugh. "Man, when was the last time you got laid?"

"Shut up. That is not what this is about. She just pisses me off. I can't deal with it."

He reined in his laughter, taking a seat next to me. "You're pining after her."

"I am not."

"You are. You have been ever since she found out the truth about the commander and you two grew somewhat closer. Everyone can tell. You're always standing up for her, you go easy on her, and you're always staring. *Always* staring," he mused.

I groaned, rubbing my hands over my face. "What do you do when the person you ache for doesn't want you? What do you do when you know you'll never be able to be with her? I'll… I'll never be *him*."

Saul frowned. "Knox?"

I nodded. "I feel like an asshole for even thinking differently about her knowing how much she cared for him."

He gave my shoulder a squeeze. "I'm not sure, but I don't think that's the case. She just needs time to move on. You, of all people, should understand that."

I winced, the comment bringing up memories I would rather keep buried. "I also don't want to be some rebound for her."

"Look, man, I saw the way she used to look at you before Knox died. There is something there, so don't try and compare yourself to him because you'll never come out on top. It's the hard truth, but it's the brutal truth. Let's say you get the chance to be with her… if you keep thinking she's comparing you to him or vice versa, you'll be miserable and second-guessing yourself at each turn."

I rubbed my eyes. "Should I give up on it then? Why make myself miserable? It could be years before she's ready to try anything with anyone. Who's to say she would even want me after all this crap?"

"That I can't tell you. You need to make that decision on your own. Everyone is different when it comes to these things. But I'm sure you'll make the right choice when the time comes." Saul stood, hiking his thumb towards the door. "I'm going downstairs. I came to tell you that everyone is gathering in the study area. We need to get this show on the road."

"Yeah. I'll be down in a few."

As I watched him retreat, I let out a deep sigh. I knew what I had to do if I wanted to get through these missions and get Haven back.

I had to let the idea of us together go and focus on the bigger picture. We have people to save.

***

The cold shoulder Haven was giving me as I walked into the study area had me gritting my teeth together. She didn't spare me one glance as I took a stance next to A.R and Saul and I wanted nothing more than to go to her, hating the way I spoke to her just moments ago, but I knew that I had to put my differences to the side for now.

"Everyone, listen up!" Saul called out, clapping his hands together to stop the hum of the low conversations.

Everyone grew silent, focusing their attention on us. Saul looked at me, cocking a brow as if he was silently asking if I wanted to start all this. Letting out a sigh, I took a step forward. "As you all know, these last few weeks have been tough. And it's all because of one man—Ghost—as we have come to know. We've lost people, family, and friends. Something that I wouldn't wish upon any of you and I am so sorry that this has happened."

I looked over at Haven, my chest tightening at how her shoulders slouched and how her eyes stared at a spot on the ground.

"But hopefully we have gotten some intel to get closer to stopping him. We found a list of women that have been sold off by your previous commander to Ghost. We plan to go after those women and see if we can save them but also hope that in our search we can find a way to find Ghost and stop him once and for all."

A light murmur broke out, the girls whispering to one another.

"We're not done!" Saul barked, shutting them up instantly.

"In doing so, we would never ask you women to participate in this knowing what he took from you all. So… A.R and Saul will be joining me along with Haven, Jay, and Nikita to go after these women. Reese will take over as the head man in charge of the MIRs and help you all to complete any missions you may have while we are gone."

Sam stood up suddenly, worry washing over her. "When will you all be back?"

I folded my arms, thinking the answer over. "Not sure. It may be a few weeks, but we will keep everyone updated while we are gone and we expect the same in return. You are in good hands, I swear it."

I didn't miss how Haven reached over, rubbing soothing circles across Sam's back who sat next to her. The small gesture gave me more hope than she'd know.

"When do you leave?" another MOT asked.

"Tonight. I know this is sudden, but we have to act fast with the information we have gathered," A.R replied.

"Is everyone okay with this?" Saul gently asked.

The MOTs and MIRs nodded as Reese stepped up, his hands behind his back before he said, "I will protect you all with my life, as will our men."

When he looked over at me, I gave him a nod of thanks.

"Well… then it's settled." I turned to A.R. "You ready?"

He pulled out his phone, clicking on a few things. "No, but your ride is."

CHAPTER THIRTEEN

Haven

Staring up at the huge jet made my skin crawl. This was the beginning of what I'm sure would be weeks of complete and utter chaos. We had no idea what we were doing or what we should expect once we got to our locations. It could go really well for us, or it could be a shit show.

Who knows.

"I have notified my contacts in Mexico that you are coming. They will provide you with everything you need, including picking you up once you land and taking you to one of my homes there where you should be safe. They will prep you on everything you need to know and how to keep a low profile. Trust no one but them. There is a code word I have written down on some notes on the jet that they will speak to you to know they are who you're looking for. *Don't forget it.* In the notes is the code to the house along with its address should you get lost. Got it?" A.R spoke, handing some things over to us.

I nodded, glancing over at Everette who remained silent.

I hated that I hurt him with my words. I was hoping that by getting him off my back, it would please me, but the cold shoulder and the way he looked before storming out of my room hurt more than expected.

"What did you tell them about us?" I asked.

A.R stuck his hands in his pockets. "Enough. They know you're friends of mine that need a place to stay low at. That's about it."

"Do these people know what you do?" Everette questioned.

He shook his head. "They know I work in some sketchy shit, but they're paid to not ask questions."

I gripped the strap that was on my shoulder. "When do the rest of you leave?"

A.R glanced at his watch. "Jay and I leave not long after you do. Saul and Nikita are last. You two better start getting on now. We need to stay on schedule."

"And what if we can't make the meet-up date?" Everette asked.

"We'll work it out. It's hard to say how each of these little missions we're going on will go, so I can't be sure that we'll make the date, but I'll send word in a few days to check in. For now, we need to keep contact to a minimum. We don't want Ghost catching any word that we're lingering close by."

I could see just how smart A.R truly was. After all, he was a notorious hitman that was always recluse. No one could ever find him unless he wanted to be found. I could practically see the wheels turning in his mind as he planned everything out for us.

"Keep Jay safe, okay?" I mumbled, dread seeping through me at the thought of one of my best friends getting hurt.

"I'll protect her with my life. You have my word."

"Besides, he's got nothing on me," Jay spoke, walking up to us with Nikita and Saul trailing behind her.

She was quick to pull me into a hug, mumbling a goodbye and to be safe. Nikita did the same shortly after and at the tight squeeze we gave one another, it was as if our hug spoke more words than we could manage.

Pulling back, I let out a deep sigh and nodding, looking over at Saul. "Keep her safe as well."

He grinned. "You know I will, little one."

"It's time," Everette said, motioning to the jet.

With one last glance and our final waves of goodbye, I followed after him. Everette was quiet as we entered the jet, causing me to try and look anywhere but at him.

It wasn't hard. This jet was so nice and expensive, it made me wonder how long A.R had been a hitman to afford something so nice and exclusive.

Eventually, Everette took a seat by a window to my right, tossing his bag into the seat next to him. He remained looking out the window, even as A.R's staff came to ask us if we needed anything.

Taking a seat opposite of Everette, I finally spoke up. "You know… we're going to have to talk on this trip."

He didn't look at me as he said, "I'm aware."

"Everette," I groaned, "Can you just let up with the cold shoulder act, please? I'm sorry, okay? I didn't mean to snap at you the way I did."

Slowly, he turned to look at me. "But you meant what you said."

I quickly shook my head no. "That's not true. I just… I had a lot happen and you were coming at me and that was just my response to try and piss you off."

"Well, you achieved that. Congratulations."

I let out a frustrated sound, grabbing my bag to pull out one of the books A.R gave me. I began to read a bit, but it lasted all of ten minutes before I slammed it shut, putting my attention back on Everette. "You know… you all didn't have to come at me the way you did. I mean for fuck's sake, A.R tranquilized me! How did you expect me to react after all that?"

He ignored me.

"Everette! Stop acting like you're five!"

"I'm not arguing with you. You want to fight again and I'm not doing it."

"I'm not trying to fight, I'm just trying to apologize, Everette, and you're acting like an asshole."

He narrowed his eyes at me. "Must I remind you that you tried to literally kill me?"

"Oh my God, you are *so* annoying. I wouldn't have actually hurt you." I grumbled, opening my book back up.

"You didn't see the look in your eyes, Haven. You weren't thinking."

I threw my book to the side, aggressively turning to fully face him. "Maybe I wasn't! Who knows, but I do know that how you all went about everything was a terrible move. I can handle myself just fine. You tracked me, followed me there, and then surrounded me like some criminal on the loose!"

He pointed a finger at me, and if he was near, it would have jabbed into my chest. "We were just trying to help you. You wouldn't let anyone in and we were worried about you."

"Again, you have no idea what I'm going through, so just stop trying to help me and just let me do my own thing!"

It was a screaming match now and any staff made themselves busy or left our part entirely.

Maybe they were hiding with the pilot—I knew I would be at the sight of us.

"If you would try and talk to me then maybe you would know that I know exactly what the fuck you're going through, Haven! I've been where you are. I know the hurt. I know that ache. I know how fucked your head gets when you lose someone you loved!"

I froze, my eyes widening slightly at the information he let slip out.

"What?" I nearly whispered.

He sighed, resituating himself in his seat. "I was married once. Happily, actually. She died right in front of me."

Fuck.

"Everette, I'm so sorry. I didn't—"

"Didn't know? Of course you didn't. Because you only think about yourself sometimes. You think that you're the only one to carry such burdens but you're not, Haven. Sorry to burst your bubble."

He went to look back out the window and if I didn't feel like a complete piece of shit, I did now.

"How did it happen?" I mumbled, tugging on a loose thread to my long-sleeved shirt.

He was silent for a minute, almost making me think he wasn't going to answer, but eventually, he spoke up. "Drunk driver hit us. I got her out, but it was too late before the paramedics got to us."

"Well… now I'm the asshole," I replied.

He let out a snort. "Kind of."

I looked out my own window, chewing on my bottom lip. "That's horrible. Truly, I am sorry to hear that. I wouldn't wish that upon my worst enemy."

Letting out a sigh, he finally turned to face me. "It's whatever. It happened a long time ago, but this is why I stress the importance of trying to talk to us. Saul? He was my rock. The one person that got me through all of it. Without him… I don't know if I would be here today."

I offered him a small smile. "Saul's a nice man."

He nodded. "One of the best. Do you understand what I'm saying now? Haven, our situations may not be exactly the same, but I know what it's like to watch someone you love leave this very earth right before your eyes—taken by someone who was careless and selfish."

I met his eyes. "You know… I don't know what I truly felt for Knox. I don't think I loved him, as weird as it sounds. We were… fresh. It was new, but I cared for him so damn much in the small amount of time we had together. It wrecked me to know that he let himself be killed because he didn't want to betray me again. God, I wish the man would have handed me over because this pain I feel? It fucking hurts."

Everette's eyes softened. "You blame yourself for his death?"

I gave him a small nod. "Every time I open my eyes, all I see is his bloodied form right there in front of me. I just stood there and watched. It was like I couldn't move. I was paralyzed with what I was seeing—what the commander had truly done. And then it hit me and this rage—this *anger*—that I've never felt before just warped through my body. It was almost as if I blacked out, but I still remember the screams and the blood that coated my body. Then I was standing in a room full of corpses."

"You can't blame yourself for what happened. I used to do the same with my wife. I kept saying that maybe if I hadn't suggested we went out to dinner and if we would have just stayed in, that none of it would have happened… that she would still be here. But Saul helped me see that I couldn't live like that. You can't either. Knox would not want you beating yourself up over this."

Hearing those words was true. I couldn't help but think about the video I watched recently that Knox left me and said nearly those exact same words. But how can I not blame myself? If it wasn't for him getting wrapped up in the shit show that was my life… he'd still be walking this earth. Instead, he's God knows where.

Ignoring his words, I looked back out my window at the scenery. "Can you promise me something?"

"Of course."

"When we get done with all this… will you help me look for the answers I need to find his body? I just need to know what they did with him. I just… I just need…"

"Closure?" Everette completed for me.

"Yeah… I need closure."

He moved, taking the empty seat next to me and gently grabbed my hand, giving it a small squeeze. "I promise you that we will figure it out, okay?"

I wanted to curse myself at the tears that stung my eyes. "Thank you," I whispered as I cast my eyes down.

"Now that our arguing is over," Everette mused, "let's pick up these books and get to reading, yeah? We have some hours ahead of us."

I took the book he handed me and flipped it open. "Hopefully this will give me some answers to all the questions we've had lately."

"Hopefully, but before we get started, can I ask you one last thing?"

I arched a brow at him. "Yeah?"

"Have you felt different since that night in the warehouse? I know it sounds silly considering what you watched, but physically… do you feel any different?"

I thought his question over. Mentally? I felt wrecked. But physically? Nothing had really changed. "I don't think so. Why do you ask?"

"I just noticed that the way you have fought lately has been off."

A frown crawled its face onto my face. "In a bad way?"

"No… in a good way. In a very *skilled* way."

It was a peculiar thought. I hadn't noticed anything different from how I had been fighting lately. I just knew that I had one mission, and that mission was to find Ghost and put a stop to him.

After a minute of thinking, I gave him a serious look. "But one thing has been different since that night actually."

His brows raised. "And that is?"

"Rage. All I am filled with is rage."

"Describe it to me."

"It's like my anger takes over and my body just knows what to do. Like I said, it's almost as if I black out."

He pointed to the book I was holding. "A.R said that he noticed a certain look in your eyes, but that the books would explain everything better than he could. Maybe this rage you have is something to do with the curse."

At the mention of it, my scar came to life and throbbed to an angry beat.

I winced, cupping my eye. "I think you're right."

CHAPTER FOURTEEN

Everette

Haven was engrossed with her books for the past few hours. Book after book, she continued reading and didn't spare me a second glance. I couldn't help but keep glancing over at her, not being able to keep my attention on my own book just by the sight of her.

Her legs were tucked underneath her, a pencil between her lips as she let the notepad she had been jotting notes on rest against her thigh. Her book was in her right hand and just the simplest sight of her reading was mesmerizing.

What the hell is wrong with me?

I shifted in my seat, shaking my head as I looked back down at one of the books I had started to read. It was information on most of the stuff we already knew. Katerina Holden started all of this, igniting the curse of her spirit that was not able to rest. It also went into detail on how Bethany Holden was able to start helping more people after she developed the scar and realized what had happened to her after getting justice for Katerina.

I had no idea all the struggles Bethany had been through, though, and it was an interesting read despite everything. She was a brave woman—one that wanted to do right by people. Nowhere in this book did it say that the MOTs had to kill their targets, which made me wonder when exactly the commanders turned to the dark side to fill their own pockets.

Suddenly Haven's gasp snapped me out of my thoughts. She shot forward, staring at the book in horror while her hands began to shake.

"Haven? What's wrong? What did you read?" I was quick to move over to her side, taking the seat next to her once more.

She stared ahead of her with wide eyes as if she was slowly trying to put the pieces together of what she had just discovered. After a few brief seconds, she turned the book and handed it to me.

"Wrath," she whispered.

Confused, I grabbed the book and looked down at the part she was pointing at.

The final Holden shall be the commander of the dead. The harbinger of wrath. The destroyer of evil. Until the next heir is born, the final Holden will consume all wrath from the souls they have avenged.

"It all makes sense," she croaked. "It makes sense why Ghost took my parents and why he wanted me."

"I'm so confused. What did you read before this?" I mumbled, flipping back a few pages to try and decipher what she was trying to tell me.

"I'm the last female Holden. The last person that can consume… that can consume pure *rage* from the souls I avenged. It states that the souls I avenged don't just move on. They're put into a different realm—one between here and whatever is truly waiting for them—to wait for me to draw upon their rage should I need it."

"This makes no fucking sense," I grumbled.

I trailed my finger over the page, skimming the words with a fast-beating heart.

The souls a Messenger of Truth avenges do not simply find their way to peace by the truth being told. Their pain needs to be harvested if they visit one of our women—that is the price they pay in the search of finding a bringer of truth. They then will be used to fulfill our women with the strength to take on any evil that is too strong to take down on their own. Until they are called upon, they will remain in a world between life and peace.

I drew back horrified. "This cannot be real."

"It would explain why I have so much rage. Before you met me, Everette, I… I killed a lot of people. I avenged so many souls. The stories the commander used to tell our recruits? About how I was some amazing component to the MOTs? It was true. Well, until it started to wear on me day after day. I couldn't tell you how many lives I have taken since being a part of the MOTs. And after I lost it and slaughtered those men… I think I tapped into that rage. I don't know how, but my scar was throbbing horribly, and it was like I just went numb and snapped. I feel as if I just blacked out entirely."

Frowning, I glanced up at her. "Because you never 'harvested' any of that rage before. You never had a reason to make you that upset. So much had happened that night and you let go."

She nodded. "But those souls haven't found peace yet. They've been stuck in some limbo and we were supposed to use their wrath to take that pain away from them so they could fully move on. We've never learned how to do that, and if I barely tapped into it that night… God knows what could happen if any MOT tried again."

It was unreal what I was hearing—reading—but I couldn't just ignore what was being said. I didn't believe in many theories or supernatural aspects of life until I was introduced to the Messengers of Truth, but Haven was proof that something so unexplainable was able to happen.

I skimmed further, my eyes locking on one particular part that had my skin crawling.

"Haven, to even touch that wrath… it says there must be a sacrifice. Does that mean killing someone?" I looked back up to her and she frowned.

"I'm not sure, but it would make sense. MOTs aren't supposed to kill, but there is always the small chance the person we go after won't come forward with the truth and death is the only way to break the soul free from this world. It eliminates what's keeping them here if the truth doesn't come out—at least that's what I understand from what I have read so far. If that's the case and MOTs before us used this method to gain this strength from harvesting wrath… I would assume the sacrifice would come after killing someone. It's a sacrifice we would have to make to free that soul."

I sat back, trying to let everything sink in. "Which is why it wasn't done much and why the new commanders never told you all. You'd be too powerful for them to control since they had you killing left and right for their own personal gain."

"Exactly," Haven replied, trying to rub the exhaustion from her eyes.

"Take a break and get some rest. We'll read more once we reach A.R's place. We need to get a better understanding of this so we can inform the others."

Haven yawned. "Agreed. Although, I'm not sure how the MOTs will take it. I trust them, but what if someone abuses that knowledge? We're trying to be better than we were."

It was always a possibility someone could, but we couldn't just sit back with all that we've learned and not tell them.

"We'll talk to Saul and the others after all this and decide as a group what is best, yeah?"

Haven relaxed some, closing her book. "Okay…"

I reached over, giving her thigh a gentle squeeze. "Rest. I'll wake you when we're near."

The next few hours I was rereading through the book that Haven had. It was as if everything I thought I knew about The Messengers of Truth was a lie. They weren't just some group of women avenging people—they were so much more. To me, it seemed as if they were more of a group offering a bargaining chip. They can help release these souls from pure hell, but they have to wait to be called upon to fully move on.

How does something like this even form? And if it was so easily formed by Katerina Holden, could it be altered in any way?

Eventually I put the book aside and checked in with Reese on how everything was holding up back at the school. The Commander was still acting as if she knew nothing more than what she gave us and the women didn't receive any new informers yet.

Maybe we could get through this without any informers visiting the girls traveling with us. It would make these missions much easier to get through without worrying about getting back home to complete new ones.

One of the attendants walked up minutes later, telling me we would be landing soon. I woke Haven so she could start to get prepared, and I could tell her nerves were starting to get the best of her.

Maybe mine were, too. I didn't know what the hell was going to happen on this trip, and if the wound on my stomach had anything to say about it… it wouldn't be good. My body was still healing—the faint throbbing reminding me that I was in over my head.

But I had to do this—even if it killed me.

"Ready?" Haven mumbled, the jet coming to a stop.

I peered outside, the unfamiliar place making me feel uneasy. "I guess so."

We grabbed our things and exited, and just as we reached the pavement, a sleek, black car pulled up in front of us and a tall, older man got out.

I didn't miss how Haven took a wary step closer to me and out of pure instinct, I placed my hand on the side of her waist, pulling her closer to me. Her small gasp had my skin heating and I gritted my teeth to stop my hand from squeezing her waist.

"Blue hawk?" The man said, causing me to relax a little.

The code word.

I nodded. "Affirmative."

He motioned to the car behind him. "We need to hurry and get you to Axton's place. There are many unwanted eyes around here that report to certain people. I'm Miguel, and I'll be helping you while you're here. Axton has informed me as much as he could, but I still don't know everything. It's best we keep it that way, okay?"

"Of course," Haven mumbled and began walking to the car, but I could tell just how much the name threw her off.

Axton Rivers was a feared man, which is exactly why Knox took on his identity while A.R was off grid. However, the simple name meant way more to Haven than this man would know.

Miguel opened the back door for her and I was quick to follow in after her. Once we were all situated, the driver took off, and Haven glanced over at me, nearly looking pale.

"You okay?" I whispered.

"Nervous," was her reply as she looked out the window.

We left the landing strip and turned onto a small road just as Miguel turned from the passenger side and looked back at us. "We will get you to Axton's place first so you can get settled in. Let me know of anything you may need and I will go get it for you. Should you need to leave the house, there will be a burner phone in the kitchen with only one contact. That would be mine. Just let me know you're heading out so we can keep a watchful eye on the house and to keep eyes on you two while you're out. I'm here for whatever you may need. Any friend of Axton's is a friend of mine. Is there anything I need to know from the two of you?"

"We don't call him Axton," Haven sighed. "We call him A.R now. Just… address him by that name please. It's less confusing for us."

Miguel frowned, clearly confused but nodded nonetheless. "A.R it is. Anything else?"

"Is A.R's place stocked with necessities?" I asked.

"Axt—A.R told me to get a shopping list from you two once we get there and I will go get anything you need."

"Good. We are not sure how long we will be staying, but I can tell you we will probably be out at night mostly."

Miguel grimaced. "Night is the worst time you could be going out."

I couldn't help but grin. "We're aware, but I promise we can also take care of ourselves."

He assessed us, tilting his head to the side. "Do I want to know who you two are exactly?"

This time Haven let out a humorless laugh. "Probably not."

Miguel shrugged. "Fair enough. Okay, I will let my men know."

Interested, I asked, "How do you know A.R exactly?"

Miguel thought his answer over carefully. "To be short, he saved my life. I owe him my own, so I do what I can to help him when he visits. He's a very closed-off man, but he is a good one. I don't ask questions; I just do as told."

Haven snickered. "And he pays well?"

Miguel belted out a laugh. "That, too."

He turned back around just as we pulled down a long driveway. We reached a gate, and the driver reached out to punch in the code. When the gates swept open, Haven and I eagerly leaned forward to get a better look at the house as it came into view.

"Oh my God," she whispered in awe.

The house didn't look like any house I knew. This place looked almost like a damn mansion compared to my house back at home. "He sure does go all out for his living accommodations."

Haven scoffed. "I'll say…"

Miguel laughed at our shocked states, motioning for us to get out. We were quick to hurry and grab our things as the driver and Miguel got the rest of our bags. We followed them up the steps and Miguel had to punch in another code to the door before we were able to enter. The minute we did, he hurried to the side of the foyer and disarmed the security system.

Placing our bags on the ground next to the door, Miguel threw his arms out. "This is it. It has everything you could possibly need, trust me on that. I stopped before we came to pick you up and got some basic things in case you were hungry when we got back, but if you'll get a list together for me, I'll go now and get that for you."

"Where's paper and a pen?" Haven asked, setting her things down as well.

"Kitchen, the top drawer by the fridge," he replied.

The driver pointed where to go and Haven took off. I wanted to laugh at her excited state, knowing she didn't have much back home with her life as an MOT. Although this was no vacation, that didn't mean we couldn't find joy in the small things.

My phone buzzing in my pocket brought me from my thoughts. Confused, I pulled it out to see A.R's name. I opened the message and couldn't help but let out a small laugh. He wasn't supposed to be messaging me, yet he couldn't help to let me know one thing.

Tomorrow is Haven's birthday. Be nice, yeah?

I looked back up at Miguel, a grin crossing my face. "Can you add a birthday cake to that list?"

Miguel smiled. "Of course. For her?" When I nodded, he grinned. "How long have you two been together?"

My smile faded some. "We're not. Just friends—partners now, I guess."

Miguel cleared his throat. "My mistake. You two just look close. I'm sure she'll love the cake. I'll do whatever I can to get the best I can find. My wife loves this one bakery not far from here. I'll see what I can do."

"I appreciate that."

Haven bounced back into the foyer with the list in hand. "Here's everything I could think of for now. Thank you."

Miguel thanked her and looked back at me. "Anything you want to add?"

I shook my head. "I trust she got everything."

"Then we'll be on our way. A.R said he gave you all the codes, so when we leave make sure to lock up. It won't take us long hopefully. Call me if you need anything or think of anything new you might have forgotten."

We thanked him and soon they were gone. I looked at Haven, letting out a puff of air. “Well, what now?”

She smiled and grabbed her bags. “For now, we unpack and then find something to eat. I’m starving.”

“Let’s be nosy?” I asked, earning a devilish grin to cross her face

“Most definitely.”

CHAPTER FIFTEEN

Haven

Everette and I were quick to look around the house, gawking at our expensive surroundings. As usual, A.R had nothing homey to this place. It was simply just a place for him to crash at when needed and he didn't bother to leave anything that could give us a glimpse into his everyday life, but I wasn't surprised by that.

Soon, we found the floor where multiple bedrooms were. Everette and I each took one next to each other and unpacked the small things we had brought to get through this trip. And as I placed away the last of my things, I couldn't help but feel relieved that we weren't at each other's throats anymore.

I was terrified with what I learned on the jet, but it gave me some peace of mind to know that maybe this rage I had been feeling lately wasn't necessarily my own doing, but something that was linked together with this curse that had plagued half of my life.

I was more shocked that Everette had chosen to open up to me some about his life—his *wife*. I had no idea the man used to be married, but knowing what I do now had me feeling like a piece of shit. In a way, Everette knew exactly what I was going through and I pushed him away like some asshole.

It just goes to show that even though I felt as if I had known him for years, I really knew nothing about him. Or Saul. Or his organization.

That needed to change.

How were we supposed to work together if we barely knew one another?

A knock on my door brought me from my thoughts and I looked back to see Everette leaning against the doorway. "I scoped out the fridge. Looks like sandwiches are what's in store until Miguel gets back."

My stomach rumbled at the thought. "That's fine with me. I'd eat anything at this point."

He beckoned me to follow him and we were quick to make our way to the kitchen. It took no time for us to make a few sandwiches and I should have been embarrassed with how quickly I inhaled them. Miguel had left a few small bags of chips for us as well, to which Everette and I dove into after our sandwiches were gone.

We were so occupied on the ride here that we hadn't bothered to eat. It was safe to say that the groceries Miguel was bringing us were more than needed.

I was sitting on the kitchen's counters, a habit of mine, as Everette filled his glass up with water from the fridge. My stomach was nearing fullness as I eyed the last small bag of chips. Did I look like a complete pig in front of Everette? Possibly. Did I care? Not one bit.

Everette turned towards the same bag of chips I had been eyeing, causing me to dart off the counter. I neared them, almost snatching them up, but he saw me coming and grabbed them before I did.

He chuckled, holding them high above my head. "Not happening, Red, I'm much bigger than you and need some fuel."

I jumped for them, but Everette's six-three figure didn't help in the slightest.

The man towered me.

"Hand them over," I growled, hopping up again.

Everette laughed once more, pushing me away with ease to turn his back to me as he opened the bag. I gasped, launching myself onto this back, causing a full-on battle to break out between us as we fought for them.

"Ow!" Everette yelped as I pulled on his ear. "You brat! Stop that shit."

"Asshole!" I countered, my fingertips grasping the bag before he snatched them away again.

If I wasn't pissed that he wouldn't even *share* them with me, I would have laughed at the handful of chips he grabbed and shoved into his mouth, parts of them cracking and breaking off into the floor.

"Everette, just share the damn chips!"

"Not happening! You can wait."

He was teasing me now, I knew that, but that didn't stop me from launching myself at him again. From the blunt attack of me nearly wrapping myself around the man like a spider-monkey, Everette nearly toppled over.

"Haven, my stomach. The wound. Stop!"

Like water was thrown over me, I immediately separated myself from him, my eyes wide in horror. "I'm so sorry, I forgot. God, are you okay?"

His pained expression quickly morphed into a cocky one as he turned the bag of chips up and delivered the rest of the oily treat into his mouth. "I lied," he replied with a mouthful.

My jaw dropped as I punched him in the shoulder. "You're such an asshole! That wasn't funny, Everette."

Rubbing his arm, he grinned. "It kind of was."

I huffed, leaning against the kitchen counter. "I hate you."

"No you don't," he replied before hopping up on the counter next to me. "Don't pout, Red, Miguel will be back with groceries soon."

Rolling my eyes, I turned to look at him. "Why do you call me that?'

"What? Red?" I nodded, causing his grin to falter some. "Well, everyone else had a nickname for you. I felt left out."

I frowned. "Who?"

He shrugged, crossing his ankles. "Saul. Knox. I guess I felt the need to join in. Saul calls you *little one* and Knox called you *darlin'*. When I saw you in our attire for the first time, I couldn't help it. It just stuck. And now that you wear your own MOT attire with one of our hoods sewn into it, it fits even more."

For some reason, that small bit of information he gave me had my chest feeling funny. I fought down a smile, tilting my head to the side. "I guess we all did get somewhat closer than I expected."

Everette met my eyes. "In a way, yeah, I guess we did."

"Funny how that happened and I barely know anything about you," I replied and propped myself up next to him, swinging my legs. "So who are you outside of The Men in Red, Everette Knight?"

"No one, really. For half of my life, The Men in Red is all I've known. Remember how I told you that this all started for me when I was at the wrong place and the wrong time? Well, I was younger and put my nose where it shouldn't have been. I was introduced to all this not long after. My father… I don't think he ever wanted this for me but he couldn't help it. My uncle was leading The Men in Red at the time and it's safe to say he was a bastard."

I frowned. "Your uncle forced you into the MIRs?"

Everette nodded. "I was taken out of high school and forced into training. I knew too much apparently and they were afraid I'd speak up about it to the wrong person. If I was participating in the act…"

"You would be too scared you would get in trouble as well if you told anyone." I realized and he nodded.

"So I did as I was told. I was sent on missions and I didn't ask anymore questions. The Men in Red are similar to the MOTs in a way. We go after some horrible men, but it didn't start that way. It's a long story about how we were originally formed, but to be short… My uncle got on the wrong side of someone and as a debt, he had to work for them."

"How did they get out of it?"

"My father put a stop to his brother's quests. My father feared his family would be hurt in the process, so he went after the man that was blackmailing my uncle and his family and stopped him. Then my father took over and decided that we had to do right by people—help those who were in similar situations that my uncle got in. Then it progressed over the years. We stopped drug dealers, traffickers, and more…"

"Wow," I mumbled. "And how do you all profit? How do you keep your organization afloat?"

"We have businesses—some of which we protect and in response those businesses give us a cut. Some we started on our own. A club, for one, is where we get most of our money."

I couldn't help but let out a laugh. "You all have a club?"

Everette snorted. "Yeah. Booze and drunk people looking for a fun night bring in a lot more profit than you would think."

"When we get back home, I have to see this club."

Everette shot me a wink. "Maybe if you're lucky."

Rolling my eyes, I relaxed some. "And Saul? How did he get into the MIRs?"

Everette rubbed the slight stubble that was growing on his face. "Saul's story is one for him to tell. But let's just say… he got on the wrong side of someone as well. Funny story, Saul actually was in law school before he joined us."

My jaw dropped. "You're lying! Goofy Saul? A lawyer?! No way."

He chuckled. "He was. Saul may act goofy as hell most days, but he is fierce when it comes to helping people. He's loyal—that's why he's my best friend. He's smart as hell, too, and one of the many reasons we've worked around the law so much."

"Which law school?"

Everette's grin spread wider. "Harvard."

I howled in laughter. "I cannot believe this. I am *so* teasing him about this later. Lawyer turned assassin. How does that happen?"

Everette's grin faltered some. "People take advantage of those who are different from them. It involved family, and that's all I can say. The rest you'll have to get from him."

To say I was shocked was an understatement. These men were nothing I expected at all, but I guess when you join something like The Men in Red, it was probably because of some backstory that you don't want to be told. I understood that.

"So you don't have a life outside of The Men in Red? You just live and breathe the MIR life?"

Everette shrugged. "I mean, before all the shit went down with the MOTs, I was busying myself in the club to help make us a living. Some of the men work there for extra cash, some have smaller jobs, and I… was the owner of a club. So, in a way, I guess outside of my organization I'm just a club owner."

I arched my brow. "No hobbies? I like to paint. Well, I used to back in New York. I would paint my informers before all this shit went down. Anyway, you have to like to do something, Everette."

He thought about it for a moment. "I like to read."

Was he blushing?

I smiled. "Me too. What's your favorite type of book?"

"I can read just about anything. I like historical books a lot, but perhaps that's just because I loved history in my short time in high school. Mystery I like a lot, too. You?"

"I love the classics. I—" I was cut short when I heard the front door open.

The two of us went on guard for a moment before I heard bags rustling and the security alarm disarming. "We're back!" Miguel called out, causing us to relax.

Everette hopped off the counter and waved me off. "I'll put these away. Go shower and get some rest."

"I still need my chips," I mused.

Everette let out a snort. "I'll make sure to bring you some after I'm done."

Fighting down a smile, I made my way back upstairs feeling the day finally taking its toll on me. I was ready for a shower and some sleep. Who knows what we'll plan to do tomorrow, but I knew it would be time to get our plans in order so we can get this over for once and for all.

Learning a little bit more about Everette was a breath of fresh air. He seemed much more comfortable with me, which was an odd feeling to enjoy so much. I could only want to know more about him and The Men in Red.

The shower was amazing, to say the least. My muscles ached, but the steaming hot water that cascaded over me during my shower helped give some relief to the ways I had been torturing my body lately.

When I was done, I pulled on some pajamas and walked out into the room only to halt at the sight. On the table against the far wall, a small cake sat with a candle lit on top. My heart skipped a beat as I walked up, seeing a bag of chips laid next to it with a note.

Happy early birthday, Red.

I grabbed my phone, my eyes welling with tears as I looked at the date. I hadn't even realized tomorrow was my birthday.

I hadn't celebrated it in years—I wasn't allowed to.

Holding the note to my chest, I slowly sat down at the table and finally let the tears fall.

CHAPTER SIXTEEN

Everette

I woke up to screaming.

Before I realized it, I was throwing the bed covers off of me as I ran next door to Haven's room. The bedroom door hit the wall with a crack as I flung it open and darted to her bedside. Haven was tossing and turning, screaming as she tangled herself within the covers of her bed.

"Haven!" I shouted, trying my best to wake her.

She fought against me, her screams growing louder as my anxiety grew at the tears streaming down her face. I grunted as one of her arms jarred my wound, causing me to try and pin her.

"Haven!" I shook her, causing her eyes to snap open as a gasp left her.

She flew upright, looking around with horror in her eyes and breathing heavily. Sweat drenched her forehead, most of her hair covering her face. "Where are they?" she whispered.

"Who, Haven?"

She blinked a few times, everything finally coming into view for her. "Everette?" she mumbled.

"I'm here, Haven. It's me." I moved to sit next to her.

She was still a bit in shock, looking around the room with fearful eyes. "You were all dead."

I frowned. "What?"

"In my dream… Ghost killed you all in front of me. Then I was next." Her voice quivered, causing me to finally ignore my no-touching rule and pulled her to my side, wrapping an arm around her.

"We're fine. It was just a bad dream—your mind was playing a trick on you."

She let out a shaky breath, resting her head on my shoulder. "It was so real."

I rubbed her arm gently. "I know, Red, but that's all it was. A dream."

"A nightmare."

Hesitantly, I reached over and swept the hair out of her face, tucking it behind her ear. She looked up at me, but what I saw had my heart nearly stopping.

Her expression grew more scared. "What? What is it?"

I gulped, not sure if my eyes were playing a trick on me. "I… I see…" I couldn't properly form my words as I stared at her eyebrow.

The MOT scar.

Her eyes widened in realization at where I was staring. "You see it, don't you?"

I nodded. "I see the scar now."

Haven flew up out of the bed, running to a nearby mirror. She looked at herself but shook her head. "I don't understand. Nothing has changed for me."

When she looked back at me, she let out a cry, running from the room. I was quick to move and follow her as she ran into the room I was staying in. Confused, I saw her looking around panicked.

"Haven, what the hell are you looking for?"

"Your body!" She cried. "Did you die?!"

I was dumbfounded. I opened my mouth to speak, but before I could stop it, a booming laugh left me.

Haven's head snapped in my direction. "This isn't funny! You shouldn't be able to see it. The dead are the only ones that can. That and... my next target."

My laughter was quick to dry up. "Well, I'm not dead, Red. I'm here in the flesh. But you think I'm your next target?"

She shook her head, grabbing at her hair. "I don't know. This has never happened before."

I walked to the bed, taking a seat on the edge and patted the spot next to me. As she sat down, I couldn't help but stare at the scar. It was so odd that all these years I knew about it, but could never see it and now was the time it showed.

When Haven looked up, she caught the sight of my paralyzed state. "It's hideous, I know. I hate that you have to see this... I don't know why this is happening."

Anger spiked through me when she dipped her head, letting her hair fall to cover her scar. "Haven, what are you talking about?"

"The scar, Everette. What else? It's jagged, repulsive, and a constant reminder of what I am. It helped knowing that you all couldn't see it, but now? Now I just want to go hide under a rock. What if normal people can see it? Why now of all times?"

Ignoring her question, I kneeled down in front of her and gently grabbed her chin, lifting it so she would look me in the eyes. "I wasn't staring because I was disgusted, Haven. I was staring because I was mesmerized. I couldn't tell you what makes it flawed or what completes it, but I know they all come together to create something so astoundingly beautiful. You, Haven McKinley, are fucking breathtaking—scar or not—so don't you *dare* go thinking anything different. Do you understand me?"

She pulled her chin out of my grasp and shook her head. "You're crazy."

I cracked a small smile. "Perhaps, but I meant every word. You're thinking too much. You look just as beautiful as you did without it." She hadn't been looking at me, but from the sniffle she gave, I knew she was trying to not cry. Sighing, I pulled her back to my side. "We'll figure this out, okay? I'll call Saul and the others tomorrow to see if anything has changed on their sides. Maybe… maybe the curse changed its way to allow us to help the MOTs better. For us to see what you are seeing—to become an asset to one another."

As the words left my mouth, Haven groaned and cupped her eye. "I think you're right. My scar is throbbing again."

Eyes wide, I said, "Then we're on the right path. Those women are here. This is good for us."

Haven nodded, wiping her eyes with the sleeve of her shirt. "Thank you. For comforting me."

I rubbed her arm. "Of course." I looked over at the clock on the side of her bed and let out a small laugh, giving her arm a squeeze. "Happy birthday, Haven."

She laid her head against my shoulder and grabbed my hand, giving it a small squeeze. The small gesture had my heart racing as she whispered, "Thank you."

***

After what had happened last night—well, early this morning—Haven and I separated and went back to sleep. Actually, I tossed and turned for a few hours from not being able to get Haven or her scar out of my head. I didn't know exactly what this all meant, but the fact the curse was trusting The Men in Red with something so valuable, it made me feel a lot better about the whole trip.

But now? We're trying to break into A.R's office to use his printer.

"This is ridiculous," Haven grumbled, trying to pick the lock.

"Why the hell would he lock it? He knew we were coming." I rolled my eyes, and Haven nodded her head in agreement.

"That's what I'm saying. I get the whole not trusting thing, but damn… a printer will be so much easier than having to write everything down by hand."

I gave her a gentle shove. "Move, let me try."

"No, I got it."

After three more unsuccessful attempts, Haven cursed before handing me her tools. I crouched down, trying my best to pick the lock but whatever A.R did to this thing… there was no getting inside.

"Maybe I should just kick it open," Haven stated, a contemplating look on her face. "Or maybe not. A.R would most likely kill me for ruining his precious door."

I snickered, trying one last time with the lock but soon gave up. "I can't get it. A.R is proving to be more mysterious by the day."

Letting out a puff of air, Haven folded her arms. "I'll say…"

I glanced down the hall. "I guess we'll just have to copy everything Saul gave us by hand." I began to walk down the hall and Haven fell into step beside me.

"So what are we doing until nightfall exactly? Memorizing the files?"

I waved my hand back and forth. "Kind of. I want us both to have copies so we can memorize faces and names. The better we know these women, the easier it's going to be to spot. Now, from the last locations on the papers is what will be tricky. It's the warehouse they were shipped to, but not exactly a definite pinpoint for where the women went after."

Haven's brows furrowed as we walked downstairs. "And so you think the warehouse is one of Ghost's locations for shipping and receiving these women?"

"Yeah… at least, I hope it is. If we can find one of his men that are there, it will give us a better starting point. Without that, we're doing this blind. Hopefully it won't come down to us having to ask too many people too many questions."

I glanced over at Haven, practically seeing the gears turning in her head. "So… find the warehouse, see if we can find one of his men, get answers out of him as to where to go next?"

"Bingo."

A clouded look crossed her features. "And if we find someone? What then? We can't just let him walk away. What if he notifies Ghost that we're lurking?"

I rubbed the back of my neck. "We'll do what we have to for the sake of those women."

She didn't reply.

I walked into the kitchen, opening the fridge to see the numerous groceries Miguel had brought us last night. We slept in late today, so the both of us had missed breakfast by a landslide. "Hungry?" I asked.

"Starving," Haven shot back, propping herself up on the kitchen counter like she did last night.

A habit of hers, I'm starting to pick up.

Looking in the fridge, I rummaged around for some things to make a quick lunch. "Want anything in particular?"

"Um… a hot ham and cheese?"

I snorted, turning to look back at her. "Are you serious? Out of all things, that's what you want?"

"Don't knock it until you try it. Actually, let me fix you one and prove to you just how amazing one can make this sandwich be."

I motioned to the fridge and moved aside so she could grab what she needed.

She was an odd little thing, but I was starting to find that it was one of the things I enjoyed so much when it came to Haven McKinley. You never knew what to expect and you never knew what's going to come flying out of her mouth.

As she got to work, she started asking about the mission.

"So when are we leaving tonight exactly?"

I leaned against the counter, watching her move around. "I let Miguel know that we would be heading out when it gets dark. I think it's best if we work quickly. We don't have much time to waste."

"And for the plan of the warehouse… are we going in blind?"

I grinned, not being able to help myself from checking her out. She danced a little when she cooked—swaying her body slightly. I can only assume that when she takes a bite of her *sacred* hot ham and cheese, she'll probably do a little happy dance.

Women.

"Everette? Are you listening?"

My eyes snapped up and I cleared my throat. "I asked Miguel if he could get blueprints of the warehouse so we can see what we're working with. He said he would try to see what he could find. If not, yeah… we're going in blind."

Haven placed two sandwiches into a pan, the buttery smell invading my senses as the pan gave a nice sizzling sound. "Well, I've done my fair share of going in blind. We can do it."

I smiled. "Yeah, I know."

Flipping the sandwiches, she glanced over her shoulder at me. "Have you ever had a hot ham and cheese?"

"Maybe when I was like five."

"Well now you're about to have it at… wait. How old are you again?"

I grinned. "Twenty-eight."

"Okay, Mr. Twenty-eight-year-old, get ready for the best sandwich of your life," she mused, placing one onto a plate before handing it over to me.

I took the sandwich, looking it over. It did look rather tasty, but to me it just seemed like any ordinary hot ham and cheese. But when I grabbed it and took a bite, my tastebuds exploded. Haven watched me intensely, seeing my brows rise slightly in surprise.

"See!" She giggled. "I told you! It's so good. It's all about the cheeses you add to it. Oh, and toasting your bread just right."

I swallowed my bite. "What cheeses did you use?"

"Not telling."

I frowned, trying to look over where she was cooking, but Haven had already put everything back into the fridge before she put the sandwiches into the pan. "You're really not going to tell me?"

"Nope."

Smothering my laugh at the grin she was trying to hide, I demolished the rest of my lunch before she even had a chance to take a seat and eat.

"Okay, so what are we supposed to do while we wait for Miguel and for night to come?" she asked, grabbing her plate and turning to lean next to the stove. "Twiddle our thumbs?"

I snorted. "We can always train."

Haven grimaced before biting into her sandwich. "That sounds terrible."

For the first time, the thought of training *did* sound like a shitshow. My wound was only…

My wound.

I stood abruptly, noticing how it hadn't ached in the slightest today. Haven noticed my abrupt shift in behavior and straightened. "What is it?"

I pulled my shirt up, looking down at my wound only to see that it was nearly healed. "What the fuck?"

Her plate clattered against the counter as she tossed it aside and quickly walked up to me. "Okay, that isn't supposed to heal that quickly is it?"

I shook my head. "Not at all. This should still be harboring a gruesome infection I've been fighting off."

Goosebumps traveled down my arms as dainty fingers trailed right above the stitches that were now starting to dissolve. Haven traced across my abdomen with wide eyes—awe even. "Is it not odd that you were able to see my scar and now you're healing with exponential speed?"

My mouth parted slightly. "This is too unreal for me to fathom. You think the curse is really doing all this?"

The scar that stared back at me was only proof. Just days ago I saw nothing but beautiful hues of blue and green staring back at me. Now I saw the scar of stories—one that told a story of its own staring right back at me as if saying *here's your proof, boy.*

Haven ran a hand through her dark hair, which had gotten longer over the past few weeks, and let out a deep sigh. "Who knows what this curse is capable of at this point. I have a feeling this thing goes way deeper than just avenging people."

I nodded my head in agreement, feeling my phone buzz in my pocket. I pulled it out, seeing Miguel had been calling. Quickly putting the phone to my ear, I answered, "Hey, any good news for us?"

Miguel sighed. "Yes and no." Frowning, I awaited the news. "To be short, the warehouse you asked for the blueprints to isn't much of a warehouse anymore. It's a club. Is that what you were looking for?"

I cut my eyes to Haven who looked as if she had gone pale.

"No… not really. Any idea who owns it?"

"Didn't say," Miguel mumbled. "I can ask around?"

I sighed. "No, it's fine. The less people we have knowing someone is looking around, the better. We'll figure something out. Thanks, Miguel."

"No problem. Is there anything else you need me to do?"

I locked eyes with Haven, an idea popping into my head. Grinning, I asked, "Is A.R funding most of this trip?"

Miguel snickered. "He said to get you anything you two needed. So yes."

"Great. We're going to need a dress. And a blonde wig."

Haven's eyes narrowed into slits.

"Um… okay. Send me Haven's dress size and we'll get on it."

I thanked him and hung up the call.

Haven stepped forward and popped out her hip with folded arms. "What the hell do you think you're doing?"

I smirked. "We're going clubbing, Red."

CHAPTER SEVENTEEN

Haven

It was official. I was going to murder Everette in his sleep. The heels I wore dug into my feet uncomfortably and I kept pulling at the end of my dress. I felt like if I even moved slightly, I'd flash everyone in my vicinity. Looking in the mirror, I wanted to scream.

Red dress, blonde *fake* hair, and pumps—which made me grow a few inches—stared back at me.

"Who are you?" I whispered in horror.

Everette's grand plan was for us to just waltz through the front doors. *No one will know*, he had said. Bull. Shit. It was clear Ghost and his men knew what I looked like. I don't know if some wig was going to hide me away.

Totally pulling a Clark Kent here.

Sighing, I grabbed a tissue and blotted the fire hydrant red lipstick before I tossed it into the trash and turned to grab my dagger. I slid my dress up so I could strap it to my thigh and stood, looking at my appearance one last time.

I hoped that the façade worked.

I threw open my door, trying my best to not let my grim expression become permanent as I went to search for Everette.

Hearing commotion from the living room, I walked in to see Everette kicked back on the couch, hands behind his head as he watched some show on the TV.

And he looked… wow.

Clearing my throat, his head snapped in my direction. Slowly, he raised to his feet, his eyes not leaving my body as he looked me over.

Everette noticeably gulped. "You look… good."

I tried not to roll my eyes. "Good? Do you know how much work I put into this to make it work?"

He chuckled. "You look stunning, Haven McKinley. As if you hung the moon and the stars. You are the shining star that will light—"

"Okay, you can stop now," I grumbled, ending his mocking tone as he stared at me humorously.

When he turned away to grab his phone, I couldn't help but take him in. Black button down, black pants, boots, and were those *rings* on his fingers?

My weakness.

"Why are you staring?" Everette mused, cocking a brow.

I wet my lips. "I… just have never seen you dress like this."

He threw his arms out to the side. "Welcome to my going out look. Don't get used to it."

I wanted to. God, I wanted him to dress like this all the time. It was different, but it was a *good* different. No MIR attire, no sweats, no jeans, and no plain shirt. This… this was a beautiful sight to see.

Who knew Everette had an edgy side to him?

When I noticed the hoop through his nose, my eyebrows nearly shot the ceiling. I rushed towards him, grabbing his chin and turned his head to the side. "Is that a nose ring?! Where is Everette and what have you done with him?"

Everette laughed, shoving me away from him. "I don't wear it much because I would prefer it to *not* get ripped out of my nose during a fight."

His cologne invaded my senses at the wrong time.

Sandalwood and spice.

He looked *and* smelled divine.

What the hell was wrong with me? One minute I barely notice he had his nose pierced this whole time and now I'm practically drooling at the sight of him.

Noticing my baffled state, he cockily asked, "Do you like it?"

Yeah. Yeah, I think I do. Because this version of Everette? Carefree-looking and just… normal? It was so damn refreshing. Although tonight we were just putting on an act to see if we could get some intel at the club, I couldn't help but suddenly feel giddy—as if I were on a mere vacation with a handsome guy.

I wiped the expression off my face and shrugged. "A bit edgy, don't you think?"

His only response was a wink as he started to leave the room.

Okay, so he totally noticed me checking him out.

Great.

"Run the plan by me again," I spoke, trailing after him.

"Miguel is here and will take us to the club. We're simply going to go in with the other people and act like we're just there for a good time. Hopefully we can pick up on some clues to see if Ghost even operates out of that place anymore. We'll scope out the women there, see if you see any scars. Then we'll leave and form a new game plan if needed."

I scoffed. "You make it sound like it's easy."

Everette opened the front door and let me out before arming the house and shutting the door behind him. He was silent for a moment as we made our way to the car.

"Honestly? I have no idea what the hell else we can try to do. It may sound like an easy plan, but when has anything ever been easy for us?"

I pulled on the end of my dress with a huff. "Touché."

Miguel was waiting for us and opened the back door to let us slide in. "You two sure this is a good idea?"

"No," we both spoke simultaneously.

Miguel chuckled. "Good talk."

I held back a laugh as he shut the door and I glanced over at Everette who seemed to be doing the same.

"We only live once, right?" I asked.

Everette snorted. "What are you, twelve?"

"It's a true saying. I was just trying to lighten the mood of… I don't know… this whole shit show of a night? Who knows if we'll walk out of there with your grand plan."

Everette looked out the window. "If I have to hear your complaints all night, God knows I don't want to make it out of there alive."

I punched him in the shoulder, earning a groan to leave him.

"Brat," he gritted out, rubbing the spot.

"Asshole," I huffed and folded my arms.

We were silent for a moment, but then he cut the silence. "When we get back can you make us your hot ham and cheese?"

Despite the scowl on my face, my heart skipped a beat at the silly comment. "Yeah."

More silence.

"Extra cheese?" His voice was still clipped.

"Sure." I bit back.

Miguel suddenly burst out laughing. "You two are something else."

I hid my smile by tucking my head, letting my hair fall around my face.

We truly were something different.

"Yeah, yeah. Turn the music up," grumbled Everette.

Snickering, Miguel obliged.

Minutes later we were pulling up to a sleek-looking club. For some reason, the hair on my arms stood up, causing me to stiffen. A second later, my scar throbbed.

The small gasp that left me had Everette craning his neck. "We're in the right place I assume?"

I nodded. "Most definitely."

"I'm staying in the car. Many people know my face and I wish to not be seen," Miguel spoke as he turned in his seat to look back at us. "Don't do anything stupid."

I grinned. "Us? Never."

With that, I threw the door to the car open and hopped out. Looking around, most of the people standing in line were in expensive clothing and looked as if not one hair was out of place. Just the sight of it all made me realize that this club was far different from the clubs I witnessed in New York.

"Ready?" Everette asked, resting his hand on the small of my back.

I gave him a tight-lipped smile. "Not in the slightest."

"Perfect," he replied before gently ushering me forward.

I nearly tripped in my heels, causing Everette to curse under his breath. "Can you not give us away the minute we leave the car?"

"Can you just, I don't know, shut the fuck up?" I snapped, trying my best to put one foot in front of the other. "I've never worn heels."

He shook his head. "I can see that."

Biting my tongue, we got in line behind the others as the line slowly started to inch forward.

I tried not to panic as the line got closer and closer to the front. We didn't have IDs on us, nor did we have anything else like some damn password, which yeah… that may be a bit much and I may have watched too many movies, but that didn't change the fact we were trying to get into the place without *anything*.

Eventually, it was our turn. A man and a woman stood at the front doors that had been beckoning people forward this whole time. When the man saw us, he raised a brow before barking, *IDs*.

But I didn't reply because I was too busy staring at the woman.

Staring at the scar that rested on the left side of her face.

An MOT.

"IDs, now," he barked once more with a thick accent.

I went to speak, but the woman came out of her shocked trance and nudged the man. "They're good to go."

With the simple words that left her mouth, the man moved aside and raised the velvet rope to let us enter. But her eyes didn't leave my own as we passed her, and I didn't even realize Everette had been gripping my hand the whole time until we were fully inside and he pulled me aside.

"Did she have a scar? Is that why she let us in?"

Millions of thoughts racked my brain, but I couldn't get the picture of that woman out of it. She had to be one of the women on our list, but I couldn't remember her face or name. Maybe the men were right and their appearances had changed drastically because of Ghost's doing.

"Haven?"

Snapping out of it, I nodded. "Yeah. Yeah, she had the scar. You're not able to see it?"

He shook his head. "No… Maybe I can only see yours?"

Ignoring the headache that was starting to surface, I waved my hands around. "Maybe, but what would you have done if she hadn't let us through? What was your big plan to get us in, huh? Because that almost blew up in our face, Everette."

"Don't be dramatic. I was just going to slip him some money."

My eyes widened. "*That* was your plan?! Look around, Everette, do these people look like they want some money? No."

He shrugged. "It was that or I'd break in, but I'd rather try the easy way first. Turns out, we had to do neither. Now, why the hell would she let you through?"

"I don't know," I sighed. "But we need to keep a low profile. She might have let us through just to tell some higher up authority that an MOT is lurking around."

Everette looked deep in thought for a moment before he spoke. "What if she just thought you were another person like her? We said that the warehouse could have potentially been turned into a club as a front, yes? What if women like the MOTs come here all the time. If he's moving women around, it's safe to say that the women we came here for might not still be here at all. I didn't recognize her from the files."

I worried my bottom lip. "I was thinking the same thing."

"There is something bigger going on here. Why would an MOT be standing guard to let selective people into some club? And why would your scar throb in the car?"

It did raise a lot of questions. Was this just some front to shuffle girls around so he could bid them off to the highest buyer? Was it some scheme to lure innocent people in to get them involved in shit they didn't wish to be? I didn't know, but I knew just from standing in this room that I didn't have a good feeling about it.

"What do we do now?"

Everette looked around with a tight jaw. "Blend in for now. We'll start getting around to intel later. Right now, we could be on their radar. We need to stay low."

I nodded. "Agreed. Should we just go get a drink and get one of those booths in the back?"

A wicked look crossed his face. "I was thinking we would merge with that huge crowd of people dancing. What better way to hide yourself than within a large group of people?"

I winced. "Please don't say you're asking me to go dance. Look at those people. They look ridiculous."

"Suck it up, Red. We have to get through this."

With that, he snatched my hand and led me to the dance floor.

The bile rose in my throat at the thought of having to dance within a sweaty group of people. I can't dance, I hate people I don't know touching me, and again… I can't dance! What did this man expect from me?

I could maybe do the Macarena. The Running Man?

Yep, we're so dying tonight.

What I didn't expect when we made it to the center of the crowd was for Everette to spin me around, pinning himself behind me.

I nearly froze as he settled his hands on my hips, moving his lips next to my ear. "Just follow the others. Move to the beat. Don't stick out like a sore thumb."

"You act like I do this for a living."

"You don't," he said as I started to slightly sway my hips. "But I do. Kind of. Club owner, remember?"

I nearly forgot the man owned his own club and probably saw this all the time.

"Relax," he gently spoke, pressing himself closer to me.

My mouth parted slowly as I felt the heat between us grow, his own body heat warming me in ways it shouldn't as I moved my hips from side to side.

Starting to get in sync with the rhythm of the music, I found my hands moving behind my head to grip the sides of his neck as I pushed myself impossibly closer to him. Everette lowered his head as I turned mine, our eyes catching while we danced to the beat of the music pumping through the place.

And just like that, it felt as if everyone slowly faded away and it was just the two of us. Moving together, hands roaming, and feelings that we shouldn't be feeling splattered across both our faces, our eyes never leaving one another.

"Did I tell you how amazing you look tonight?" Everette mumbled, leaning in closer.

I tried to speak, but it was as if words wouldn't come out and my brain refused to function because of his close proximity.

Somehow, I managed a nod.

"Because you, Haven McKinley, are breathtaking. I mean that."

Gaining my composure, I gave him a weak grin. "Like the shining star that will light the night?" I teased, repeating his mocking words from earlier.

He let out a husky chuckle. "Most definitely."

I turned my head away from him, my heart feeling like it was about to beat right out of my chest and for the first time in a while, it felt like I couldn't breathe—my chest tight with some emotion I couldn't quite understand.

"Don't you see?" he spoke next to my ear, his breath fanning down my neck. "All these men can't keep their eyes off you."

I looked around, seeing people staring. "They'll freak out when they realize I'm not a real blonde."

His chest rumbled with laughter. "I quite like the dark hair. Blondes are overrated."

I mockingly gasped. "Jay will have your balls for that."

"Yeah… don't tell her I said that."

I giggled, my hands lowering to rest over the tops of his that had been gripping my waist.

In a quick movement, Everette jerked me around to press his front against my own, causing a yelp to leave me at the motion—leaving me nearly breathless for the second time tonight.

This time I couldn't get away from those hues of blue that nearly pierced my soul with one gaze. He stared at me like he wanted to see if he could figure me out, which made me want to shy away and put as much distance between us.

But my body refused to let that happen.

My arms shook slightly as I moved them around his neck, falling back into the beat of the music, and his hands began to trail a little below my hips, causing goosebumps to raise on my skin. At the feeling of Everette pressed against me, hips to hips, my eyes fluttered shut as I let my head fall back slightly, already getting lost within the music.

I haven't felt this way since—

My eyes flew open and I jumped out of his grasp to put a good few feet between us. Breathing harshly, I ignored Everette's concerned expression. "I think we've blended in enough," I mumbled.

I blew out a breath of air, cursing myself for letting my guard down. I let my guard down once with Knox.

I can't let that happen again.

CHAPTER EIGHTEEN

Everette

What I did was idiotic, I knew that much, but I couldn't find myself to hate anything about what had just happened between us. I saw that look in her eyes—the look that gave me a stupid amount of hope that I should have let go of a long time ago.

She pulled me from the dancefloor to the outskirts of it and rubbed the back of her neck awkwardly as she refused to meet my eyes. "What now?" she asked softly now that I was able to hear her better.

I sighed, glancing around us. "We start asking questions."

"Let's not be obvious, yeah?"

I frowned. "I'm not going to just walk up to someone and demand to know where Ghost is. Do I look like I'm stupid?"

"Maybe you won't have to ask," she replied, looking behind me.

I contained my frustrated groan, trying to be casual as I turned to my side a little and glanced at the people Haven had been looking at. The woman who had let us in was with some man and was pointing towards our direction.

"Cover blown?" Haven's voice sounded alarmed as she took a wary step back.

"Cover blown!" I spit, grabbing her hand as the two took off after us. "Run!"

We maneuvered through the crowd of people, trying our best to not knock people out of our way, but when some people got in Haven's way and made her trip, a rage swept through me as I shoved them to the side, causing them to fly to the ground.

"Way to *not* be suspicious!" Haven shouted, regaining her footing.

"We're way past that, Red!"

We took a sharp right turn when other men darted in front of us. I ran towards a set of doors just a few feet away and pushed through them, making my way into what looked like the kitchen to the club.

"Care for an appetizer?" Haven asked as the kitchen staff let out a screech at our running figures.

"Don't have the appetite!" I jumped forward, sliding over a kitchen counter to which Haven copied.

The staff was scrambling around us—one person dropping a tray of food in shock as I ran around another side of the counters they were trying to get to. Just as I neared the back door, three men ran in through it, stopping us in our tracks.

Haven ran into my back at my sudden stop and let out a curse when her eyes locked on the men in front of us. I quickly turned to go back the other way, but the men chasing us from before had caught up to us.

"Well, well, well… if it isn't Everette Knight. I thought you were dead," the man spoke.

I should have known I was too notorious, hood covering my face most days or not.

"Takes a lot more than a sword wound to keep me down," I gritted out, pulling Haven closer to me.

"And who's this pretty lady? Someone says she has a certain… scar?"

I swallowed, trying my best to come up with some plan.

Haven rested her hand on my shoulder. "Babe? Who are these people?"

Sticking with her sudden idea, I sighed. "Nothing, sweetheart." I looked back to the men surrounding us. "Look, I'm just here with my girl to get away from the shit storm that was happening in the states. We didn't come here for trouble."

The man who had been speaking before chuckled. "You expect me to believe that?"

Dropping the act, I shrugged. "It was worth the shot."

"Why are you here?" the man asked, the doors behind him opening to a handful of women.

They were all dressed in the same uniform—a short top that I could only say resembled a bra, a long skirt with a slit all the way to their hip, and a dagger strapped to their thigh. A mask covered their nose and down, but from Haven's grip tightening on me… I had a feeling they weren't just some random women.

They were of the MOT bloodline.

"Business," was my curt reply.

"You have the scar, how?" a woman spoke up, directing her attention to Haven.

"Because I'm one of you," Haven replied. "And you're all being taken advantage of."

The man suddenly burst out laughing. "That's why you're here? To what, save them?"

My hands slowly started to drop to my sides, eager to rip out the two daggers stuck behind my back and wedged between the waistband of my pants. There were too many of them, so how we were to get out unscathed, I had no idea.

"Sorry to say, but you won't be leaving here with this information. Take them!" he ordered, and the women darted forward.

I was quick to grab my daggers just as Haven freed the one from her thigh. "I think it's time to let it out, Haven!" I shouted, darting forward.

I had no idea if she understood what I meant, but at the sound of the grunt that left her as she easily moved her way around the women, I had a feeling she did.

The rage of a Holden.

I was praising whatever had sped up my healing process because as I swung my weapons, my body didn't ache with a torturous pain that made me sick. Now, I was out for blood.

This time around, I was protecting the woman who had been determined to come on this mission with me, and I'll be damned if anything happened to her on my watch.

I smacked the hilt of my dagger into one of the women's head, causing them to drop unconscious as I moved on to the next. Haven flew past me, sliding to her knees as she dug her dagger into one of the men's stomachs. Ripping it out, she spun and entered a fight with an MOT.

With the numbers dropping, two men came at me. I held my ground at first, trying my best to not let them gain any ground as I delivered blow after blow. However, someone hit me from behind, causing me to stagger forward as another drove his knee up and smacked it underneath my jaw.

My vision went in and out as I collapsed to the ground, a metallic taste crawling into my mouth as the ceiling came into view.

I heard a rage-filled scream as they raised something and thrust it down towards me, but before it touched me, it was knocked from their hands.

Through a blurry vision, I saw flashes of red darting around, a metal sound clanking over and over as the screams rose.

Then it was silent.

Blinking a few times, my eyes finally locked on a heavy breathing Haven, her eyes dark as she held a cast iron skillet above her head, and her hands shook with blood scattered across her body. She looked over at me with wide eyes, as if she couldn't believe what had just happened.

Trailing her eyes back to the unconscious men around us she spit out, "Rapunzel *that*, bitch." Then she tossed the skillet onto the ground and dropped to her knees beside me.

"Everette? Everette, are you okay?!" She cupped the sides of my face. "They're all out cold. We need to go. We have to get out of here. Can you walk?"

I groaned and managed a nod. Haven helped me to my feet, and I winced at the throbbing underneath my chin. "I think he nearly dislocated my jaw," I mumbled.

She threw my arm around me, helping me to the back door and leaned me up against it. She then sprinted across the room to retrieve her dagger—which must have been knocked from her hands during the fight—and padded back over to me barefoot.

Placing my arm back around her, she sighed. "Let's just get you home. Your mouth is bleeding."

"I think it's just my tongue. He nailed me pretty hard."

When we made our way into the back alley, Haven looked up at me. "You're lucky he didn't break some of your teeth. Are you stupid? Taking on that many men at once?"

I gave her a weak grin. "Says the woman who just took out four men with a frying pan."

She lowered her eyes. "I think I killed those men. I just… I saw you go down and Everette… I blacked out again. When I came to, I was standing over you with that fucking cast iron."

"Your instincts kicked in. You couldn't help it."

We walked a little further before she stopped. "No… It was the *rage* that kicked in. I felt it clawing at me when we started. Like it was begging to be released and then you… I… I gave in. And I don't remember what happened next. Just the aftermath. My dagger must have been knocked from my hands and my instincts just grabbed whatever was available."

We started walking again and I looked down at her, seeing a streak of blood dripping from under her wig. "Haven, your head is bleeding."

"I'm not important right now. We need to get you back to the house"

I scoffed. "You're always important to me, do you understand that?"

She remained silent for a few seconds before saying, "What do we do about those women? They clearly didn't want to hear us out. I mean, we had to knock them unconscious to get away from them. They would have killed us."

I managed a shrug. "Maybe they are in the same situation as you. Just like with the commander. They are doing all that they were taught. Maybe they don't know any better, so that's why we can't give up on them just yet."

Haven's jaw ticked. "We didn't even get any intel on Ghost or how to help those women. Our plan sucked." She let out a humorless laugh. "What do we do now? They know you're here with an MOT sneaking around. Those men are dead. Surely those women are going to report back to Ghost if he's the one commanding them around. They're literally just as trained as the normal MOTs. One hit me so hard, I actually got scared for a moment. They were created to be monsters."

I dug into my pocket. "Let's take it one step at a time." I pulled out my phone and called up Miguel. "We'll figure this out, I promise."

At least, I sure hope so. Because it's the first time in a very long time that I, Everette Knight, had no damn plan on how we were supposed to proceed. We were in foreign territory with no one but ourselves for help. How do we stay alive for this?

CHAPTER NINETEEN

Jay

I always wanted to travel the world. Hell, I remember times when Nikita, Haven, and I would get a huge map and circle all the places we wanted to visit once our scars disappeared. If only I would have known what a fraud our organization was, maybe I would have saved myself the heartbreak.

Because Russia? It was nothing without my girls by my side.

A.R and I had reached Russia just days ago. I was awestruck to witness a country outside of the states, but I couldn't fully appreciate the trip knowing what was in store for us.

And A.R? I wanted to murder the man. He was incurable.

"I said no. Once we get the whereabouts from my contacts, we'll make a move towards the location the women were last seen at. I don't have time to make mistakes," he grumbled.

I rolled my eyes. "You're such a pain in the ass. I can't sit around and wait any longer. We have a mission here."

"I'm well aware. Must I remind you that I don't even have to be helping you all? I'm doing this for Haven and her parents."

I folded my arms, falling back further into the living room couch I was sitting on as A.R looked at some papers. He looked so pampered in his huge house and expensive suit. Just the way he sat, which was one leg folded neatly over the other, made me clench my teeth.

I cocked a brow. "If you're screwing us over, I will cut off your dick, even if it's the last thing I do."

He hummed, his eyes never leaving the paper before him. "You seem to have some fascination with my dick, care to explain?"

I scoffed. "As if I'd be interested in you."

He chuckled. "Didn't say you were."

My fists clenched. "I actually hate you. And it takes a lot for me to hate someone."

"Consider me honored."

I stared agape at him. Did nothing get under this man's skin?

His phone buzzing brought him out of his paper trance. Grabbing it, his brows furrowed when he read the message. I eagerly leaned forward, waiting for him to say something. Was it one of his contacts? Was it time to finally start our mission?

Calmly, he sat his papers to the side and stood, loosening his tie. "Get ready."

"It's time? Is it actually time to move in on the location?"

He pulled his tie off, raising a brow. "Well? This is all you have been bitching about. Get a move on it. I'm going to get changed. Meet me at the car in ten."

I waited no time before darting through the huge house to where my room was. It was as if I couldn't get in my MOT attire quick enough as I ripped my clothes off and pulled everything on. I strapped my dagger into place on my thigh and grabbed my spare to tuck in the back of my pants.

Giving myself an encouraging nod in the mirror against the wall next to me, I took a few deep breaths and quickly exited the room.

By the time I made it to the car, A.R was already inside.

Such a gentleman.

I got in and noticed his dark clothing and designer shades. "You really go all out with spending money, huh?"

A.R grinned, placing his arm on the back of my seat as he backed out of the driveway. "Don't worry about it, princess."

Ignoring the nickname, I looked out the window at our surroundings. "Where are we going exactly?"

A.R turned onto the road, speeding down it. "I'm getting us as close as I can. I particularly travel the most I can on foot, but this place is a good distance away from us. It's a building that has been known for Ghost to use as a post for some of his men. Ghost is… well, let's say he lives up to his name. He's practically a ghost. He has everyone do his bidding and no one sees him in action. Ever. This post is apparently used for information, which means he has men stay there in case someone needs to get word to him."

My brows drew together. "So we're just going to ambush those men who gather information for… more information?"

He snorted. "Something like that, yeah."

I rubbed my arms, not liking the idea. "I know I was eager to get out, but look… as an MOT, I plan days in advance before I go after a target. When I do take off one night, I know everything about them, all the way down to what they eat for breakfast. We're going in blind here, Axt—A.R."

"I do, too, which is why we didn't go in guns blazing the first night like you were so willing to do. I got the intel from my contacts and now we're going to find those men. This is the best we could do with what the commander had. It has been years since she sold those women off. Who knows what we're really getting into."

I gulped, feeling like I was about to heave up my dinner. "I'm just nervous."

A.R sighed, reaching over to give my thigh a small squeeze. "I'm not going to let anything happen to you, okay? You'd totally haunt me in the afterlife."

I couldn't help but let out a small laugh, appreciating the jab to get my mind thinking about something else. "I *so* would. I'd hide all your hair products."

He drew his hand back as if I burned him. "You wouldn't dare."

I threw him a wicked grin. "Even the gel."

He gasped. "Not the gel."

I snickered, looking at his perfect dirty blonde hair. It was longer but gelled back to give him that sleek and elegant look.

A.R was the definition of a player. He was a pretty boy. I didn't know his story, but I knew he liked to pamper himself. He was fit, had killer blue eyes, and a sharp jaw and broad cheekbones that could make a girl swoon.

"You're staring again," he pointed out.

"Thinking of all the ways to cut your hair while you're sleeping."

He grimaced. "Remind me to hide all sharp things when we get back to the house."

I laughed once more, looking out the window to see him pulling over near a rocky path. "We're stopping here?"

"Yeah, this is where I'll keep the car away from prying eyes. We'll travel on foot from here."

He leaned back to grab a bag out of his back seat. I watched him curiously as he unzipped it and pulled out a small pouch. Opening it, he pulled a small piece of tech out and stuck it in his ear before grabbing another one and handing it to me.

I gently took the small thing from him, staring at it warily. "What is this?"

He deadpanned. "Isn't it obvious? It's an earpiece. We'll be able to hear each other while we're working."

I raised a brow. "Why would we need this if we're going to be with each other?"

He smirked. "Because we're not. You, my dear friend, are going to distract the men while I get high up in the building to lock my sights on them."

My mouth parted slightly in shock. "You're abandoning me? No way!"

He sat back, looking genuinely surprised. "Are you really scared right now? To me you seem like the most fearless one out of all of the MOTs."

I winced. "That's Haven. You got the wrong girl, pal."

He shook his head. "No, I don't think so. I believe you can do this, okay? Or else I wouldn't have let you come with me to Russia."

As I put the piece in my ear, I rolled my eyes. "You didn't exactly have a choice in the matter."

"Oh, I did. I could have easily convinced Saul to go with you, but I didn't. I wanted someone who would hold their own. Tell me, Jay, can you hold your own?"

"Of course, but—"

"No buts. I know you can, and you know you can, so stop stalling. I've already worked this all out in my head. I scoped out the place last night while you were sleeping. There is a building, yes, but it's abandoned next to a shipping yard where Ghost's men operate. If you can stall them enough for me to get to my gun I have waiting up there, you have nothing to worry about."

I think I went pale. "So I'm going out in the open as bait? Those men will kill me on sight."

He shrugged. "Not if I have anything to say about it."

"Fine, but what happens after that? You can't just kill them all. We need answers."

A.R didn't reply as he zipped the bag up and tossed it back into the rear of the car. He grabbed a few other things, stashing ammo and other stuff along his body. Eventually, he grabbed his handgun and cocked it, turning it to the side as he examined it. "I make an example out of one to get the others to fall in line. I'll tell you what you need to do when we get there, but if we wait any longer, we're going to lose our opening."

With that, A.R got out of the car and shut the door behind him. I blew out a deep breath, smacking the dashboard. “Fuck, fuck, fuck!”

I closed my eyes, reminding me of why I had to do this.

Justice.

***

A.R ditched my ass the minute we neared our location, which isn’t surprising. He had warned me we were going to be separated, but as I stayed crouched behind a shipping container, my heart started to beat harder and harder.

I could hear the men talking in Russian. There were about five of them in navy cloaks walking around, taking note of their surroundings.

I couldn’t believe I allowed myself to be the damn bait.

Checking my watch, I noticed it had been around ten minutes since A.R had left me. That had to be enough time for him to get into the building, right?

As if the universe was confirming my suspicions, the earpiece made a high pitched sound before A.R’s voice flooded through it. “All right, princess, I’m in position. I count five men about twenty feet away from you. Don’t talk to me, just listen. We need you to be as quiet as possible. The minute I tell you to, I want you to run across to the other container to your left. Hide there and wait for them to get a bit closer.”

Why? I wanted to scream. Isn’t the bait supposed to just hop out and say *hey assholes! I’m here! Come and get me!*

“Okay, three…two…one… now!” I held my breath and took off into a sprint before I dove into a roll, hopping upright beside the container he mentioned.

“Good girl,” he mused, causing me to shoot him the bird.

His laugh confirmed that he saw it.

“Now look out in front of you, you should be able to see them better.”

I did as I was told and assessed the men. He was right, this position gave me a better viewpoint of the men that were walking around. Two swords stuck out from behind their backs.

These were definitely the men Haven had talked about.

"The tall one with the limp in his step? He's clearly hurt. If they try anything you need to take him out first. The one to his right? Dark hair and wearing a mask? He's the most built, he's going to be the strongest most likely. The other three are dogs following the leaders, which are the two men I pointed out. They'll cower the minute they hear my gun go off. They're a flight risk, so don't let them get away."

I was impressed, to say the least. I could tell A.R did this for a living.

I moved my hands, motioning for him to continue. "Now you know what I do. Get out there and make me proud."

With that, the static line went off.

I gulped, mentally preparing myself for what could very well be my death.

You're a bad bitch, Jay.

With that, I stood and unsheathed my daggers as I walked out into the open. The minute they saw me, their swords were out and ready.

"Hold!" the one with the mask yelled.

I spun my dagger in my hand. "No can do, fellas!"

The man with the limp stepped up beside his fellow 'leader'. "What do you want?"

By the way they assessed my attire, they knew exactly who I belonged to. I grinned at the thought and tilted my head to the side. "Justice."

The masked man laughed. "You were stupid to show up here alone."

I smirked. "Who said I showed up alone?"

As the words left my mouth, there was a whistling sound before the masked man toppled to the ground, blood pouring from his body.

"Make one move and you're all getting a bullet between the eyes," I warned, cutting my eyes to the three men who staggered back like they were going to run.

Just like A.R said.

I pointed my dagger at the man with the limp. "You there, stay put."

I walked closer and got a few feet in front of him. "Where is Ghost?"

"I can't disclose that information and you know that. I'll be as good as dead."

I hiked a brow up. "You're as good as dead right this moment if you don't speak up."

He noticeably gulped, looking around for my hitman that was hiding somewhere. Little did he know that A.R was just as good as staying hidden as the man he followed.

Letting out a shaky breath, he said, "Ghost went back to the states about a week ago. He heard Haven McKinley was dead. Now he wishes to take control of the other MOTs."

My anger spiked. "Why?"

"Why does Ghost do anything he does? He wants power. Craves it. He already has MOTs working under him. If he gets more, he'll be unstoppable. He'll have an army."

I clicked my tongue. "And why did he wait until my friend was dead?"

The man let out a humorless laugh. "You all truly know nothing do you? Haven McKinley was the *only* person that he feared. He wanted to control her—wanted to control the gifts she had. But that doesn't matter now because she's dead. When we ransacked that warehouse to get her, she… lost it. It scared the shit out of him. The commander promised Haven to him, but he clearly didn't get that. Now he's after the next best thing."

Knowing this man was there when Knox died, knowing he helped cause my best friend so much pain, made me sick with rage.

"And the women the commander sold to him? The ones Ghost bought like they weren't even living, breathing human beings? Where are they?"

His jaw clenched. "You'll have to be more specific. We see a lot of women that your commander sold off."

I stepped forward, our faces only an inch apart. "The ones that were shipped right to this fucking shipping yard! Don't act like you don't know. There were ten of them. Some as young as sixteen."

He shook his head, fear seeping into his tone as he said, "I truly don't know! I was put on this post just recently. I really don't know."

I urged him for more information. "Where can I find the answers that I need?"

He looked pale, knowing that he was in too deep. "There's another post that has been known to have the MOTs working there. A torture chamber, as some of my men used to say who actually got to witness it. It's heavily guarded, though, but it's about two miles from here. Stay on the main road and take the one that goes off into a fork. The right trail will lead you there."

I nodded my head. "And you're not lying to me?"

"What do I have to lose at this point?"

I tilted my head, surveying him. "Your dignity," I muttered and drove my dagger into his stomach. My heart clenched as I heard three shots break out, taking out the men behind him. As the man fell on me, I held him up, putting my mouth next to his ear. "That's for Haven and Knox."

Ripping the dagger out, I shoved him away.

Revenge is always best served cold.

Fuck you, Ghost.

CHAPTER TWENTY

Haven

Late in the night, I woke up sweating.

I could still hear the screams of my friends, the mere sound of it raising the hairs on my arms. And all I could see was Ghost standing there with a wicked gleam in his eyes as he slaughtered them all in front of me.

I had run to the bathroom, emptying my stomach from the thought of losing any of them, and each time I heaved, flashes of their bodies filled my mind.

The last person Ghost had brought in front of me in the nightmare had been Everette, and it gutted me to watch him plunge a dagger into his stomach repeatedly—just like the Commander had done to Knox.

I had no idea why he was always the last to die in front of me—why it was always the thing that woke me from the nightmare. I wondered if it was the curse trying to tell me something or trying to warn me about something that was in store for us.

I didn't know what Everette was to this curse, but I had a feeling he played a more important role with each day that passed.

Perhaps that's why I lingered in the hall outside his room shortly after just to make sure no one had gotten to him. I lasted all of ten minutes with my back resting on the door with racing thoughts before I made myself go in and take a seat next to his bed in an empty chair, trying my best to not wake him.

Now, I stared at my book with tired eyes. I read the same lines over, trying to get a better understanding of this rage that was starting to consume me. But even after I read the words a hundred times, I still couldn't grasp it all.

It seemed like some fantasy book that someone would read for a thrill.

Setting the book down, I looked at the pile next to me. Apparently, I still had so much to learn and I needed to figure out what exactly Ghost wanted from me.

"Haven?" a groggy voice spoke.

I turned, seeing Everette slowly rise from his bed.

Dammit.

"Hey," I replied, gently closing the book.

"What are you doing in my room? It's nearly three in the morning."

I didn't know how to answer that. Fear maybe? Fear that someone would come and take him from me in his sleep. I hated the idea that Ghost could now possibly know he was alive. Just looking at Everette made me wince—the underneath of his chin was so bruised.

It had been almost two days since we last went out and I was determined to let Everette get some rest, even when he declared he was fine.

"The house was too quiet," I lied. "Didn't want to be alone."

He frowned before letting a yawn escape and he moved over, patting the spot he had just been lying in. "Come on."

A small, smart part of my brain told me not to accept the offer, but the other side of it told me to sprint to the spot. After a small internal battle, I sat my book aside and moved over to the bed.

It felt almost natural with how easy it was to slide under the covers and lay next to him, turning so I could get a good look at the man who now seemed to be all I think about.

He faced me, propping his head up with his arm. "What's on your mind? What's the real reason you're sitting next to my bed like a creeper."

I mirrored his position and let out a sigh. "I'm just worried about the possibility of Ghost knowing you're alive."

He reached out, tucking a strand of hair behind my ear. "Worrying about me, Red?"

I let out a snort. "Apparently so."

"Why do you do that? Worry about the unknown?" he asked.

I looked at him like he had two heads. "How do you not?"

He pursed his lips for a moment before he said, "I learned a long time ago that I have to live in the present. If you don't, your mind is always elsewhere. It affects everything you do—it consumes you. I'm not saying it's easy, but sometimes you have to cut yourself some slack."

I let out a dry laugh. "Cut myself some slack," I repeated. "That's harder than it sounds."

He nodded. "Yeah, but sometimes it's needed. You can't keep thinking about all of the what ifs. You just have to do your best in the present and hope it sets the future up nicely."

I fell back onto his pillow and stared at the ceiling. "Everette Knight, the man of many wise words."

He chuckled. "Don't get used to it."

Turning my head, I caught his gaze. "Isn't it odd? How at one point in life we kind of hated each other and now we're lying in the same bed together?"

"That's bonding over trauma for you," he mused.

I belted out a laugh. "I'll say."

Our laughter quieted down as we locked eyes once more. "Have you slept any these past two days?" he asked.

I gave him a sheepish grin. "If I say yes, will you not ask any more questions?"

"Haven, you need to sleep."

"I can't," I mumbled. "I keep… I keep having that same damn dream you woke me from. I hate it."

At the thought of it, tears brimmed my eyes and I was quick to cover my face. Everette gently grabbed my arms, trying to pry them away from my face.

"Hey… hey, what's wrong?"

I hiccupped, trying to hold back the tears as I nailed my eyes to the ceiling, refusing to look at him. "I can't lose anyone else, Everette, I just can't."

"Hey, come here," he mumbled, pulling me closer to him.

I let him pull me into his embrace and wrapped myself around him, tiredly dropping my head on his chest. "I'm *so* tired," I croaked.

"I know, Haven, I know. Hopefully, this will all be over soon." He gently played with my hair, causing my eyes to flutter shut as the last of my tears fell.

"This is so embarrassing," I mumbled, sniffling as I tried to aggressively wipe my tears away.

He rested his chin on the top of my head. "No, it's not. It's good to let your emotions out sometimes. You can't keep them bottled all the time."

I closed my eyes again. "I just want to forget. I just want one moment of peace because I feel like I'll never get one."

"Is there anything I can do?" he asked, rubbing my arms.

I looked up at Everette through tired eyes. "I wish."

He stared at me for a moment, his eyes drifting across my face. Gently, his thumb brushed over my cheek… my bottom lip. The gesture made me go back to the night in the manor when he gave me my dagger back.

"Haven?"

"Hm?"

"I'm going to kiss you. And we're not going to talk about it until we're ready. We're just going to forget for now, okay?"

My heart skipped and no words came out of my mouth. Everette searched my eyes for an answer, but I laid there frozen in his arms.

"Everette... I don't..." I couldn't find the right words and it felt like my mind was racing at a terrible speed, all my thoughts jumbling together in one big mess.

"All you have to say is no, Haven," he whispered.

But that was just the thing.

I didn't want to and that scared the hell out of me.

Because the last person I ever kissed was Knox. And he died not shortly after. I felt that everything I touched withered away and if I played into this moment, I knew it wouldn't just be something we could forget—that I could forget.

Not with how he looks at me or how my heart speeds up when I hear him laugh or see him smile. Or how his simple words can make me feel better within seconds. Or... Or how I felt so damn safe in his arms.

It was stupid.

This idea was stupid.

But I couldn't form the word to tell him no.

Slowly, my hand raised to cup his cheek. "Okay," I whispered, "let's forget..."

His hand sunk into my hair as he pulled me to meet his lips and I couldn't stop my toes from curling at the feeling of his lips pressed against my own.

Everette groaned, kissing me back with more force as he rolled us over to where my back was against the mattress. I threaded my hands through his hair, loving the feeling of it between my fingers as I gave it a small tug, earning another groan from him. His hands skimmed down the sides of my body, causing a shiver to dance down my spine when his fingers slid underneath the hem of my shirt.

I parted my legs, allowing him to move between them before I wrapped each one around his waist, pulling him closer. We broke apart for air, but Everette continued his torturous kisses down the base of my neck, nipping at a spot that had desire swirling within my core.

At the roll of his hips into my own, my head fell back with a moan. And at the sound of it, Everette's grip on my waist tightened and he did it again, causing me to grab the back of his head and smash my lips to his.

Something shifted within me as if everything faded away and the ache and pain that haunted me vanished. Right here in his arms, I felt free.

I relished it.

But what I noticed most was that here, in this moment, my rage was gone. That horrible feeling that gnawed at me *each* and *every* day since that night in the warehouse was completely gone.

"I got you," he whispered between kisses, peppering them down my neck.

As the words left him, my grip on him tightened, and a calming feeling washed over me again as if he shielded me away from the horrors of our world.

And now I felt like I knew why the curse had shown him everything—why for some odd fucking reason that it helped him heal.

Because he was supposed to heal *me.*

He was what would push me back into the light each time that it got too dark—would wake me from the nightmares.

My scar throbbed at the thought and my eyes instantly stung.

I tried to blink the tears away, letting my fingers roam Everette's form, but my hands shook as I fought back the sob that was trying to escape my chest.

Everette pulled back, cupping my face gently. "Haven, are you crying? We can stop. We can—"

I grabbed his hands, smiling up through my tears. "Just shut up and kiss me again."

I probably looked and sounded like a lunatic, and he most definitely wanted to question it, but he leaned back down and gave me a gentle kiss.

Then one on my nose.

Each eyelid.

My forehead.

"Talk to me, Red," he begged.

I let out a shaky breath, locking my arms around his neck as he stared down at me with a small smile. "You'll think I'm crazy."

He cracked a grin. "I already think that, so…"

I laughed, trying to shove him away, but he shook his head and pulled me back to him. "I'm listening, I promise."

I gulped. "Have you ever felt at peace with someone? Like everything fades away when they're near?"

He nodded. "Here. Right now. And just a few minutes ago? It was weird, but I felt like everything was just so… free?"

I let out a shaky breath of relief. "Me, too."

He tilted his head. "And that made you cry? I was about to start doubting my amazing kissing skills."

I let out a sound between a laugh and a sob. "I just… I have a strong feeling that we're where we're supposed to be in life. We are on the right path, maybe? I don't know, but something about this… it just feels right. Is that crazy? Am *I* crazy?"

He shook his head. "No, not at all because I've felt that way for a while. It was like a small part of me always had some sort of connection to you and I just couldn't let it go."

I chewed on my bottom lip. "And the worst part is that I don't feel guilty for feeling this way. Aren't I supposed to? With Knox dying so recently, I just feel like an asshole for even letting you touch me."

Everette frowned, laying back beside me. "Everyone heals in their own way, Haven. You can't hate yourself for the way you feel. On the plane here, you said you didn't think you loved him?"

I shook my head. "No… no I didn't. There wasn't enough time for that. But I did care about him. A lot. But A.R seems to think that Knox did love me and that makes me feel so shitty. Even shittier when I am the one responsible for his death."

Everette laced his fingers through my own. "Maybe he did. There's no time stamp on love. It's different for everyone, but Haven… Knox had known about you way longer. What you felt, you felt in a shorter time than what he had so it wouldn't have felt the same for him. That's why you can't justify love that way. And you're not responsible for his death. He made that choice and he was happy with it."

I snuggled into Everette's side, my hand resting above his heart. "At the club? When we were dancing… I didn't mean to flinch away like I did. I just got scared. Because the last person I felt even slightly the same about was Knox. And you see where he is now. I just feel everything I touch *dies* and when I let my guard down and allow any amount of happiness into my life… it gets ripped right out of my hands."

Everette rubbed my back. "I'm not going anywhere, Red."

Wanting to change the subject, I asked, "My tears kind of killed the mood, didn't they?"

He laughed. "A little, but this night turned out better than I thought it would, if I am to be honest."

Biting my lip, I tried to hold back a smile. "Maybe we can continue later."

He looked down at me with a raised brow. "Haven McKinley… you can't tease me like that."

I grinned back at him. "Just you wait and see."

CHAPTER TWENTY-ONE

Everette

I woke up from the light shining through the windows, causing me to squint my eyes as I took in my surroundings. But when I felt a small weight on my chest, I froze, remembering the events that had happened early this morning.

Haven.

The kiss.

Looking down, Haven was asleep on my chest with my shirt clenched between her hands.

My chest ached at the sight of her there, something I had only dreamed of. I almost thought last night had been a dream, yet here she was… holding onto me like her life depended on it.

I cracked a cheesy smile as a slight snore left her, her mouth partly open. It made me feel greedy to know that she finally had gotten some sleep in my arms, and if outside was any sign… it was most definitely nearing lunch or past it. But I couldn't bring myself to wake her.

Instead, I stared at the slight features on her face that made her look even more stunning, regardless of her messy bed head. I let out a soft laugh, my eyes trailing over her freckles, the MOT scar, the small indention she had on her chin (which was hardly noticeable unless you were up close with her and that I figured was from a fight years ago).

I couldn't help but run my hands through her hair as my mind drifted to why we were really here at this moment. We had a mission to uphold, one we were failing at already. The other night went to absolute shit and I nearly left that club with a busted jaw.

But Haven had been there. She stopped them from killing me and I would forever be in her debt.

It was mind-blowing to me how our roles were so quickly reversed. At one point in time, it was my mission to make sure she stayed alive. I had thought I was doing it because I needed her to get us out of the contract between the MIRs and the MOTs, but now I understood that it was far from the truth.

I was simply drawn to the woman.

And now the roles were reversed and she was the one pretty much keeping *me* alive. My ego was hurt knowing that I couldn't stand my ground long enough to keep her safe the night at the club, something I had experienced for the second time in my life, yet I was starting to understand one thing.

Haven McKinley was her own savior.

Seeing her stand over me with rage consuming her was a frightening sight, but the fact that Haven simply just witnessed me go down and it made her jump into that rage without another thought… I didn't know what the hell to think.

Haven stirred, ripping me from my thoughts, and a soft whimper left her as she stretched, blinking her eyes a few times.

"Good morning, Red."

She tilted her head, her surprised look morphing into a goofy smile. "Good morning."

I think my heart stopped a little at the sight.

My God, I was becoming *such* a simp.

I couldn't stop the grin that crossed my face. "Hungry?"

She yawned, snuggling closer into my side. "Can we just stay here forever?"

My body said *hell yes*, but my mind stated it was time to get some fuel in us before we planned out what our goal would be tonight. "As lovely as that sounds, we need to get up and get some food in us. I believe it's way past noon."

Haven groaned, placing her face onto my chest. "Idontwanna," she mumbled, her words muffled into my shirt.

I snickered. "I'm sorry? What was that?"

Her head raised. "I don't want to."

"What about breakfast for lunch? I'll make some pancakes."

Her eyes narrowed some. "With chocolate chips?"

I pushed the hair out of her face, cupping her cheeks. "If we have some."

"Oh we have some, I made sure to put them on the list."

I chuckled, my hands sliding down her arms, feeling goosebumps rise from my touch. "Then you'll have it."

Another yawn escaped her as she sat up and she rolled her neck side to side. "I may have only slept for a few hours, but I think that was the best sleep I had gotten in a while."

Feeling the need to touch her, I sat up and wrapped my arms around her waist to boldly place a kiss upon her shoulder. "If your snoring was any indication, I would say you're correct."

Haven gasped, turning her head to look back at me. "I do not snore!"

A deep laugh rumbled within my chest at her pink cheeks. "Oh, you so do. I have blackmail on you for days now. I think you even drooled a little bit."

She was quick to push herself out of my arms. "You are such a liar."

I leaned against the headboard and folded my arms with a lazy grin as she padded across the room to the bathroom. My eyes swept over her form, just now noticing the short shorts she was wearing that had me shifting in bed.

God, I could still remember her breathy moans last night as I rolled my hips into her own. The sight of her head falling back had me nearly in a frenzy to make it happen over and over until she was panting beneath me.

When a certain part of me awakened at the thought, I quickly shut that train of thought down and threw the covers off me before I pitched a tent right here for Haven to see.

She walked out of the bathroom just as I got up. "I'm going to take a quick shower. Meet you downstairs in a few?"

"Sounds good."

I expected her to walk out, but instead, she walked up and planted a kiss on my cheek. "Thank you for being so considerate last night," she whispered.

"Of course."

When she finally did leave my room, I rubbed my face with a heavy sigh.

"Cold shower, Everette, cold shower," I muttered.

***

"I'm just saying, I think we're at a dead end. I mean, how are we going to find those women? We can't just waltz back up into the club," Haven mumbled through a mouthful of pancakes.

I bit into a piece of bacon, chewing it as I thought over my answer. "I don't know, but we can't give up that easily. Today we're supposed to touch base with A.R sometime so hopefully they have good news for us. If the only lead we have is the club… our only option might be to go back. I know it sounds terrible, but that's all we have at the moment."

Haven grimaced. "How do you expect us to get in?"

"Let me think about it, I'll figure something out. Trust me, I've dealt with worse before. We're getting too into our heads. We need to think about this just like we would in New York. What do you do when you're learning about your target?"

She shrugged a shoulder. "I pretty much stalk them."

I pointed my fork at her. "Exactly. Maybe we can catch one of the MOTs leaving the club and follow them. If we can get one of them, or maybe even one of the men that works for Ghost, alone, then we can try and get some answers."

She grabbed her OJ and took a sip before cutting her eyes to me. "Okay. If that's what you think will work, then I'm game. It's not like we have anything else to go on."

Placing my fork down against my plate, I folded my arms. "But I'm going to say something you're not going to like."

She froze, narrowing her eyes. "What?"

"We need to get some training in today. I think we indeed went in too blind last time, but now that we know what we're working with, we can prepare for that."

She cursed. "Fine."

I shoved the last of my pancakes into my mouth and stood from the table with my plate. "Meet me outside in fifteen."

She scoffed. "I don't even get half an hour to let my food digest? I'll have you know, it's terrible to do things like that on a full stomach."

I let out a snort. "I think you'll manage."

"Fine, but don't bitch when I throw up on your shoes."

Shaking my head, I placed my plate into the sink and headed upstairs to change. By the time I threw on some basketball shorts and sneakers, I could hear Haven cursing from the room over as she got dressed.

Snickering, I grabbed my swords and headed back downstairs to the huge yard out back. A.R was an interesting man, one of which I couldn't quite figure out yet. He liked expensive things, that was obvious, but I didn't know why he had to have all this. I mean, the house had like six rooms.

And the backyard? It was gigantic. The house sat on a hill, overlooking a certain field that, from here, I could see had multiple targets in it. I guess even A.R had to train just as much as us.

Except he liked to use guns.

"Okay, I am here—early might I add," Haven called out, causing me to spin around.

I tried to hide my grin as I assessed her attire. A sports bra and shorts. Spandex shorts? I don't even know what to call them, but I damn well know they had my friend downstairs a little *too* excited for the training session.

I cleared my throat, motioning her forward. "We'll start with hand to hand first."

She paused, using her hand to motion for me to spin around. Raising a brow, I slowly did.

I nearly jumped when I felt her fingertips trailing across my back. "I never got to ask you what these flames represented," she mumbled, dragging her finger across one that swept down my back to the side of my rib cage.

I feel like I definitely got bonus points for not putting on a shirt in the form of Haven's wandering hands.

"I did it as a reminder that sometimes you have to push through hell and eventually it will all be behind you—that there is always something ahead of you to fight for."

She hummed. "And that's why it's at your back…" she murmured. "I like it."

I spun back around. "I'm glad. Now? Training?"

She shook her head. "Right. But you mean *torture session*," she corrected.

I rolled my eyes. "Sparring with me is not that bad, Haven."

"But it is! You always have me on my ass and it hurts for days."

"Maybe you need to work a little harder to stay off it then."

She gasped. "What is that supposed to mean?"

I belted out a laugh, realizing how terrible that sounded. "I just meant in training, Red."

She scoffed, placing her hand to her hip. "I was starting to think you were calling me fat."

I grinned, dragging my eyes over her form. "With a body like that? Definitely not."

She looked away, a pinkish tone gracing her cheeks. "Whatever, let's just get this over with."

We spent the next few minutes practicing certain foot placing techniques and other basic things that Haven reminded me at least twenty times that she didn't need to revisit. After a few minutes, we moved to hand to hand, and I had to admit… the woman paid attention in training.

I could remember our days back in the manor's courtyard when we sparred and she always gave away her next move with certain ticks. It was so easy to put her on her ass that I began to think of it as a game to piss her off.

How many times could I knock Haven off her feet until she stabs me? It was fun while it lasted.

But now? Those tics were gone, and I could barely catch sight of her next move as she moved around me with a fast pace and just as quick punches.

When she pulled her next move and swiped my feet out from under me, a sound of victory that I had never heard from her bounced off the trees around us. "I finally did it! Man, Everette, you are slacking!"

I tried to laugh, but with the wind knocked out of me it came out more like a wheeze. "Help me up, you goofball." She took my hand with a wide grin and jerked me upright. "Damn, woman, are you trying to rip my arm out of the socket?"

She faked a pout. "Everette? Are you getting too old to keep up with me?"

I ran my tongue over my bottom lip at the expression I so desperately wanted to wipe off her face.

Maybe I was going too easy on her, even Saul said so.

Without giving her a chance to react, I dove for her. Haven screeched as my body slammed into her. She tried to fight back, but I had her pinned to the ground in seconds and it only took one of my hands to pin both of hers above her head.

Breathless, she looked up at me with wide eyes as I trailed my finger across her neck. "If I would have had my dagger on me, it would have been right… here," I mumbled, pressing harder into her jugular.

She gulped under my touch and my body became too aware of our position as I straddled her waist. I leaned down, placing my mouth next to her ear. "Rule number one?"

"Don't lose focus," she whispered, her voice catching as I nipped at her ear.

I leaned back a little, a cocky look plastered on my face. "How's that for being, what was it? *Old*?"

She shifted her hips slightly and it immediately wiped the look from my face as her eyes heated. Haven reached up, grabbing the back of my neck to lower my head. My breath caught in my throat when there was a whisper of her lips on mine before she abruptly flipped us.

When my back slammed into the ground, Haven held a triumphant grin with her hands planted on my chest to hold me down. "You lost focus."

A sound similar to a growl left me as I reached out and grabbed the back of her neck and smashed my lips to hers.

This kiss was different from last night. It was rough. Raw. Filled with need and desire for one another.

I couldn't stop the groan that left me if I wanted to. Haven's nails were digging into my back as I sat us upright, my arms circling her waist as I pulled her as close as space would allow. And before I knew it, I was laying her on the grass and letting her wrap her legs around me as I rolled my hips into her own.

Just as I expected, her mouth left mine as her back arched and her head was thrown back in pure pleasure. I couldn't take my eyes off her as

I lowered my mouth to the valley of her breasts, trailing dangerously low and cursing this damn sports bra at the same time.

When I nipped at her through the fabric, the sound that left her was like music to my ears. Hands skimming her waist, I trailed one finger beneath the waistband of her shorts, seeing her eyes flutter open.

"Please," she whispered.

Groaning with pleasure at the sound of that, my hand dipped under her waistband fully and past the thin lace she was wearing beneath. My fingers found her core and I looked up at her with a wicked grin when I found her *soaking* for me.

When I found the spot she was crying for me to touch, her back arched as my thumb brushed against it. "Fuck," she breathed out.

My free hand flattened against her stomach. "Stop moving or you'll wait," I ordered, watching her instantly try to stop her fidgeting.

"Everette, stop fucking around," she growled out.

I let out a husky chuckle as I moved back up her body, taking my time to take in every inch of her. "I like my name on your lips, especially when you're begging."

Haven raised her hips, which only caused me to pull my hand back slightly and for her eyes to snap open, shooting me a deadly glare. "Don't tell me you're a tease."

I thrust a finger into her core, causing her mouth to fall open with a breathless moan, stopping whatever complaint was about to come out next. I lowered my mouth next to her ear once more. "No. I just like when you do as you're told."

The small intake of breath made me realize she liked the thought of that more than she let on.

Snickering, I moved my hand slowly, enjoying the look of pure ecstasy on her face. She was a responsive little thing, moving her hips with the slight rhythm I set. Oh, how she bit her lip when I added another finger, whimpering underneath me.

A part of me thought I could just get off watching her writhe underneath my form. It was a sick thought, knowing that just her listening to the smallest of commands made me grit my teeth together with an inexplicable amount of pride.

But when her breathing picked up and she started to grow restless, I knew she was close.

I picked up my pace, smashing my lips to hers and finally let her hands dive into my hair as I nipped at her bottom lip, causing another gasp to leave her. My tongue met her own, fighting for dominance that she let me have instantly as I worked her to the edge.

And when she came, she clung to me, a beautiful sound leaving her body as her hands shook slightly against my neck.

Carefully, I pulled back, staring down at her with a newly possessive and dangerous feeling when she finally opened her eyes to look at me. "I never thought I could witness something so beautiful."

Haven was quick to hide her face in the crook of my neck as I removed my hand. "That was… wow."

I'll say.

"Let's get you cleaned up, Red. We're both covered in grass," I mused.

She halted my movements, biting her lip. "Do you want me to…?" she stated.

I frowned. "No, Haven. I will never expect anything in return. Understand? I was more than glad to give you what you wanted."

Her blush was becoming one of my favorite things.

"I think we suck at training," she mumbled, her eyes not able to meet my own.

I let out a laugh. "We do."

But believe me when I say this was the best damn training session that I've ever participated in.

Maybe I need to make Haven train more often.

CHAPTER TWENTY-TWO

Nikita

I belted out a laugh as Saul devoured yet another croissant. "Saul, if you eat any more of those, you're going to be sick."

He waved me off, sticking the last bite into his mouth. "I mean, is everything better in London? The food is to die for. Croissants in the states are never this good."

I giggled, tucking my feet under me. We were in some apartment of A.R's that he had set up for us. It was nice and cozy, but I missed my friends dearly. However, I couldn't have gotten a better person to come on this mission with.

Saul had made me laugh at least a hundred times since we got here, if not more. We were on day four and I was having to remind myself that this was a mission and not a vacation.

The first night, we got food and stayed in to come up with some sort of plan that would lead us to the women we were searching for. The next night, we set off to the location that the women were last seen at. We had come up short, the place abandoned, but that was until Saul snooped around and found an old office within the place.

There were plenty of papers to give us leads as to where Ghost could have sent the women. For the past two days, Saul had been overworking himself to try and decipher a lot of the files.

He had confided in me that he once was in law school and paperwork didn't bother him in the slightest. To hear that Saul himself had been in law school was like having cold water being thrown over me. But for some reason? It suited him. As I watched him work these past few days, I knew that had he not joined The Men in Red for whatever reason it may have been, he would have killed it as a skilled attorney.

"Maybe we need to take you to Paris next," I teased, and his eyes nearly rolled into the back of his head at the thought of it.

"That sounds absolutely marvelous, Kit Kat."

Yes. Kit Kat. Apparently, Saul likes to hand out nicknames like Halloween candy, because he was quick to give me one. I hated it at first, telling him to think of something different, but he refused and by the third day, it had grown on me.

"Okay, so what I have gathered is that one: Ghost's men are literal fools when it comes to keeping things confidential because who would just leave all these papers? And two: there are apparently posts that his men operate out of from all over the globe. Ghost's reach extends way further than we originally thought."

I thought about it, my face twisting in curiosity. "Or it's a trap. I mean, I would think Ghost wouldn't just leave important files lying around that could potentially give him away."

Saul nodded. "I thought that, too, but the last paper with the latest date has a note on it. Someone was onto them. I don't know who, but it had Ghost a little riled up. What if that person or group found this post and his men had to flee before getting all of their things?"

I contemplated it. "That's true. It's very possible."

Saul sat back at the other end of the couch and tossed his pen that he had been scribbling on the paper with to the side. "Case closed."

I smiled to myself, looking him over. "What made you want to become a lawyer?"

His smile faded as he directed his attention towards the floor. "I mean, I've always had the grades growing up, but I didn't know I wanted to be a lawyer until I was about to graduate high school. Uh… my brother was the reason I decided to. He was convicted of something that he didn't do. It broke me to see him sent away to prison knowing that he was one of the best souls there was—he would never do such a thing. So I decided when it was time to start applying to places, that's what I was going to do. I didn't know how I would do it, but I was determined to get him out of there. I got a full ride to Harvard and the rest was history."

The urge to reach out and comfort him shot through me. The pain etched into his face at the confession made my fists clench. I understood somewhat what it was like to want justice for someone wrongly convicted—to want to put the right person behind bars. The person who was responsible for causing so much heartache. The sad thing was that situations like that happen all the time and it wouldn't stop.

"But you joined The Men in Red?" I asked, pulling on a loose thread to the couch to try and distract myself.

"Yeah," he mumbled. "There was an incident at the prison where my brother was sent to. It was his third year there, just when I was about to actually start my journey as a lawyer. He was killed, to be short. And I went into a downward spiral. My head wasn't in the right place and everything just slipped from my fingertips. I met Everette shortly after that and he was the person who helped me get back on the right path. I didn't know what he did at the time, but we grew close. Then when he knew he could trust me, he offered me a spot in The Men in Red. I just thought since I couldn't do right by my original plans, at least I could do this to help someone out. So I joined and put my sweat and tears into helping those in similar situations. It may not have been by following the law, but I did it."

When Saul finally looked at me, my heart clenched at the unshed tears in his eyes. Finally getting the courage to move closer, I crawled across the couch to his end and rested my head on his shoulder, taking his hands into my own. "I'm so sorry you had to go through that, Saul."

Saul rested his chin on the top of my head. "That's all right, Kit Kat. Stuff happens. You just have to learn how to continue on."

"Don't you wish we could just live in a world full of peace? Where there are no horrible people?"

He nodded. "Every damn day."

I chewed on the inside of my cheek for a minute before asking, "What was he like? Your brother."

Saul let out a weak laugh. "He was someone who would give you the shirt off his back if you needed it. He didn't have much money, but he would give to those who needed it more than him. He would even go to the boy's and girl's club on the weekends to volunteer. I remember stopping by sometimes and seeing him playing basketball with some of the younger kids and his face when he was there at that moment? Man, he just lit up the whole room. Those kids loved him."

"He sounds amazing."

"He was. I could remember when we were little and he just seemed so cool in my eyes. I wanted to go with him everywhere. His friends hated it, but one day when this guy said to leave his *pathetic* little brother at home… he looked that man dead in the eyes and said that it was me and him or not him at all. He also may have given that guy what I used to call the death stare, which could make any grown man squirm, but that's beside the point." He chuckled, shaking his head. "He was my idol."

Just hearing him talk about his brother made tears fill my eyes. June's death was still a fresh wound, one that I don't think I would ever recover from. She was taken too soon and taken by the hands of evil so a point could be made.

How someone could be so cruel was beyond me.

She was so young.

"That kind of reminds me of June. She was younger than me, but she always held such a fiery attitude that she seemed like the older sister in most eyes. She was a loyal sister and one that would do anything for those she loved."

Saul sighed, tucking me under his arm. "I'm sorry for your loss. No one should have to go through what you did."

"Neither should you…" I tailed off. "But like you said… stuff happens."

Saul let out another strained laugh. "What doesn't kill you makes you stronger, right?"

I patted his chest. "I sure hope so."

He suddenly slapped his thighs, making me sit up straight. "All right, enough of this sappy talk. We have a mission to get prepared for."

I nodded, watching him go to stand, but before he walked off I grabbed a hold of his hand. "Saul?"

"Hm?"

"Thank you for trusting me with that story."

A smile found its way on his face and he gave me a deep nod. "Thank you for listening."

With that, I let go of his hand and he left for his room. Sitting back, I resumed chewing on the inside of my cheek nervously.

It was a strange feeling to see how many new people had entered my life recently and that we had all grown close in a small amount of time. But I always believed that you cross paths with certain people for a reason.

Because sometimes you need them just as they needed you.

To better one another.

To hold one another up.

To have someone to understand you.

A best friend.

Despite the circumstances, I was glad that I crossed paths with Saul and the others. It made my life look a little less chaotic with knowing that someone else could understand my upbringing.

I now understood why Haven always sought out someone that could understand her. It used to confuse me, because Jay and I understood her perfectly, but having a perspective outside of the organization that had consumed our lives for so long was a breath of fresh air.

It was like stepping out of the dark into the light for the first time. Everything was a little less scary and life was much more clear.

Shaking my head, I grabbed the files from where Saul had left them and hoped to see if anything could lead us to where Haven's parents were taken. It was a long shot, but I had to try.

We can't let Ghost win.

Not this time.

CHAPTER TWENTY-THREE

Haven

I leaned towards the phone eagerly waiting for A.R's call. He sent a short message today that he would be contacting us with new information that Jay and him had found out. In response, Everette and I had been lingering all day by the small burner phone A.R had left us.

Despite our impatience, it was easy to say something had shifted between Everette and I.

After training earlier today, I didn't know how to act around the man. I never thought I would lend myself over to him so quickly, but after last night and today… I was feeling things I shouldn't have been.

But I couldn't find it in me to be mad at myself.

What happened between us had been amazing. And this new electricity circling us? It was a delightful feeling—one that I had never felt before around a man.

At one point in time with Knox, I felt as if he had been that person I was seeking. The person to understand me, better me, and just *be* there for me. Knox may have made me feel many things, but I would be lying if I said he made my heart beat the same way Everette did.

With Everette, it was different. It wasn't just sexual tension or a desire for one another. It was something more. Like we were meant to be at this point in life together.

And now everything was just finally coming together.

Did that make me sound like a terrible person? Probably.

With Knox's sudden death, I felt as if I would have never been in this position so soon. When I first noticed my change in viewpoint towards Everette, I almost felt like I was betraying Knox. But how can you betray someone you didn't get a chance to love?

What if this was my chance at such a thing?

Or maybe I was a fool still seeking something to complete me. But the curse wouldn't have given me such signs, I would like to think, if Everette wasn't someone that could be good for me.

Everette held an important place in my life, and I was beginning to think I was finally narrowing down what that could potentially mean for me.

Peace, perhaps.

"What are you thinking about?"

I looked up at Everette, trying to push the thoughts away. "Nothing. Just hoping A.R has good news."

We were in the living room, the smell of the lasagna Everette had fixed for dinner still lingering around downstairs. The sun had just set, meaning night was upon us and we would have to set out soon if A.R didn't call in time.

Everette blew out a long breath, his head falling back against the couch. "I hate this waiting game."

"Me too." I sighed, tossing my legs over Everette's thighs and kicked back, placing my arms behind my head.

If I wasn't so stressed out by A.R's awaiting news, I would have laughed at our positions. It seemed like such a casual thing for us. Sitting here lounging as Everette stared off into the distance in thought, his thumb rubbing small circles over one of my legs.

"Do you remember that karaoke night Saul made us have?" Everette randomly asked.

My brow etched up. "How could I forget? I felt like I got hit by a train the next morning."

Chuckling, Everette shook his head. "That night was terrible in so many ways. But you know what pissed me off even more?"

"What?"

"You trying to kiss me and I don't even remember it."

Laughter rumbled within my chest. "Drunk Haven is a feisty thing apparently."

His face twisted in a grimace. "I'll say. I'm never one to be scared of someone's next move, but after seeing Knox's face that day on video… I thought the man was going to kill me."

I tilted my head to the side as I grew more curious. "Why bring all this up?"

"I just… I just feel like an asshole, kind of. As if I just moved in on his girl and all I can see is his face in that video."

"Yeah, I understand. But we really weren't anything, if I am to be honest. We fooled around once. That was it. Everything was just happening at the wrong time and as I have told myself multiple times… we just didn't have time to become anything more."

Everette looked as if he wanted to say more on the matter but decided against it. Instead, a small smile crossed his features. "At least I got to know him a bit better. He was a good man, Haven—that I can't lie about. A little stalkerish in my eyes, but a good man somewhat."

I snickered. "Aren't I a hoot? I got involved with a man who stalked me for weeks."

"He had the right intentions with trying to help your father, he just went around the wrong way of doing it. Plus, I think after watching you for so long, he grew infatuated with you."

A cold shiver traveled up my body at the thought. "And I played into everything."

Everette nodded. "But like I said… he was a good man. He'd never dream of hurting you."

"I know… but can I ask you something?"

"Always, Red."

"Why did his men and your men join forces within the last few days he had left?"

Shifting with a look of discomfort, Everette leveled me with a serious stare. "Because we swore to your father that we would do anything to keep you safe. That was easier to do if we joined our men and grew our numbers. The Men in Red have a fearful title already and if our numbers suddenly grew… I guess we thought it would give a more threatening look, but also some peace of mind."

I understood the protectiveness of my father, but I didn't understand why he was so hellbent to make both of these organizations swear to protect *me*. What did my father know that we didn't?

"I get that you wanted to protect me, and I thank you for that, but what made you, at that point, agree to what my father was asking? You didn't owe him anything. You didn't owe *me* anything."

Everette looked as if someone gutted him. "Your father had a lot of contacts. He also knew how to keep stuff from getting back to the commander to some level. I asked him if he could get my sister and family somewhere safe where she couldn't find them. The day he went missing… he was supposed to tell me where they were."

My jaw nearly dropped to the floor as I shot up. "Which means you have no idea where your family is?"

He was hurting, it was so clear, and I had been so engrossed in what was happening in my own life that I didn't even bother to see it.

"I don't. He was supposed to change their numbers, get them somewhere safe, and update me once it was done."

"Everette," my voice quivered, "I'm so sorry. I had no idea."

Shrugging me off, Everette exhaled. “It’s okay. Because I’ll find them one way or another. I already talked to A.R about it to see if he can look into it, but we’ve been a bit busy.”

It was heartbreaking to hear that he couldn’t get in touch with his family, so I couldn’t imagine what they must be going through. “Have they not tried contacting you?”

He shook his head. “No, which is what worries me. I know they have my number, so why haven’t they called me? Texted?”

I rubbed his arm as I tried to think of something—anything—that could comfort him, but I came up short, my mouth opening and closing like a fish out of water.

Before my brain could find any words to speak, the phone began ringing.

Quickly, Everette answered. “Hello?”

“It’s me,” A.R’s gruff voice spoke.

“It’s about damn time. We’ve been waiting all day,” Everette replied, rolling his eyes as he leaned back into the couch, resuming his gentle circular motions now on my thigh.

I gulped, trying to focus on the conversation, but Everette’s touch was like an electric shock—it awakened everything inside me.

“Well I’ve been busy,” A.R snapped, and I could hear Jay yelling in the background for him to ‘hurry the hell up’.

They bickered for a good minute before A.R cursed. “Ghost is back in the states.”

I paled. “What?”

“He’s not near any of us, which is good for us to try and complete our missions, but not good for the women and men back home. Apparently, he’s trying to cook up some plan to take over the MOTs. He thinks that if he got the rest of the MOTs to work under him, he would be unstoppable.”

Everette’s jaw clenched. “I need to inform Reese. Have you told Saul and Nikita yet?”

"I plan to call them after I get off with you two. But besides that, I do have some good news."

I grabbed the phone from Everette, earning a glare. "What is it? Did you find the women?"

He made a strange noise, as if he wanted to say something, but didn't know how to say it. "Well… kind of?"

"Kind of?" Everette barked. "What the hell is that supposed to mean?"

There was rustling on the other side of the line before Jay's voice came through the speaker. "It means we did find them but those little shits are brainwashed like no fucking other. One literally cut my forearm and A.R had to stitch me up. Might I add that he most definitely should *not* become a doctor. His line work is ass."

I would have laughed had this not been so serious. "And? Are you okay?"

"Well, I'm talking, am I not? Yeah, I'm fine. But those women? They refuse to listen to anything we say. After we got the information on Ghost and him being in the states, the same man gave us information where we could find some of the women. Well we found them, or most of them. Then it became a shit show. Now they're locked in the basement until we find some sort of plan on what to do."

A gasp broke through my lips. "You locked them up?!"

"Well, what were we supposed to do, Haven? They were trying to kill us! Luckily A.R had enough tranq darts on hand to take down a whole army. We can't kill them or let them go back to Ghost."

I looked to Everette who seemed just as stunned as I was.

"What the fuck?" he mouthed to me and I could only shake my head in response.

"You two are never going on a mission together again," I grumbled, running my hand through my hair and feeling utterly exhausted by this whole thing. "Try to talk to them. Be honest. Explain everything without having weapons drawn."

"You don't think we've tried that?" A.R snapped. "They are the literal definitions of lunatics. One bit my shoulder. My *shoulder*, Haven. I think I may need a tetanus shot."

At this, Everette belted out a laugh. I gave him a shove, glaring at him in warning.

"I don't care what you have to do, but you better figure it out. You can't just leave them down there like that."

A.R grumbled something inaudible under his breath before giving the phone back to Jay. "We'll try," she said. "Anything on your end?"

"Our first night failed. We're going to try again, but it's not looking good for us either. We had an encounter with some of those women and they're deadly."

"Clearly," she muttered. "We need to go but we'll be in touch. We're all going to have to meet up soon, whether we have these women or not. We have to get back to the states."

The feeling of defeat washed over me at the words. Mainly because I knew how much truth was in them. The MOTs were always saving people—avenging them—but for the first time… we might have to accept defeat and move on to prevent something even worse from happening. Maybe if we can't get these women, but we're able to stop Ghost, the women could eventually be free.

"Agreed," Everette replied. "Just call us when it's time."

After our short goodbyes, I looked over to Everette with tired eyes. "Why do I have such a bad feeling about this?"

He grabbed my hand, placing a soft kiss upon it. "We'll figure it out."

For some reason, I highly doubted that.

***

Hiding behind a dumpster at two in the morning wasn't how I imagined this night to go. Actually, I had thought it would be minimal stalking and trying to get a location pinpointed for another night.

Everette had other plans.

"This is so stupid," I snapped, the smell of trash making my stomach twist in disgust.

"Are you seriously complaining right now? I know that you of all people have dealt with much worse missions," he shot back.

I clenched my teeth, peering around the side of the dumpster to see the loading dock we were near. Sitting behind the metal bin made me think about the night I threw Joshua Taylor's body into a dumpster and moved on with my life. At that point in time, I thought my life was tough. Clearly, I hadn't experienced how tough life could truly get.

"I wonder why those women came here?" I mumbled.

We had left the house after A.R's call and headed out to wait near the club to see if we could catch any of the women leaving in hopes to follow them to another location that, preferably, housed other MOTs.

Everette sighed. "I don't know, Haven, why don't you walk out and ask them?"

I scoffed. "Someone's in their asshole mood tonight."

He didn't reply as he let out an annoyed sound and set his sights on the dock that was next to a gigantic boat. Earlier, we saw two MOTs enter—their attire was hard to forget.

I mean, how could one fight in that? Apparently, it didn't faze them, but there was so much exposed skin. I could never. I'd be cut to pieces.

I snuck a glance at Everette again, hating the silence. "Okay, this is where you say I'm a brat or something after I call you an asshole."

"I deal with brats at home," was his gruff reply.

Eyes widening in surprise, I couldn't help but take that in a different way.

Okay, a sexual way. But who could blame me? The man was sex on legs.

"If we make it out of here alive, that sounds interesting," I tried to tease, but he wouldn't budge.

Suddenly feeling nervous, and a little rejected, I looked back at the dock. What had gotten into him in a span of an hour? I understood that I was a bit annoying at times, maybe a lot, but he never seemed to have cared before.

"Okay, what is up with you?" I asked impatiently.

"I'm just not wanting this to blow up in our faces."

I placed my hands against the cool feeling of the dumpster, leaning towards him to get a better look at his face in my crouched position. Eyes trailing his face, I realized the fine lines of stress and flushed cheeks.

"Why are you staring at me like that?"

I quickly placed my hand against his heart before he could push me away—it was racing. "You're scared. Panicking even."

Everette was never scared.

He gulped, gently shoving my hand away. "Yeah, well our last meeting with these women didn't go too well."

"You're always cool and collected. What has gotten into you?"

Suddenly the beautiful blue hues of his eyes found my own. He looked so conflicted and the urge to reach out and comfort him shot through me like a vine. "You, Haven. It's you. I used to not think of anything when doing something like this, but now all I can think about is you getting hurt and never forgiving myself."

All my previous teasing made me feel like a piece of shit. I was so used to Everette being such a brood towards me that this caring side of him was something I wasn't used to. In fact, I wasn't used to anyone really feeling such a way about me. There was always the protectiveness of my friends, and even Knox, but this? It was almost a whole new world to me—the look of pure torture on his face at the mere thought of me getting hurt.

"I can take care of myself, Everette."

He sighed, cupping the sides of my face with determination. "I'm well aware. Trust me, *I know*. But that won't ever stop me from worrying about you. I know this is all new between us, and I don't know where my head is at most days, but I know that the thought of you being in any danger causes an ugly side of me to show itself. I don't mean to be short with you, I'm just trying to mash this feeling down," he whispered the last part, placing his forehead to mine. "Do you understand?"

Falling short on what to say, all I managed was a nod.

"Good," he whispered once more, placing a soft kiss on my lips.

My eyes shut, savoring the feeling of him.

But the kiss was over before it even started because of the yelling coming from the boat. No—*screaming*.

We jumped, startled by the sudden screaming that ricocheted around us. Peering around the side of the dumpster, Everette hovered over my small form, pulling me close to him. A few women exited the large boat, anger etched across their faces.

"Bring them in!" one of the women shouted.

I froze, fearing that our cover was blown yet again, but when two men came around the side of the boat, holding someone who looked as if he was brutally beaten, I looked to Everette with wide eyes.

"We need to act fast," I stated.

Everette let out a shaky breath. "Stay close."

CHAPTER TWENTY-FOUR

Everette

My heart raced. My stomach dropped. And I felt as if I had gone pale as Haven and I snuck around the dumpster and neared the boat. Usually situations like this never phased me, but now with Haven near? I hated it.

I had failed her the last time.

I won't let that happen twice.

We ran with determination, practically diving onto the boat as we flattened our backs on the side of it, wedged between the boat's wall and a small railing. One wrong move and we would plummet into the water.

When we settled in our spot, the boat began to move.

Fuck. We were going to be stuck out in the middle of nowhere with a bunch of people who'd like to see us dead.

The screams grew louder, ripping me from my thoughts, and I knew those exact screams. It was the screams of pure torture being brought upon you while you sat on the brink of death. That man could be dead by the time we reached him.

One could only hope he wasn't one of the good guys.

"We need to move," Haven growled, her knuckles turning white with how hard she was clenching her fists.

"I know," I muttered, taking in a deep breath before I started to shuffle down the side of the boat since we had no room to turn around fully.

Haven followed my movements and when we reached the end, I peered around the corner, not seeing a soul out back. Eyes locked on the back door of the boat, I nodded. We can do this.

I stepped out in the open and darted towards it with Haven hot on my heels. We unsheathed our swords and darted inside. Going in blind was something I hated, but we were wasting time and that was time we couldn't afford to lose. If the boat had left its port without us, there was no telling if we would see the women again.

Then the idea of trying to help them at all was gone forever.

The inside of the boat was surprisingly hollowed out with only a few crates sitting inside. However, there was a circle of people in the middle of the open area and a man on his knees in front of them as an MOT dragged her blade across his back.

They had yet to notice us, which was honestly in our best interest considering Haven and I had skidded to a stop at the sight, horror washing over us.

"Tell us where they are!" the woman ordered, digging her blade deeper.

"Eat… shit," he grumbled.

My face fell at the familiar voice.

Miguel.

"Get away from him!" a deep voice shouted in rage and it took me a second to realize it belonged to Haven.

Before I could stop her, she had freed one of her daggers and sent it spiraling through the air.

The dagger embedded itself into the back of the MOT, sending her flying to the ground and screaming in pain.

Eyes wide, I looked at Haven who… didn't even look like herself. Her eyes were darker, her hands shaking in pure rage when she darted forward.

"No!" I yelled, trying to run after her, but as gunshots sounded, I had to dive out of the way to avoid being hit.

My back hit the side of a crate and fear poured over me as I craned my neck to lock my eyes on Haven. But she moved expertly, her swords swinging in ways I couldn't even fathom. Sparks flew as bullets were knocked out of the way by the steel she wielded and with the closer she got, the paler the men and women grew.

There had to be around fifteen MOTs that flooded the room and ran straight towards her. The sight finally kicked me into gear as I forced myself to get up and move towards them.

Haven held her ground, her swords slicing through the men as if she channeled her own rage into them, giving them a life of their own as they worked with their master to slaughter those who dared to cross her.

My view of Haven was blocked when an MOT ran in front of me, swinging her sword. Our weapons clashed midair and the steel winked under the low lightening of the boat. I took the opportunity to raise my foot and kicked her back, knocking her off balance slightly.

"You don't have to do this!" I yelled, our swords clashing once more. "We're just trying to help you all. We can free you from this hell you live in every day."

"We don't want your help!" the woman sneered, twisting her sword away from my own and swung it once more, nicking my forearm.

My jaw ticked, my anger spiking as I jumped back with a fast-beating heart. "I don't want to hurt you."

Her eyes darkened. "Too bad we don't want the same thing."

A hot, stabbing pain shot through my abdomen suddenly and I gasped, hunching forward at the unexpected feeling. Just as I did, a blade passed over my head and missed me by a few inches, a soft wind breezing over me from the sharp motion of it.

I looked down expecting some type of blade to be sticking out of my stomach, but there was nothing in sight. It was purely an ache where my newly healed scar resided.

That would have killed me had I not bent over.

Getting my head back into the game, I spun around to find out another MOT had snuck up behind me, clearly trying to behead me with the glare that was on her face.

The two women circled me and my mind raced with what to do. I couldn't kill these women, but I had to do something. But at the thought, a memory surfaced from the night we had told Haven the truth about everything.

Kill? No. Harm? Abso-fucking-lutely, Haven had sneered to Knox that night.

Around us, the screams grew worse, but none of them belonged to Haven and the mere thought of Haven killing all these people before we had the chance to save them made me kick into action.

A growl ripped through me as I thrust my sword through the air, slicing the abdomen of one of the women. She howled in pain, dropping to her knees and I shifted on my feet to face the other one.

When my eyes locked on her, I saw that she had somehow gotten Miguel in that short moment and her blade to his neck. Miguel regarded me with wide eyes. "Move and I'll gut him."

I halted, my stomach started to throb again. But it was at that moment I realized it wasn't my stomach, but my wound—my wound that was now a *scar*.

The scar of the cursed.

"Let him go and let's talk. You can stop all of this." I motioned around me to the people lying dead around us. "Stop this, please."

With all the commotion, I hadn't realized Haven was nowhere to be found and that made my skin crawl. Not because I was scared she was gone, but because I feared what the hell she was about to do.

The woman looked around at her wounded or dead friends and her bottom lip began to tremble. "Stop her then!"

I raised my hands in a small surrender. "She will once you let him go. He has nothing to do with this."

A shadow breezed past us, causing us both to stiffen.

Haven was still in here somewhere, but she was calculating her last move.

A predator hunting its prey.

Miguel groaned, fading in and out of consciousness, and I felt sick knowing this man who had only tried to help us was now paying for it in one of the worst ways possible.

The woman suddenly screamed, jumping backward and letting Miguel slump to the floor. Looking behind her, nothing was there.

A shiver ran up my spine and the hairs on my arms stood, my scar throbbing again.

This time when I looked at the MOT, I finally saw a small figure standing directly behind her… but it wasn't Haven. The left side of the person's face was present, the MOT clearly not seeing what I was, but she could feel the presence of the person.

An informer?

The lights flickered and an eerie vibe flooded the room as if it was a scene pulled straight out of a horror movie. The floorboards creaked as someone started walking up from behind me.

The MOT locked eyes on who it was, gulping. She looked as if she wanted to run, but she was paralyzed in fear.

"You dare try to cross me?" Haven spoke, walking up beside me, but it didn't sound like Haven.

The voice was lighter—younger even.

"All we have done is try to find you and help you all, but you continue to abuse the power we so graciously gifted into your blood."

Realization settling in, I realized the person standing behind the MOT wasn't just any informer. There was a scar leading down the side of their face, but it wasn't exactly a scar. It was a wound.

A bloody one.

"I… I am only doing as told," the woman sobbed. "She said if I didn't, then Ghost… Ghost would come for us. They said to find the woman that came with the MIR from the club. The man we were trying to get answers out of knows where they stay."

"Who?" Haven barked, but as she spoke the informer behind the woman moved her mouth at the same time—as if the two were speaking in unison.

"Her name is Lydia and she's our leader—Ghost's right-hand woman. She saw two people at the club and said they were a threat that needed to be taken care of."

I frowned. "Have you not put the pieces together? We're who she is searching for. Did you ever bother to think why?!"

She swallowed hard. "I can't disobey her. You might as well kill me. If I go back there, I am as good as dead."

"Then go with them," Haven, or whoever was controlling her, spoke. "Help them save the real women of The Messengers of Truth. We are here to avenge and to better this world. We are not here to bow to some pathetic *man*."

She swallowed, nodding. "Okay. I'll do it. I swear. But please don't send me back there alone."

Haven sighed, looking around. "We didn't kill our women. Well, not any MOTs. Ghost is playing you all. Some of you contain the gene, a gene that revolves around the scar on your face. You have been lied to and you clearly do not understand your true purpose in this world. He's throwing in fakes to grow your numbers because MOTs are rare." Haven's head snapped to the side slightly, as if she was listening for something. "You all need to go. Now. Get your friend and go. Not everyone on the boat was down here. Danger is lurking."

I hurried to get Miguel up as the MOT rushed to my side to help.

"And Everette?"

I looked over at Haven, her eyes still dark. "Welcome to The Messengers of Truth. I see you understood my warnings."

My eyes narrowed. "Who are you?"

She laughed. "I thought you would have figured that out by now." She bent in a mocking bow. "My women call me Katerina."

I paused. "How are you doing this?"

"Read the books. Bethany Holden can explain it better than I can."

"And how do I play a part in this? I have no MOT blood."

She hummed. "We made an exception. There always must be a balance. And with what I need Haven for… there has to be light to balance out the dark. Now, go!"

Haven suddenly jolted forward, clawing at her neck as if she couldn't breathe. I left the MOT and Miguel and ran to her.

"Haven?! Haven, are you okay?"

She coughed, shoving me away. "Go!" she croaked out. "Gasoline…"

I didn't even realize the smell that was coursing through the air. Cursing, I helped her to her feet and ran to put my arm around Miguel. He put his arms around the MOT and myself, leaning on us. We started to leave the boat as quickly as we could with Haven staggering close behind.

When the boat suddenly went up in flames, I heard Haven curse. "Go! Now! We don't have much time before this thing explodes. You have to jump."

I looked around in a panic. "MOT, grab that!" I pointed beside her at the small life raft. She was quick to grab it and hand it over. I put it around Miguel and gave them all one last nod.

Then we fled out the back and jumped before freezing water submerged us.

CHAPTER TWENTY-FIVE

Haven

I kicked my feet, clinging onto the life raft Miguel was currently passed out in. "I bet Jay and the others are sitting peacefully on land right now," I spoke, my teeth chattering.

"Not funny," Everette replied, shivering just as much as I was.

The MOT from the boat, now known as Hailey, looked as if she would pass out at any second.

We had been stuck out in the middle of nowhere for what felt like hours. The boat had exploded and sunk into the deep sea not shortly after we had jumped from it. It all had happened so fast, I couldn't even remember exactly how it went down.

I blacked out once I saw Miguel in the middle of that torture circle and when I came to, I was on my knees coughing as Everette sat in front of me. The look on Everette's face said he knew more, but it wasn't the time to tell me. All I knew is that I smelled gasoline and my scar throbbed in warning, telling us to get out of there.

"Have I mentioned," Hailey's teeth chattered, her long blonde hair floating on top of the water as she tried to keep herself upright, "that I hate the ocean?"

I looked around, but it was so dark that the only thing giving us any light was the moon shining down over us. The stars twinkled when I stared up at them like they were laughing at us.

"What do we do?" I asked, looking to Everette.

"Die," he grumbled. "The water's temperature is raising concern for me."

My forehead fell against the raft. "You are no help."

Suddenly something brushed against my leg and I screamed, clawing to try and pick myself up to get somewhat on the small raft. "It's a shark! I'm going to die!" I sobbed.

This made Hailey freak out as she thrashed around, poor Miguel's body jostling from our motions.

"Enough!" Everette yelled. "If it's a shark you're only making this worse by your splashing!"

I suddenly stilled, my heart feeling as if it was about to explode out of my chest and sink just like the boat had.

Everette rolled his eyes, moving his head around to try and get a better view of whatever lurked below us. After a minute, he sighed. "I think it's just some fish."

"Oh thank God," I breathed out, lowering myself back down into the water fully.

Hailey sniffled. "W-we're really going to die out here, aren't we? We're in the middle of nowhere."

I couldn't help but scoff. "Well maybe if you all weren't having a *torture session* this wouldn't have happened."

She glared at me from across the raft. "I had no choice."

I mocked her, moving my hand like a puppet only for Everette to kick me. "Ow! Asshole!"

"Stop being a brat. You of all people should know about following orders. At least she did the right thing in the end."

"Yeah, because she had no other options," I grumbled underneath my breath.

Hailey suddenly let out a weak laugh. "I don't like hurting people, you know? I was ripped from my sleep at the age of sixteen and was drugged before I was thrown into a car. When I woke up, a man named Ghost was standing before me and told me I had a new purpose. He said that he *owned* me and if I tried to escape, he would kill me. I was—still am—terrified of that man."

I straightened a little at her confession. "Were you taken with any other girls?"

She nodded. "There were nine others."

Relief like no other flooded through me.

We at least got one of them.

Thank God.

"I'm sorry," I mumbled. "It's just been a long week and the women working by your side didn't make it exactly easy."

She managed a shrug. "Whatever. Can we do this later? I can't think when the idea of some shark about to gobble me up is on my mind."

I shifted my attention over to Everette who looked so tired. Scooting closer to him, I rested my head on his shoulder. "I'm sorry for causing all of this. If I wouldn't have blacked out… maybe we wouldn't be here."

"You couldn't help it, Red. But like Hailey said… let's just deal with all that later. We need to try and figure out what to do."

Hailey spoke up. "I'm afraid there's nothing we can do. We can hope the waves wash us up to a shore, but I fear we won't make it that long."

Dread ate at me. If this was it, then what would happen to the others? What would happen to the MOTs? Jay? Nikita? Saul? I hated the feeling of defeat, but with every passing minute and each time our eyes grew heavier, I began to lose hope.

I sniffled, raising a shaky hand to Miguel's pulse. It was weak, but it was still there. "He doesn't have much longer," I began to cry. "And because of me… another person is going to lose their life."

"It's okay, Red," Everette croaked. "It's going to be okay."

But he knew it wasn't. We should have just gone down with the boat, at least then our deaths would have been quick.

"Everette if this is our time. If this…"

He shook his head, covering my mouth. "Don't."

I blinked away my tears when I saw unshed ones in his own eyes.

Trying to ignore the subject at hand, Everette started talking to Hailey to try and keep her awake, but I eventually tuned him out as something caught my eye in the distance. It was dark, but I could see the moon's light making out something. "There!" I pointed. "What's that?"

The two of them looked towards where I had pointed and Everette squinted his eyes a little before they widened in surprise. "Oh my God, it's another boat."

After that, we were all screaming, waving our arms around frantically as the boat finally came into view out of a cloud of fog.

At first, they didn't seem to see us, but we continued our screaming, and when a sudden flare went up into the air and we heard yells from the ship, I sagged against the raft in relief while tears of happiness brimmed my eyes.

"Hang on a little longer!" a voice was finally audible. "We're coming!"

Everette grabbed my hand that was gripping the raft and squeezed it. I knew that simple gesture was enough to explain what he was thinking.

We're okay.

I'm here.

It's not our time.

I squeezed his back, managing a small smile and thanking God above that I didn't make a fool of myself earlier from what my brain and heart was about to unleash on him. But I couldn't stop thinking that we could have died right here tonight if it wasn't for the boat heading our way and the only thing I had been thinking at the time was how I didn't want to die with any regrets—didn't want to die without telling Everette what he now meant to me.

***

Everette rubbed my arms over the thick blanket one of the fishermen had thrown over my shoulders when they pulled us on the boat. My teeth were still chattering, but at least I wasn't confined in the water any longer.

They were taking care of Miguel as we sat here trying to warm up and I desperately hoped that he would pull through. As far as I was concerned, Miguel didn't deserve any of this and he was ready to die without giving up our names—the names of two people he barely knew.

"Here," one of the boat's men said. "It's some broth that should warm you all up a bit. We have someone getting some more food for you now."

The three of us icicles took the broth greedily after we thanked him. I had no idea what it was, but since I was freezing and hadn't had anything in my stomach the past few hours, it was nearly a gourmet meal to me.

The man, who I assumed was the captain of this ship, took a seat in front of us with a raised brow. "What happened to you all? Why were you stranded like that?"

He looked to be in his early forties, his beard having a few greys shining under the lights around us and his eyes looked as if he had seen many, many years at sea.

"It's better if you don't know," I mumbled. "But we are grateful for your help."

The captain frowned. "Well, you have swords strapped to your back and you all are wearing some weird clothing. Pardon me for being a bit worried about who I just let onto my ship."

Everette leaned forward, sticking his hand out. "I'm Everette and this is Haven and Hailey. What we are a part of we cannot say, but I promise you that the minute you get us to some sort of land that we will be out of your hair."

The captain grimaced but shook Everette's hand. "Harold's the name, and I'm captain of this ship. It's not often that I find three people dangling from a raft on my trips."

Everette let out a weak laugh. "It's not often we find ourselves in a body of water. I appreciate what you do, though… my dad was a fisherman."

This made me more interested in the conversation as I sipped my broth, leaning closer with curious eyes.

"Really now? Well, what did he do?"

Everette looked around. "He was a captain as well. Crab fisherman to be exact."

Harold hummed. "Interesting. You didn't take after him, I suppose."

At this, Everette belted out a sarcastic laugh. "Actually, I took after him a little too much. But um… not in the fisherman type of way."

There was a sad look on his face—one that told a story that even Harold didn't try to pry out of him. I only could imagine how his father started as a fisherman and became a fearful leader to a group of assassins. It was a strange thing to ponder on.

Some men brought us food, interrupting the conversation before anyone else could add to it.

The smell of whatever the stew contained was to die for, or perhaps that was because I was starving. My stomach was bellowing angrily at the thought of food sitting right in front of me, yet I didn't make a move to dive in. I was too focused on the feelings Everette was clearly trying to mash down.

Hailey, on the other hand, was eating so fast I thought she might throw the food back up later. The sight of it made my heart ache and I couldn't help but let my mind wander to what her everyday life was like. If she was a slave to Ghost, what's to say he didn't properly take care of her?

I doubt he did.

I bit my lip, bringing the piece of bread they brought with the stew to my mouth. Everette continued to talk to Harold as he ate while my mind wandered elsewhere.

I tried to wrack my brain for what had happened when I blacked out, but it was a fuzzy mess. I just remembered that feeling of a fiery rage swarming me when my eyes locked on Miguel. I leaned into that feeling and that was the last thing I could recall.

Then I had woken up to many men and women dead around me.

I gulped, shakily resting the bread on the side of the bowl. Did I kill MOTs? My own kind? I couldn't place the women's faces to know if they contained a scar or not, but if their attire was similar to Hailey's… I'm certain I did.

What if some of those women were the exact people I was supposed to be saving?

"Haven, did you hear him?" Everette's voice snapped me out of my thoughts.

"Huh? No," I shook my head, "I'm sorry, what did you say?"

"They said Miguel will be fine. He's resting and has some wounds, but it looks as if his ribs are the worst. Broken. He took a beating before they brought him onto that boat."

My jaw ticked. "I'm glad he's going to be okay."

"Now, we'll reach a port in a few hours. That's the best I can do for you and then you're on your own after that," Harold spoke, resting his hands on his hips. "You all don't seem like the bad guys, so I really hope you pass on this act of kindness, yeah?"

I tried to hold back my snicker. If only he knew. "Of course."

Harold then glanced back at Everette with a smirk. "You said your dad was a fisherman, yeah? Let's hear your best shanty."

My eyes widened with humor as Everette nearly paled. Nervously fidgeting, he began to shake his head. "I uh… I don't know many."

Harold and the men all began hollering something inaudible as they beat their fists on a nearby surface, setting a beat. Everette clearly knew what was happening as he let out a deep sigh, setting his bowl aside as he stood, the blanket falling from around his shoulders to the ground.

It was small, but I could see the smile he was trying to hide. He was enjoying it more than he let on.

After a minute of the banging of the crew members, Everette held his hand up. It went deathly silent as they stared back at him with anticipation.

Then he started to sing, hunching forward a bit as if he was about to tell a scary story. "There once was a ship that put to sea. The name of the ship was the Billy of Tea. The winds blew up, her bow dipped down. Oh blow, my bully boys, blow…"

"HUH!" The men joined in. "Soon may the Wellerman come…"

I laughed, clapping my hands together as men began stomping around, singing their hearts out. The look on Everette's face warmed my heart—a smile so big that it lit the whole ship.

Soon, one of the men grabbed my hand, pulling me from my seat as the shanty shifted into a new song, not missing a beat. I had no idea what it was called, but they chanted something about a drunken sailor and my body just fell into it as we danced around, my worries washing away as I was spun into Everette's form.

He caught me, smiling as if he had just won a million bucks, and took my hand to spin me once more. My head fell back in laughter as I moved around the deck with him. Even Hailey had gotten up, loosening up a bit as she began to smile and repeat the lyrics with a man leading her around.

As I looked at the tattooed flames peeking out from Everette's collar, it made me realize how true his statement about them had been. You may go through hell some days, but you can push past it and leave it at your back to take on a new day. You can't stay stuck in the past because it would be like standing in hell every damn day.

You have to take the good moments where you can get them.

Everette caught my smile as I gazed at him, his getting even bigger as he dipped me and placed his lips to mine in a lip-bruising kiss. I smiled into the kiss, clinging to him with a sudden burst of happiness that shook me to my core.

Never had I felt such a feeling after having a day that we did.

The men cheered around us at the sight of it and I couldn't help the schoolgirl giggle as he pulled me back up, wrapping his arms around me.

Hailey walked up to us, beaming a smile. "I feel like I'm ready to take on the sea now after all that."

I snickered. "Whoa there, cowgirl, you were ready to throw Miguel off that life raft just an hour ago at the thought of a fish swimming around you."

She puffed out a laugh. "Says the woman who made me scared in the first place."

We all chuckled, the adrenaline from the recent moments starting to wear off. As the men began to disperse, patting Everette on the back as they did, Hailey turned to us with a serious look.

"Everything okay?" I asked.

She looked around, a small smile gracing her lips. "Yeah. Now it is. Thank you for getting me out of Ghost's reach. I know I was a bit stubborn back on the boat, but it's hard to go against something that was beaten into you from a young age. I'm willing to do whatever I need to in order to help the two of you."

"Believe me when I say that I understand what it's like to be brainwashed into believing something. The only thing we can do now is face the future head on. We can save those women you were shipped to Ghost with."

She chewed on her bottom lip. "I sure hope so. I'm going to go get some rest."

Everette and I watched her walk away with somber expressions. When Everette looked down at me, I rose to my toes and placed a kiss on his lips. "You should smile more," I whispered as I ran my thumb over his bottom lip. "It looks good on you."

He kissed my forehead, giving me a small squeeze. "You too, Red."

CHAPTER TWENTY-SIX

Jay

I paced A.R's office with a gut-wrenching feeling as the call went to voicemail once more. The look on A.R's face had me feeling nauseous with each passing second. Once again, he dialed the number and waited for the line to pick up.

Nothing.

I dropped into the chair across from his desk, tears brimming my eyes. "Do you think something happened to them?"

A.R sighed, pushing the burner phone aside. "I don't know. They could just be on a mission right now."

I looked down at my trembling hands, hating the fact that we were hundreds of miles away from our friends and couldn't do a damn thing about it.

From a young age, the MOTs were trained to mash their feelings down. Trained to be emotionless, yet I could remember the nights when

I would crawl into my bed at the manor and finally let the day take its toll on me. I would claw at my chest because I couldn't catch my breath and had to work through a panic attack on my own.

This almost felt like that.

I didn't want to show A.R that type of emotion because it felt as if I wasn't allowed to. Just hearing Haven admit to me before we left for our missions that she was *scared* was something that throttled me. Haven was someone I looked up to—someone I admired. Before the Messengers of Truth took its toll on her, I used to envy the way she could bottle everything up—how she so easily compartmentalized so many things in her hectic life.

She used to be something dark and dangerous, which I believed was the result of being abandoned at such a young age and forced into the organization. Everyone knew of her and everyone wanted to be her. But when she entered her early twenties, something shifted in her. It was like she finally came to be aware of the things she was doing and the people she was killing. She began to hesitate more often and I soon realized that Haven McKinley was *feeling* things.

It made me feel more human to know she was.

And now? Now knowing that even she was scared was something I had to slowly start to come to terms with. Because if Haven was scared, we all should be scared. She wasn't one to easily admit such a thing.

"Hey, are you okay?" A.R asked, rising from his seat.

I shook my head, trying to choke down the tears. "No… I'm not. I'm so sick of feeling like that at every turn we take, something is waiting to try and end us all. And now Nikita and Saul aren't answering our calls. We've been at it all day and night. They should have reached us by now."

A.R squatted in front of me, gently taking my hands into his own. "You're shaking."

I let out a dry laugh. "Yeah, that's what happens when you feel as if you're about to lose your mind."

He frowned, his forehead creasing in thin lines from, no doubt, years of stress. A.R was easy to figure out after spending a few days with him, surprisingly. He was a man used to a life of being a recluse and living alone while having to fight his own battles at every twist and turn. In a way, he was similar to us, but yet so different. The emotions I experienced seemed almost foreign to him with the way he looked me over as if he didn't know what the hell to do with a crying woman in front of him.

Or perhaps that's all men.

"We'll figure out what is going on with them, okay? We can't start thinking the worst just yet. If we don't hear from them by tomorrow morning, I will send my contacts after them."

I tilted my head back, ushering the tears to not fall. "But what if we're too late?"

A.R sighed, his thumb rubbing small circles over my palm. "We'll figure it out."

I pulled my hands from his grasp, wiping angrily at my traitorous tears. "I just find it concerning that they would message us that they found something. Something that could not only lead us to more of those women that were taken from us, but also something that could lead us to Haven's parents. A.R, I just know something bad has happened, I can feel it in my gut."

He pushed himself up, placing his hands on his hips. "Has your scar throbbed?"

I stared up at him confused. "What?"

"Has your scar throbbed at the thought of Nikita and Saul being in danger?"

I thought it over, realizing that I haven't felt anything of sorts from the curse. "No… it hasn't."

"Then I am going to assume that they are just on a mission and cannot contact us at the moment. If they found something big, they may be staying low for a few days. Your curse will notify you when someone you or someone you care about is in danger. Until then, I can't worry about it. We have to keep moving forward."

I chewed on the inner side of my cheek nervously. "How do you know all this?"

He sighed, taking the chair next to me. "Like I told Haven, when her father started bringing me in on certain things within the organization, he had me read a few books that were written by Bethany Holden herself. Still to this day, I don't understand most of it considering I don't know what it's like to have such a curse, but I do know a few things. Like the way your scar is almost like a beacon to help lead you in the right direction. It will warn you and confirm some of your wary thoughts, amongst other things. The books helped me get a better understanding of you women so I could help Haven's father accordingly. It's why I told Haven to read them."

At the thought of my dear friend, I gave him a pleading look. "Can we at least call Haven and Everette? I just need to know that they're okay as well."

A.R motioned to the phone on his desk. "Be my guest, Jay."

I flew up from my seat to grab it. I clicked on the number that was to their burner phone and put it on speaker. It rang a few times and as it continued to ring, my heart sped up. "Come on," I mumbled. "Pick up. Pick up."

Suddenly, the line stopped ringing and there was a rustling noise on the other side. "Hello?" Everette's gruff voice broke through.

"Everette!" I nearly yelled. "Are you all okay?"

I heard a door close as he let out a tired sigh. "Yeah. We had… a shit show of a night but we're managing. Is A.R with you?"

"Yeah, he's here."

A.R stood from his seat, his eyes narrowing as he walked closer. "What's up?"

"Last night we had a problem. Haven and I followed some women from the club to this boating dock. I don't know how they found out, but they got Miguel, A.R."

A.R's jaw ticked as he grabbed the phone. Despite his calming demeanor, I could see the frustration in his eyes. "Is he dead?"

"No… he made it. We got him off, but it's easy to see that people are catching onto us as well as the people helping us. Everyone needs to be cautious—even more now with all this shit happening."

A.R visibly relaxed at the sound of his friend being okay. "Good. What exactly went down?"

"They were trying to get him to tell them where we were, but the stubborn bastard wouldn't give in. It's safe to say the night ended with an exploding boat and Haven and Hailey clinging to a life raft with Miguel and me."

My eyes widened. "Who is Hailey? How did you all get back home?"

"Hailey is an MOT that worked for Ghost. It took some convincing, but she came back with us. We just got back not too long ago. It was a long, dreadful night. I don't know how long we were in the water for before a ship of men found us and helped us get back to land. Once we did, Miguel finally woke and called in a favor to get us back home. He's fine for now, but he's pretty busted up. You should call him."

"I will," A.R mumbled. "How's Haven holding up?"

Everette was silent for a moment before saying, "She's dealing. When we got back to the house she crashed. I'm letting her sleep before I fill her in on everything that happened."

This pulled a frown from me. "What do you mean?"

"Haven… blacked out in a way? When she saw Miguel, she lost it. And then… fuck, I don't even know how to explain this without just coming out swinging. I'm pretty damn sure she channeled so much rage that it somehow gave a connection with Katerina Holden herself. Katerina channeled her like an informer would and the way Haven moved about that place and slaughtered people… I've never seen anything like it. I mean, the woman quite literally dodged bullets as if she was some damn superhuman."

A.R groaned. "Did she not read the damn books?!"

"She has read some. But the only thing she has had time to digest was the rage of the MOTs. What do you know about this?"

I think my body was in shock at what Everette had just admitted. Katerina Holden came to Haven's aid? She channeled Haven? How is that even possible?

A.R sat the phone on the desk, his palms flattening against the sides of it as he closed his eyes. "Haven is a Holden, which means she has connections with all previous Holdens. If you would have read the damn books like I told you to, you would have figured this out. The Holdens have always been able to communicate with the dead. It wasn't until Katerina showed signs to Bethany about the truth to her death that she took further action to speak with her. Bethany performed witchcraft pretty much—something so dark that she cursed her generations to come. As a result, she was able to see Katerina and when she drank whatever concoction she whipped up to make this possible, the MOT curse was born."

My jaw was on the floor. "What the hell? You're telling me this all started because someone who had the ability to communicate with the dead, like a medium, performed witchcraft? And now we're cursed because of it?"

A.R nodded. "Bethany was fixated on getting down to the bottom of Katerina's strange death. Katerina had given her signs in any way she could, but it was still hard to do without communicating with Katerina herself. After she performed what she needed… she finally saw Katerina again. In the books, Bethany says that prior Holdens can channel their bloodline if needed, but it takes so much energy to do so. Haven must have really dived into her rage last night."

Everette cursed. "She did. I have seen her anger grow over the last few weeks, but nothing like last night. Is this going to continue to get worse for her?"

"I'm not sure," mumbled A.R. "But I do know that the longer Haven keeps that rage in, the worse it's going to get. In my opinion, as gruesome as the outcomes may be, it's a good thing she's getting it out. It's been building for too long." His eyes flicked over to me. "And I'm starting to see the same thing in the others."

I looked at him confused, my brows pulling together. What the hell was he trying to say? That I was losing myself to this curse?

A chill swept over me as I took a step closer to him. "What are you saying, A.R?"

"That the MOTs will slowly lose their mind if you don't give into the rage that was burned into your fucking soul, Jay. Haven harbors most of it because she's the last Holden, but that spills out into the rest of you when hers is filled to the brim. Do you see how Ghost brainwashed those women to do just that? To release hell at his command? He knows and he's winning the battle. If you all don't start to learn to use your rage accordingly, you'll kill everyone around you. If you can master it, you can stop any *enemy* around you. Understand?"

Everette cleared his throat. "I think I'm going to wake Haven. She needs to hear all this."

A.R's eyes didn't leave my own as he ended the call. He took a step closer, our chests touching. "I saw the way you stabbed that man the other night. Even through a small scope, I could see the fire burning in your eyes. You're filled with just as much rage as Haven fucking McKinley because you never let yourself *feel*. Your previous commander made it that way for a reason. Eventually, she would have used you all for even worse things. Fortunately, she was stopped in time. But Ghost is picking up where she left off."

I staggered back, my breath hitching. "You need to tell me everything you know. Now."

He motioned to the seat next to me. "Then sit. We have a lot to discuss."

CHAPTER TWENTY-SEVEN

Haven

I curled up on the couch, my heart racing with a panic it had never felt before. Everette looked sick to his stomach from what he had just told me and Hailey looked just as shocked as I felt. I was woken from my sleep about an hour ago by Everette saying that he needed to tell me something that couldn't wait.

He was right. It truly couldn't.

"So… this rage we read about… it will be our demise if not used properly?" I asked, my eyes meeting his.

Everette gulped. "Yeah. From what I gathered from A.R, this curse is exactly that. A curse that was put on your bloodline for generations for years to come. Bethany Holden just made something useful out of it, the organization, to try and contain it. Whether she knew what she was really doing or not, it makes life hell for you all either way. And according to A.R since you were never properly trained on the matter, you're full of this horrendous rage and *you* harbor most of it because you're the last Holden—the last person with the original bloodline of the curse. When you're full of it… it leaks into the others around you with the same gene."

I rubbed my face. "But I haven't seen the others act out?"

He rubbed his thighs nervously. "But I have. That night that we all came to get you from that warehouse when you were after Ghost's men? I saw that rage seeping through Jay and Nikita. They killed without a second thought. Granted, they now know the curse won't take its wrath out on them if they kill outside of their target, but it was like they didn't even think of that and their bodies just acted. You would think they would hesitate since they are not used to killing outside of said targets, right? It wasn't a calculated kill like they were used to."

Hailey let out a shaky breath. "I've seen that before as well. Ghost used to make us train to be these… cold blooded killers. But when some of the girls got so angry, it was like they were unstoppable and I just remember him having this wicked look as if he knew exactly why and now it makes sense. If Ghost is trying to get to the others in your organization, and if he originally wanted you, he's trying to get the utmost potential out of these women. Out of *us*. He truly is building an army. But what I don't understand is why? What's his angle?"

Everette pondered on the thought. "I would say power, but he already is a powerful man. I mean, hell, even A.R couldn't take him down. So what's he really after if not more power?"

I tried to search my brain for that answer, tried to place the pieces together, but we were missing so much that nothing was adding up. We were just finally starting to learn the truth behind this curse and it all seemed so impossible that I didn't know what to believe.

After a minute, Hailey sat up, her eyes wide. "An heir."

Our heads snapped in her direction. "What?"

She ran a hand through her hair, frustrated. "Ghost used to talk about how one day he would expand 'the family'. I always just thought he meant by adding more MOTs or new men. It didn't make sense then, but Ghost is in his forties. He's never been married. Has no children. So who is going to continue his lineage after he goes? Who will take over the business? Any person with a lot at stake will start to think about that stuff. He wanted Haven originally, right? The last Holden. Does it make sense yet? If he can't have her because he thinks she is dead, then he's trying to get the rest of the litter to see who compares. He definitely wants power, but he wants to continue what he started in doing so."

I felt as if I was about to hurl. "If I were to have children, it would continue the bloodline. But if another MOT has a child, it still would… they just wouldn't be, what? As powerful?"

Hailey nodded. "It would be a guessing game if any other MOTs' children would get the cursed gene—far more rare than a Holden. If he could find someone who could harbor rage just like you, he might think that could do the job. He doesn't want just any MOT to have his child, he wants one that's strong enough to harbor the rage."

Everette cursed, staring straight ahead with a horrified look. "It all makes sense."

My mind was in haze as I took everything in. The commander never favored me because she thought of me like one of her own, she favored me because she knew what my body could potentially earn her.

I covered my mouth as nausea rolled over me. "I have been nothing but a pawn," I croaked, flashes of Ghost trying to force himself upon me for some sick plan to expand his lineage.

Everette flew up from the couch. "I'll be damned if that man *ever* tries to put his hands on you!" he snarled.

When my stomach flipped, I darted from the couch and ran from the nearest bathroom. Throwing the door open, I dropped to my knees and hurled into the toilet. The thought of that man wanting to take me, and the fact that the commander was so fucking willing to give me over, made my skin crawl.

She was ready to sell my fucking body to that monster.

My hair was suddenly pulled back from around my face as Everette crouched down next to me, using his free hand to rub circles over my back. "I got you," he whispered.

I couldn't help the sob that left my body. "She was ready to sell me! To sell my body!"

Everette didn't say anything as he pulled me against his chest, holding my head there. I clenched his shirt between my hands, my tears seeping into the material as my chest rose and fell at the horrid cries leaving me.

"I'm not going to let anything happen to you, Haven. I swear it on my life," he breathed, his grip tightening on me as if I'd vanish from his grasp in seconds.

I tried to regain control of my breathing, trying to remember how easily I used to stop the tears from ever leaving my eyes, but it was pure torture with the feelings coursing through me.

After a minute of Everette just holding me, I finally gathered my thoughts and was able to peel myself off him. Taking in a deep breath, I looked at him. "I'm sorry. That just… that wrecked me more than I thought it would."

Everette's face hardened as he cupped my cheeks. "Hey, you don't ever need to apologize for basic human emotions, Haven. Do you hear me? Don't ever apologize to me for that." I sniffled, leaning back into his touch as he pressed a hard kiss to my temple. "If what the commander planned was true, I'll kill her myself."

Tears brimmed my eyes again. "What hurts me the most is that she was so willing to give me away to him. I was someone she used to say she thought of as her own daughter. How screwed up is that?"

Everette rubbed my arms. "She was a fucked up person, Haven. She thought of no one but herself. Regardless of what she said, she was just trying to get you to trust her. She knew you missed your mother and she used that against you."

My eyes shut, embarrassment washing over me. "I know."

He heaved out another deep sigh and patted my arm. "Let's get you in bed."

I let him pull me from the floor and walked with him down the hall. Hailey stood when we entered the living room again, a pained expression plastered across her face. "I'm sorry. I didn't know that would upset you so much. I wouldn't have said anything if I knew."

I waved her off. "Don't be. I'm glad you mentioned it because that would have never crossed our minds. It makes a lot of sense, so thank you."

She bit her lip, not knowing what else to say. Everette gently steered me towards the stairs before looking back over his shoulder at her. "There is a guest room down the hall that you can use. I'm going to sit with her for a bit."

A small part of me hated being treated like a child, but another part of me loved the fact that he was so protective and caring of me.

It was new and something I definitely had to get used to, but I couldn't bring myself to say anything as he walked us up the stairs and to my room. I parted ways with him, walking to the bathroom to brush my teeth. I had already showered when we first got back, but just thinking of another hot shower made me want to strip right there.

I eyed it, brushing my teeth slowly.

Cutting my eyes back to the bedroom, I couldn't help but want one thing.

To forget.

I finished brushing, turned the water off, and grabbed a towel to wipe my mouth as I slowly thought over if this was what I really needed. Glancing up in the mirror, I stared at a familiar face.

Dark bags, pale skin, freckles, and a scar that fucked my life up.

Hell yes I did.

Looking out the door curiously, I saw Everette sitting on the edge of my bed while he scrolled on his phone.

Building up my confidence, I walked out of the bathroom to him. When he noticed me standing in front of him, he leaned back as he tucked his phone into his pocket, his eyes glazing over me. "Ready for bed?"

I slowly shook my head and grabbed his hand to pull him up from his spot. He looked frazzled for a minute until he saw the look in my eyes and his own instantly heated. "Are you sure you want to do this right now?"

I didn't reply as I led him to the bathroom, dropping his hand once we stopped in front of the shower. I opened the door and turned the water on, letting the steam invade the bathroom as I turned to face him. Eventually, I grabbed the ends of my shirt and pulled it over my head before I tossed it to the side.

Everette's eyes glided over my body appreciatively before he stepped forward, tugging me to his chest. "Last time I'll ask. Are you sure?"

"Whatever it leads to, I'm fine with," I mumbled, my lips a hair's breadth from his own. "Help me forget."

Goosebumps traveled down my arms as his fingertips ran down the sides of them, his eyes never leaving mine. Slowly, he grabbed the waistband of my shorts and began to lower himself to ease them down my legs. One foot at a time, I stepped out of them with a fast-beating heart.

Everette began to place tortuous kisses up my thighs as he grabbed ahold of the lace covering me right where he seemed to desperately seek. As he pulled them off, I reached around me to unclasp my bra.

Standing bare before him, Everette moved back up my body with a dazed look. "Fucking beautiful. Every damn inch of you."

I think I could watch this man pull off his shirt every day just because of the way his muscles flexed, his abs growing more defined with the simple gesture.

The steam of the shower had fogged every mirror and glass panel in this bathroom by the time Everette stripped his clothes off. Greedily, I looked him over, my eyes widening a bit at one specific part of him.

He let out a husky chuckle and tugged me to him. "Like what you see?"

"Seen better." I lied, causing him to pull open the door to the shower and shove me in.

I gasped under the hot stream of water, pushing my hair out of my face when he stepped in, and I suddenly felt the sting of the cold tiled wall where the heat had yet to hit and Everette's figure locked me in place there.

"Seen better, huh?" he murmured, his nose trailing up the side of my neck, causing heat to pool within my core.

I clutched at his shoulders. "You'll have to perform better since your looks are failing," I breathed out, earning another deep chuckle from him.

"You really shouldn't have said that, babe."

I grinned up at him when he finally moved his face in front of my own. "And why's that?"

His hand skimmed up my waist, suddenly caressing one of my breasts. A slight moan left me at his touch. "Because I'll fuck that attitude right out of you."

Yes, *please*, I wanted to scream.

"But not tonight."

My eyes snapped open. "What?"

It was his turn to grin. "Brats don't get rewarded when they catch an attitude. Did you learn anything from last time? Teasing me is not the way to go, Red."

His finger trailed over a nipple, causing my breath to hitch in my throat, my back arching. "Please, Everette."

He lowered his mouth to my ear. "Begging won't get you anywhere, even as much as I love to hear my name on your lips."

"Then I'll do it myself," I challenged, causing him to stiffen.

"Go ahead then," he replied, backing away from me. "Show me what you got, Red."

I was frozen like a deer in headlights. Was he being serious?

He chuckled. "Where's the feisty girl from a few seconds ago?"

The mocking tone in his voice had my teeth clenching. Not backing down, I slowly began to trail my hand down my body, enjoying the way his eyes darkened and how his fists clenched at his sides.

He made a move toward me, but I shoved a hand to his chest. "Uh uh, you wanted to watch," I teased, watching his jaw clench and unclench.

Moving his hands up in a slow surrender, he backed away to see how far I'd take this. But when the first moan left my lips at my own doing, it was like something in him snapped.

In a flash, he had me pinned against the wall, his lips bruising my own as he worked them against me with so much pent-up hunger, that it had me pulling him to my body as if I couldn't get enough.

I didn't think I ever would.

His hands grabbed my hips and he caught me as I jumped, wrapping my legs around his waist and pressing me back against the wall harshly with one hand holding me up as the other moved to smack against the wall right next to my head.

His kiss was driving me wild and my mind reeled at the thought of him and the way he made my body light up under the simplest of touches. I couldn't help but roll my hips into his own with my need to feel him. His arousal brushed up against me, causing us both to moan into one another's mouths.

Everette ripped his mouth away from mine, trailing kisses down the base of my throat and nipped ever so often just hard enough that I knew I would have love bites tomorrow. A part of me liked the idea of it, which was a disturbing thought.

"Fuck this," he grumbled and began to lower us both to the floor. "This shower is big enough for what I plan to do to you, Red."

With my back against the tiled floor, my eyes widened as Everette leaned back, the water cascading over him like some damn sexy scene from a movie. He ran a hand through his hair, his eyes staring at me hungrily as they trailed down my body. My chest rose and fell heavily as he wiped the water from his face with a groan and descended back upon my aching body.

He placed wet kisses down the valley of my breasts, moving over to capture one of my breasts in his mouth. A whimpering noise left my throat as my back raised from the ground and my hands laced through his hair.

He moved to the other, causing my mouth to part slightly as a silent moan made its way through me. Eventually, his hands slid down my sides, one trailing over my thigh to my core as I squirmed under his blazing touch.

The minute he touched the aching part of me, I couldn't gather words and I lifted my hips in a silent plea. This time, Everette didn't wait before he plunged a finger into my heat and I cried out with the pure ecstasy of it.

"Fuck, Red," he breathed, "I don't think I'll ever get enough of the sounds you make."

My face twisted as Everette added another finger, working me in ways that had me seeing stars. I barely managed to open my eyes as he removed his hand. When he locked eyes with me, he grinned. "You're not getting off on my hand this time, Red."

I didn't have time to reply as his head ducked and he began to kiss down my belly, causing my toes to curl with anticipation when he reached just below my navel. His breath fanned over me, and I looked down just in time to see his eyes flick up, a look I couldn't quite decipher in them.

Then he lowered his mouth.

I gasped as my hands found their way into his hair again. Between the steaming water pouring over his back, dripping onto my body, and Everette's greedy tongue, I was panting by the time he barely had begun.

When my back arched again, I threw out one hand to slap against the shower's glass.

Everette took and took from me, greedily lapping his tongue with a hum in his chest.

"Everette," I breathed out.

His grip around my thighs tightened before he lifted one of my legs and tossed it over his shoulder to get better access to continue his wicked ways.

I whimpered as he continued to tease that fucking sweet spot of mine, realizing how close I was to jumping off that hill into a feeling of complete and utter bliss.

"Everette, stop," I spoke, trying to push him back.

He shot back, his eyes wide. "Are you okay? Did I do something wrong?"

I gulped, my core aching without his touch. "No, but I'm not doing this alone this time."

He was confused for a moment until I grabbed his hand and pulled him to me. He quickly understood what I meant when I palmed his length, starting to move my hand slightly.

Everette groaned, his forehead falling against mine as his eyes slammed shut. His grip was nearly bruising on my hips, but I couldn't get over the look on his face that my own touch was causing.

"Not alone," I whispered.

His eyes opened and his jaw ticked. "Eyes on me," he mumbled.

When his hand moved beneath my reach, he found my center. I paused for a second at the feel of his finger entering me again, but when his voice boomed around me and demanded me to open my eyes up, I didn't even know that they had fluttered shut.

We moved in rhythm, our pants growing harsher and our bodies finding a perfect sync that I hadn't even known was possible.

And when we both began to shake, our bodies peaking together, Everette slammed his mouth against mine.

And we were completely and utterly fucking spent.

CHAPTER TWENTY-EIGHT

Everette

Haven slept peacefully in my arms while I laid wide awake. It had been a few hours since our time together in the shower and I didn't know whether to feel extremely happy, or terrified. Was I allowed to feel both?

I was in a state of mind of believing this was all a dream, but I also knew that what was happening between Haven and me was so damn real. It was like nothing I had experienced before and I think that was what scared me the most.

I hadn't felt this way with someone since my wife and a small part of me felt like I was betraying her. We were married for three years and it was some of the best moments in my life. But Haven was slowly starting to fill that hole in my heart and I tried not to beat myself up over it. My wife would have wanted this. She would have wanted me to move on and find someone that betters me.

And Haven does that.

I felt as if I hadn't smiled in years until she entered my hectic life, and the thought of having something so real with her made my chest swell with pride. It was something I had craved for weeks and yet I thought it would never be in the cards for us.

How wrong I was.

And the thought of losing it all? It made me sick to my stomach. Hell, I was protective over her before anything had happened between us, but now that it has? I had to remind myself that Haven was more than capable of protecting herself, but that small possessive side of me never wanted her to leave my side.

I couldn't lose anyone else.

Couldn't lose her.

It would be the death of me.

Knowing that getting some shuteye wasn't happening anytime soon, I slowly unwrapped Haven from my body and inched out of the bed so I wouldn't disturb her.

Instinctively, Haven reached out at my absence but found my pillow instead and hugged it to her, going still once more. I couldn't stop the smile that crept onto my face.

I think I was falling in love with the woman.

Shaking my head, I left the room and padded downstairs into the kitchen.

What I didn't expect was for the kitchen light to be on. On guard, I crept around the corner, peering in to see Hailey stirring a spoon into a cup with tired eyes.

"Can't sleep?" I asked, walking into her view.

She jumped slightly at my sudden appearance, but quickly recovered and shook her head. "So much has happened in the past twenty-four hours that my mind can't rest."

I huffed in agreement, grabbing the coffee pot and a mug from the cabinet to pour my own dose of caffeine. "I feel the same way."

She leaned against a countertop and let out a heavy sigh. "I didn't mean to make Haven upset earlier."

I waved her off. "Don't worry about it, we're just glad you said something. Whether that's the truth behind Ghost's motives or not, it's a good thing to know about so we can prevent him from getting to Haven or knowing she's alive still."

Hailey nodded, stirring her coffee once more. "I still feel like an ass."

I brought my mug to my lips to take a gulp of the steaming drink that was becoming my addiction lately. After a minute, I tilted my head to the side. "Haven… just has a lot going on. She's not upset with you, I promise."

"Okay…"

There was an awkward silence that settled between us. When we first had gotten back to the house after Miguel, Haven had given Hailey some of her clothes to wear. Hailey was just a few inches shorter than me, so Haven's pajama pants that Hailey was wearing were too short on her legs, causing me to dip my head to hold back my grin.

My small little killer.

When I looked back up, Hailey was looking at me curiously, so I arched a brow. "What?"

"Have you told Haven you're a part of the curse yet?"

I shifted uncomfortably. "No, not yet. She already had so much to deal with tonight that I didn't want to add to it."

She took a drink of her coffee before saying, "You should tell her soon. It's important and can help you both in the long run."

"What do you mean?"

Hailey placed her empty mug in the sink, casting a look over her shoulder. "If you two can distinguish threats now with the help of the scar, you could be unstoppable. It's why Haven was so quick to dismantle those men in the club and you weren't. Our scars jolt us, in a way. Tells us when to move, when to act, and when to be cautious. You learned that on the boat."

I frowned. "You were in the club?"

She laughed. "Yeah, and you got your ass handed to you."

Snorting, I folded my arms. "Unfortunately. But apparently you did, too."

Hailey let out a weak laugh. "I was one of the last girls Haven had knocked out. I wish I would have known then that you two truly weren't a threat. But you know… following your leader blind and all that."

"Haven relates more to you than you'd think," I replied. "You should talk to her when you get the chance."

"I'll keep that in mind, thanks."

I nodded and before she left the kitchen she halted. "There's… there is a meeting that the women and I were supposed to be at tomorrow night. They will all be there. Something about information we needed to know. I'm not quite sure what it will entail, but if you want a shot at getting to the women that came here with me, this is your chance. We don't all meet together usually. It's at the club and the cover is a Halloween party. Private party. So you'll have to be smart to get in."

My eyes widened at the information she gave. "Thank you… I'll tell Haven."

She sighed. "Just be careful? Those women are ruthless. Not all still have a moral conscious like I do. I would come with you, but I just can't risk it."

"Of course, I completely understand."

With that, she said her goodbyes and walked off to her room.

The party may be our last chance to save the women before we had to leave.

***

Sleep never came. By the time Haven wandered down to the kitchen, I had already cooked a brunch that was big enough to feed a family.

I was stress cooking.

Is that even a thing?

Haven let out a long yawn, walking up behind me. My chest warmed as she wrapped her arms around me from behind and rested her cheek against my back. "Good… afternoon?"

I chuckled and flipped the last pancake, placing the spatula down. I spun around and wrapped my arms around her, pressing a kiss to her temple. "Afternoon, Red."

She grinned up at me with a goofy look. "Are those chocolate chip pancakes?"

I bit my lip to hold back my own smile. "Maybe."

Arching a brow, Haven peered around me at all the food. "Do I always get pancakes after bringing you to your knees in front of me?"

Now I was wide awake, and so was my friend downstairs. "It can be arranged." I smirked.

She batted her eyes and then spun out of my arms to snatch a piece of bacon from behind me. "Eh, the pancakes aren't that good anyways."

I feigned a hurt expression, watching her eyes light up with humor. As she shimmied away from me, my hand struck out to smack against her backside. She jumped with a yelp, her free hand coming to cover it and I threw my head back laughing.

"Asshole," she grumbled.

"Brat," I shot back with a wink.

I grabbed two plates, filling them to the brim with food, and walked them over to the table she was sitting at. Placing one in front of her, her eyes lit up again.

"Thank you." She smiled and grabbed a fork.

Feeling the need to touch her has become a normal thing that I have come to terms with. I dropped a kiss on the top of her head and took a seat across from her. As we dug in, Hailey walked in, sniffing the air.

"It smells amazing in here."

Haven swallowed her bite of food. "It's all Everette. He may seem like a total brute, but he's quite the cook."

I rolled my eyes at her commentary and continued to chow down. My mind thought back to what Hailey had told me just a few hours ago and I knew I needed to tell Haven soon so we could work out a plan on what we wanted to do.

Hailey took a seat at the table with her plate of food and sighed, flapping a napkin over her lap. Haven and I cut our eyes to one another at the sight of it. When Hailey noticed our bewildered stare, she gave us an odd look. "What?" Haven shrugged, acting as if she saw nothing, and stuffed a bite of pancake into her mouth. I did the same, causing Hailey to scoff. "Can I not eat with a napkin over my lap?"

"No," Haven mumbled with a mouthful of food. "It's just that we're not the classiest people so we don't see that very often."

Hailey grimaced at Haven. "I see that."

"Hey! What's the supposed to mean?"

"Nothing." Hailey giggled. "It was just branded into my brain that us MOTs, well Ghost's MOTs, were supposed to uphold the utmost class. Strange if you weigh in the fact that we're literal killers, but hey… who am I to judge? It's just a habit, is what I'm trying to say."

I placed my fork down, folding my hands together. "Habits are hard to break, I get it."

"Well Ghost can kiss my ass," grumbled Haven. "If you don't want to act like some classy woman then don't. I don't."

I smothered my laugh as Haven shoved a huge bite of her food into her mouth, the syrup from the sweet treat getting all over the sides of her mouth.

Yep, *she's mine*, I wanted to say.

"I like your perspective on life," Hailey mused. "But it will take some time for me to get rid of old routines."

I went to speak, but the burner phone that resided in the living room began to ping with an incoming call. We were all quick to hop up from the table, knowing what that meant, and dart over to it.

"Hello?" I picked up, worry washing over me.

Are we too late? Is it time to leave?

There was rustling on the other side of the line. "You need to get home!" Jay yelled, sounding as if she was on the run.

Haven paled. "What happened?"

"It's… shit," Jay cursed as the sound of gunshots broke out. "It's Ghost. He knows we're onto him. He found out what we are trying to do!" There was the sound of grunting, and I winced at the cracking sound.

"Are you fighting someone right now?" Haven's voice rose an octave.

"I had to call you all and warn you! Yes, I just killed a man. Not important. Fuck!" It sounded like the phone toppled to the ground and more male grunts were heard along with gunshots. Another rustling sound. "I have to go. Get home now. If they found us, they will soon find you! We're outnumbered without our women and men from back home. We haven't been able to get a hold of Nikita and Saul, Haven. It's not looking good."

My fists clenched at my side. If anything has happened to Saul or Nikita, I will raise hell for Ghost.

"How did they find you?"

The line started breaking up, but we heard the word 'tracker' before the line went dead. Our heads snapped to look at Hailey.

"You're being tracked!" I snapped. "Did you know this?!"

Hailey quickly shook her head, panic washing over her. "No! I swear it."

Those women that Jay and A.R had were all tracked. I mentally cursed, hating myself for not thinking Ghost would try such a thing.

Of course he would.

"When she was taken, they probably drugged her and implanted it," Haven mumbled, walking around Hailey and started to assess her. "Most trackers are in the neck or arm, at least that's what the commander said."

I arched a brow. "The commander put a tracker in you all?"

She shook her head. “No. She thought about it, but when we all were against it, she compromised with putting trackers in our cars.”

Haven and I quickly began to prod around Hailey’s form, pressing down on her skin gently to see if we could feel anything.

“Found it,” Haven grumbled, pressing her hand to the back of Hailey’s neck. “If you press down hard enough back here you can feel it.”

I moved, pressing down. I didn’t feel anything at first, but when I pressed harder and moved my finger slightly, I finally did.

“Oh God,” Hailey cried, her hands beginning to shake. “I’m going to get us all killed. I swear I didn’t know.”

Haven was quick to grab the sides of her face. “You didn’t know so pull yourself together. We only have one of you, so maybe Ghost hasn’t caught on yet. We might have time to–”

There was a loud bang from the front door being kicked in.

Haven’s head whipped in that direction and when the scar on my stomach throbbed in warning, we all jolted into action.

“Fuck. Weapons, now!” I yelled, running for the stairs.

Hailey followed us up them, and by the time we reached our rooms, I could hear men and women yelling.

“Shit, shit, shit!” Haven cried, grabbing her swords.

“Daggers, Haven, where are your daggers?!”

She ran to the other side of the room and snatched them up. I grabbed them from her and gave them to Hailey before I took one of Haven’s swords.

Hailey had already slammed the door shut and had begun to drag a dresser in front of it. I ran to her when I caught sight of it and began to help her barricade the door.

“We can’t fight them off,” Hailey breathed out. “I know the team of men and women Ghost sends out after people. Trust me on this. We have to find a way out.”

Haven opened the window and looked down. “It’s a drop, but if you do it correctly you shouldn’t break anything. The best move would to be try and scale down it a little farther and then drop. Maybe this will give us a head start."

I nodded, motioning for her to go. She started to crawl down after tossing her weapon to the ground. I turned to Hailey. "Have you scaled up or down any buildings before?"

"No… never. Most of our problems were on the ground with two feet."

I sighed. "Okay, then I'm going to go first so you can follow me down."

Just as I began to put one leg out the window, the door burst open, sending the dresser toppling over.

"Hurry!" Haven screamed.

Dread washed over me when men flooded the room.

I couldn't just leave Hailey.

I looked down at Haven, my heart feeling as if it was breaking in two. "The club," I mouthed to her. "Run!"

She sobbed, stumbling back with her sword as something stung the side of my neck. "Run…" I tried to shout again, but everything began to grow dizzy.

And then it was black.

CHAPTER TWENTY-NINE

Haven

Sobs wracked my body as I ran, trying to outrun the men that would no doubt be coming after me soon enough. I saw the dart strike Everette's neck, I saw him topple back into the room, and I heard Hailey's screams.

My stomach flipped and I had to stop for a brief second to throw up. Heaving, I managed to straighten myself and continue my sprint to God knows where. I had no phone. No idea where I was. Nothing.

I'm fucked.

After running what felt like a few good miles, I ducked behind a random dumpster to an old building to try and catch my breath.

Fisting my hair, I couldn't get Everette's pained expression out of my mind. The look on his face when he knew he had to stay behind. I hiccupped through my cries, trying my best to get my head straight, but I had no idea what I needed to do.

I knew I shouldn't have gone first.

It should have been me.

I let out a shaky breath, looking down at the shorts and shirt I was wearing. Everette's shirt. "Fuck," I cried once more.

I couldn't stay here for long. I had to get moving. If someone saw me running around in nothing but these clothes and a sword in hand, I would easily be spotted and my location shot straight to Ghost's men.

I stuck out like a sore thumb.

Just as I began to get up, I heard the crunching of tires on gravel. I froze, peering around the side of the dumpster to see a familiar sleek, black car pull up. It stopped, the door opening, and out hobbled Miguel.

He held his side as he looked around. "Haven?"

I let out a sob of relief, coming into view. "Miguel? How did you find me?"

He visibly relaxed when he saw me. "I was at home resting when I got the alert that the house's security had been breached. I notified my men immediately. I didn't get to the house in time, but one of my men that was out said he saw 'a lunatic of a girl' running with a sword down the road. I assumed it was you."

I rushed to him. "They took Everette and Hailey!"

Despite Miguel still being busted up from the other night, his eyes darkened with rage. "Who?"

I wet my lips. "Have you ever heard of Ghost?"

He cursed. "That's who you've been fucking with this entire time? Are you all stupid?!" He switched over to Spanish, spitting words at me angrily. After a minute, he sighed. "Get in the car. We need to go because if they got those two, they're going to be after you soon enough. You're lucky it was one of my men that saw you and not the other way around."

I followed his orders and practically flew into his backseat, thanking God that A.R had contacts here in Mexico. We would have been screwed so many times if it wasn't for this man.

"Do you have any idea where Ghost could have taken them?" Miguel asked as he began to drive.

"No… well, before Everette was taken he mouthed the word club to me. I don't know what he meant, but he obviously knew something I didn't."

He glanced at me through the rearview mirror. "And you think you need to go there?"

"I don't have a choice. I will not leave them behind. I'll die before that happens."

Miguel grumbled at the thought of it. "Please refrain from doing so. A.R would gut me alive if I let anything happen to you, that much was clear."

I blew out a breath of air. "How are you holding up?"

"After being brutally beaten? Great." Sarcasm dripped from his words.

"I'm sorry that happened to you."

He shrugged. "It comes with the job, I suppose. But now that I know who you all have been after this whole time, I could wring your neck. Any smart person knows not to mess around with Ghost. His reach is too far to risk anything with him."

I clenched my fists. "I know. He's already taken too much from me, I won't let that be happening again. But technically, he wasn't our main goal. Saving a group of women he stole from us was."

"I'm assuming Hailey was one of them?"

I nodded. "Yeah, but I'm afraid at this rate, I won't be able to save the rest."

It felt all too familiar, this feeling of heartache just when I get one ounce of happiness. I was beginning to believe I was cursed, despite the one I already harbored. It was as if the moment I played into any sort of happiness, it was ripped away from me.

After the night Knox and I once had… he was ripped from my grasp before I really even got to know the real him. And now I was just starting to create something so amazing with Everette and I didn't know what fate had in store for him.

If he… If Ghost kills him, he will wish he was the one that was dead.

At the thought, a fiery rage swept through my body and my scar throbbed. I couldn't control it as it continued to grow and grow, flashes of Ghost's dismembered body littering my thoughts.

Suddenly, I realized I was gripping my sword with white knuckles as I ground out, "I need a favor."

***

It was dark outside, a cold and eerie breeze swooshing through the air around me. My hair picked up lightly in the wind and blew around as I stared across the street at the club. It was booming with music, but unlike last time, only a few people filtered in and out of the building.

All in costumes.

The mask that clung to my face was an unusual feeling, but the rage clawing inside me wasn't. I surveyed the building once more, seeing people standing at the front doors to usher people inside and out just like last time.

I guess my uniform would get me in.

Hailey's old uniform for Ghost clung to me like a second skin and I hated every bit of it. Miguel had sent his men to the house only to find it practically turned upside down and empty. They retrieved Hailey's uniform from her room and brought it to me at my request.

It still smelled like the salt of the sea, but I didn't give a damn at the moment. I just knew I had to exhaust any opportunity to get me into this damn place.

With every step I took, that angry beast inside me reared its ugly head.

Kill them, it chanted. *Kill them all.*

I pulled on that familiar feeling, sighing in pleasure as it warmed my entire being. When I got in line, people shuffled away from me nervously, clearly knowing what the uniform represented.

If there was one thing I knew about tonight, it was that I wasn't leaving until I had the answers I needed. I would make them all pay—MOTs or not—if they participated in taking someone I cared deeply about away from me.

I wouldn't let that happen twice.

Making my way to the front of the line, the woman and man took one look at me before raising that familiar velvet rope to let me through. I walked in and looked around at the Halloween party going on. People laughed and danced, throwing their heads back with delight.

Little did they know it was about to be a fucking blood bath.

Someone walked up to me, motioning me to follow them. I did so, my fingers itching to grab the sword on my back. I had hesitated even bringing it, but I did remember a few of the women I first encountered had some while the others wielded daggers.

I stuck with the one thing gifted from Everette that I had learned to love.

We walked away from the main floor, twisting and turning down a few halls before we came to a locked one. The man slid a keycard into a small box on the side of the door and it clicked before sweeping open.

The minute it latched behind us, I looked around to see it was another hallway. Gritting my teeth, I wasted no time before unsheathing my dagger from my thigh and grabbing the back of his shirt to jerk him back. I slashed the dagger across his throat and kicked him aside, sauntering further down the hall.

If the cameras on the ceiling were any indication, I would soon be having men swarm into the hall in three… two…

The door at the far end burst open and three men ran towards me. Ignoring the warning my scar gave, I pulled out my sword with a dangerously exciting feeling.

Then I lifted that wall I had mashed down to stop my rage from exploding.

And then hell broke loose.

I dove forward, sliding to my knees with a war cry as my sword slid up one of the men's abdomens, gutting him all the way up to his throat.

Blood splashed over me as I spun, thrusting my sword into another just as he reached me. Using his body as a shield, the third man's gunshots missed me easily and the bullets easily lodged into his back.

Grunting, I threw the man backward so he would knock the third man off balance. I shifted around him with the few seconds I had and jerked my steel through the air in one sharp motion. The man's eyes widened as he grabbed at his throat, dropping his knees.

Pushing my hair out of my face, I tried not to think about the sticky feeling of the blood coating my skin and stepped over their motionless bodies to venture further down the corridor.

I reached a door and turned the doorknob, noticing it was locked. From here, I could already hear the panicked whispers from whoever was on the other side. I stepped back a few feet, my anger spiking and raised my leg, letting it kick right at the handle with so much force that the wood chipped as the door burst open.

I sauntered in, seeing women dressed similarly to me as they all quickly stood from the table they were sitting at.

They couldn't see the psychotic grin that crawled onto my face as I spoke, "Trick or treat?"

CHAPTER THIRTY

Haven

The women were slowly crowding together, not knowing who had just walked through their doors covered in blood. It was like everything was slowly going in and out and I knew that my rage was close to taking over as black spots began to dance in my vision.

"Who are you?" a woman spoke as she made her way to the front of the crowd.

I hiked an eyebrow up. "You haven't caught onto that yet?"

The woman remained silent as she assessed me, taking in the uniform that I was wearing. After a minute she spoke, "You took Hailey. That's her uniform."

I grinned. "I did."

"Pity," she sighed. "She was the weakest of us all."

My rage reared up again, causing me to blink a few times to try and get my head in the right place. I couldn't let go just yet. I had to reign it in.

"Yet she was the last one standing after I slaughtered all your women, *Lydia*." I snapped, causing the redhead to freeze slightly.

It was clear she was the leader here, the women cowering behind her.

I moved closer, my hands itching to swing my promising steel out just to show them who they truly were screwing around with, but I refrained and inhaled deeply. "Call Ghost. Now."

Lydia's eyes widened. "I can't do that."

I huffed. "Of course you can. I know that you're Ghost's right-hand woman, so let's just cut to the chase, yeah? Call him and I'll spare you all."

Lydia gulped at the threat yet made no move to stop me from walking closer until we were face to face. The women around her cowered away and I wanted to laugh at how quickly their demeanor changed once they knew who had the upper hand.

"Who even are you?" Lydia seethed, trying to regain her composure and masking her face with a hardened look.

I ripped down the mask to reveal my face. "Call Ghost and tell him Haven McKinley is alive and wishes to speak to him."

At the sound of my name, the women gasped and took even more steps away from us. I couldn't help the pride that filled my chest with the sight of their frightened forms.

Cowards.

Lydia's hands shook as she got out her phone and quickly dialed a number. After a few rings, it picked up. "What, Lydia? I'm busy. I just got some good news and wish to deal with it."

At the goosebumps that covered my arms, I had a feeling that he was talking about Everette and Hailey. Possibly Nikita and Saul. Just thinking about that man getting near my family made my blood boil.

I could rip that man's throat out with my bare fucking teeth.

"Sir… Haven McKinley wishes to speak with you."

There was silence for a few moments, but then he nearly whispers, "She's dead."

"She's not, sir. She's standing right in front of me after having slaughtered some of your men. She's the one that was running around with the man in the red cloak."

And I'll do it again, bitch.

"Put her on."

She handed the phone to me with a vicious look on her face. I grabbed it, rage boiling through me. "Ghost."

He let out a sigh that almost sounded like it was filled with pleasure. "Do tell, my little killer, how have you escaped the wrath of the curse?"

I bared my teeth as I spoke. "Not even a curse could put me six feet under."

"Apparently so…" he trailed off. "What do you want?"

"A deal."

A wicked chuckle drifted through the line. "Oh, how I like to make deals. You wish to make a deal with the devil?"

I rolled my eyes. "You took some important people from me. Let them go, with proof, and you can have me. That is all I will bargain."

"Deal," he was quick to say. "Everette and Hailey, I assume, is who you're wishing for?"

"And the others. Saul and Nikita."

He clicked his tongue. "Okay. Fine. My men will take you to the docks where my boat is currently holding Everette and the one who betrayed me. If you wish to see them alive again, you will follow the orders of my men, understand?"

"Yes," I gritted through my teeth. "But if you pull anything, you will wish you hadn't."

"Noted. As for Nikita and Saul, I'll call my men now. But the minute I have you in my grasp, you will call them off. They will not be coming after you or our deal is gone. I will kill them all in front of you with a smile on my face if they do."

My heart ached knowing he indeed had them, and I wanted to scream at the thought of what they were going through because of me. "Deal."

"Good. Lydia? Take Haven to the docks. That's where Everette is being held. Haven will take his place on being shipped to me tomorrow. If she acts out in the slightest, slit her throat."

My jaw ticked as women swarmed me, forcing me to my knees as they brought my hands behind my back and began to tie them there. I had to fight down the rage begging me to come out and I had to ignore the throbbing of my scar as it warned me to not do this.

I had to.

For Everette and the others.

I will not let anyone else's deaths be on my hands.

Lydia grinned down at me, tilting my chin up so I could look at her. "You're one stupid bitch."

Grinning, I shrugged at her. "Keep thinking that. Because one day, I *will* get free. And you will be one of the first I come for after I slit Ghost's throat."

I didn't have a chance to see what she said next as something was pressed into my neck and darkness took me.

***

I woke with a groan and a throbbing headache. Turning my head to the side, I saw through my blurry vision what seemed like a boat's interior. There was a slight rocking motion that confirmed my suspicions.

I moaned with pain, trying to move, but realized my arms and legs were tied down to the chair I was sitting on.

When my vision finally cleared, I saw the men sitting across from me with hard looks. My heart dropped as I realized I never got the proof I needed to see if Ghost freed Everette and I began to struggle in my seat.

"It's no use," one of the men with red hair spoke. "The more you struggle, the more it tightens."

I growled. "Where is Everette? I was supposed to get proof."

He laughed. "You are stupid for ever getting into a deal with Ghost but for once… he upheld his side of the bargain. We knocked the man and woman out and dumped them somewhere in Mexico. But if they live… that's up to them."

My heart felt as if someone reached into my chest and ripped it out. I knew that making a deal with Ghost wasn't one of my smartest decisions, but I hadn't even given it any thought to the condition Everette and Hailey might have been in before he let them go.

They could be dying somewhere.

I gulped. "And Nikita and Saul?"

He waved me off. "The ones in London? Yeah, he let them go, too."

Something wasn't right.

I studied the man's face and slowly it sat in. "Ghost never had Nikita or Saul, did he?"

He cracked a grin. "You're smart, I'll give you that."

Fuck.

I peered around me, taking in the boat's surroundings. "Have we left the port?"

He narrowed his eyes. "No, but we will soon when Ghost arrives. He decided to fly in when he first got Everette, but now he's even more excited that he's got the grand prize. If I was you, I would have run for the hills and forgotten the others. It was idiotic. There's no telling what that man has in store for you."

I scoffed. "And that's why you work for Ghost. You're just as shitty as him. I don't leave people behind. Cowards—all of you."

The man suddenly stood, his eyes darkening. "The fuck you say to me?"

When he neared me, I spit at his feet. "You're a coward," I repeated with venom lacing my tongue.

He grabbed my chin roughly, my cheeks squishing up from the force of it. "I can show you just how shitty I could be. You'd like that, wouldn't you?"

Black dots entered my vision as his hand moved to the top of my shirt, trying to push the material aside. My head snapped to the side and

I bit down on his hand, clamping on his skin hard enough to have him yelping in pain as I drew blood.

He struck me in the jaw so hard, that it sent the chair flying backward, which was a wrong mistake on his part.

The wooden chair I had been strapped to broke under my weight once it smacked into the ground and unknowingly freed my legs. Once I was up and free, I unknowingly dove into my rage. It swept through my body like a cold chill and before I knew it, I heard bones breaking and saw blood splattering across the walls of the boat.

I dropped the piece of wood from the chair that I had wrecked the man with and turned to the man with dark hair who had been silent the whole time. He stood as if watching his friend be killed so effortlessly was nothing he cared about.

I breathed heavily. "Your turn?"

He shook his head. "We need to go. Now. Before the others come." I narrowed my eyes, wondering if this was some trick, but his next words took me by surprise. "I work for Miguel. I've been a rat in Ghost's organization for a long time so Miguel could work around him. Today's my final day thanks to you. I planned to get you off sooner, but you have a mouth on you."

"Get used to it."

Ignoring my words, he motioned for me to follow him. I couldn't help but ask, "Is Everette really safe?"

"Free? Yes. Safe? No. He was beaten pretty badly before Ghost left him and Hailey in a field. We have to get you taken care of first and then we can go searching for him."

Do not cry, Haven McKinley, suck up your fucking tears.

"Why did Ghost not just ship me off? Is he that stupid to think his men could actually hold me for long?" I asked as we ran through the huge boat, nearing an exit.

The man laughed. "No. But he assigned the wrong men to keep you. You're lucky he chose me or this could have ended differently. Ghost wanted to see you in person because of the sick plans he has for you. He was afraid that your friends would get to you before you reached the states again. This was his way of making sure you didn't leave his sight once you were back there."

"Sick plans?"

We reached the door and he peeked out, looking to see if it was clear. "Haven, that man was looking to force himself upon you. He had spoken about it for weeks prior to your apparent death. He wants an heir. Why? I don't know, but when he first came to get you from the states… that's what he wanted. When he heard you died, he looked to seeking the next best thing."

I wanted to hurl again.

Hailey was right.

"And you work for Miguel?"

He nodded. "Yes. I have for years. He reached out to me when he didn't hear from you after the club to keep an ear out about your name. It helped when Ghost's command came through to strap you down and keep you secure until he could reach you. The name is Mateo."

He kept looking out the crack of the door, and I wanted to kiss Miguel right about now. How many times is that man going to save my ass? He needed a pay raise.

Eventually, Mateo ushered me forward. "Run like hell."

And so we did.

We sprinted down the dock, my chest yelling at me with the drug that the women used against me still pumping through my veins. I wasn't one hundred percent yet, but with how easily Ghost lied… I couldn't let that deal happen now, regardless of any of the chaos it may cause. That man was already dead in my eyes.

As long as we could get to Everette and Hailey, I didn't care.

We reached a gravel parking lot that contained a few cars, probably owned by the men that escorted me here, and continued our sprint across it.

I could hear commotion from behind us and my heart sped up as men started to come out of nowhere after us. There were too many and I felt as if we were already defeated.

"Run!" Mateo screamed.

"I'm trying! This drug still is playing on my body!"

I pushed myself, trying to find that familiar tug of rage, but I wasn't able to grasp it again. Feeling dumbfounded, I tried to push myself past my limits to keep up with the man in front of me.

Just as the people behind us grew closer, shouting orders in Spanish, I saw a black jeep speeding into the parking lot. It slid to the side, the back doors opening as two bodies dove out of it.

They rolled to their feet and swords were drawn as they met us. I gasped, seeing the familiar beautiful dark-skinned man that had become one of my closest friends and the fair-skinned brunette who completed a part of me.

"Touch the little one and I'll gut you all!" Saul yelled, running past us.

Nikita looked at me with a fire in her eyes. "Get in!"

I didn't wait before I dove into the back with Mateo hot on my heels. I could see Nikita and Saul slashing their way through the men who first reached us and when they realized the others were still catching up, they spun on their heels to hop in after us.

We were all crowded in the small jeep as the driver sped off and I was practically perched on Mateo's lap, but I couldn't care less as my eyes didn't leave the two of my best friends. "Thank you," I sobbed as Nikita wrapped her arms around me. "I thought I was going to be a slave to that horrible man."

"Never," a voice croaked and my eyes snapped up to finally see who was in the front seats.

Hailey was driving and Everette was in the passenger seat with a weak look on his face. He smiled at me with tired eyes and I couldn't stop myself from diving forward and pulling him to me. I placed a harsh kiss on his lips, earning a groan from him. At the sound, I pulled back, resting my forehead against his, my hands cupping his cheeks. "I'm sorry."

The others didn't question the show of PDA between us as his eyes closed and we took a moment to just breathe one another in.

We're okay.

We're breathing.

We're here with one another.

"You saved us once again, Red," Everette whispered, pressing a soft kiss to my lips. "Even if you went around the most idiotic way of doing it."

I let out a sound between a laugh and a sob. "I couldn't let him take you from me. I would die before that happened."

Everette finally met my eyes, our foreheads still touching, and it nearly broke me to see the tears in his eyes. "Thank you," he breathed. "But I would have given my life for you if that meant you could escape him. Don't *ever* pull that shit again and try to make a deal with him. Do you understand me?"

I quickly nodded, not in the mood for arguing, and couldn't help but press another kiss to his lips. "I promise."

When we pulled apart, I looked back at a shocked Nikita and Saul. Saul's shocked look morphed into a cocky grin. "It's about damn time!"

The sudden seriousness of the situation was quickly gone as everyone, aside from a confused Mateo, broke out into laughter.

CHAPTER THIRTY-ONE

Saul

Seeing my best friend look at Haven as if she was his entire world was something I never expected, but it warmed me in so many ways. How many times had I hoped and prayed that this man would find love again? Hoped to never see that hurt and aching look cross his face after the loss of his wife?

I knew for a fact that Everette Knight loved Haven McKinley with everything in him. There was no doubt about it. Just the way he looked at her was something strange to witness. Long gone were the broody, jealous stares and now sat a look of pure awe of the woman before him.

And Haven wasn't much different.

I glanced over at Nikita as our laughter faded and she grinned up at me, pure happiness etched across her face at the thought of her friend becoming happy again. Despite this horrible day and despite what Haven and Nikita have gone through, it was easy to see how the women loved each other endlessly.

"Where am I going?" Hailey asked, speeding down a random street.

The man that entered the Jeep with Haven leaned forward and pointed. "Take this next left. We'll go to Miguel."

Everette's brow raised. "You work for Miguel?"

"Yes. I'm Mateo, and Miguel made me a rat in Ghost's organization for a while. But after helping Haven get free, it's safe to say I won't be going back."

Everette's face hardened. "Thank you. I don't know what we would have done if Haven was taken."

I snorted. "Something stupid, of course."

The group let out a laugh at the comment, and Haven finally spoke up. "So how did you all find me? And how the hell did you two get to Mexico?"

I sighed, trying my best to wrap my hand around the whole situation. "Your sword was pinpointed to this location. We never took the tracker out of it. And the same with Everette and Hailey. The dagger Everette had given you a while ago still contained the same tracker he used to track you with. Hailey had stashed one of the daggers—his—under her clothing to hopefully use later on. When we noticed the two of you in different locations, we put the pieces together."

"Okay… but how did you get here? How did you know to come?"

This time, Nikita spoke. "Saul found papers in this old warehouse where we thought that some MOTs would be. It was abandoned like everyone there had left in a hurry. After Saul did some more digging, he found out that they did indeed leave in a hurry. A.R had been after Ghost. It was him that sent Ghost into a panic and he cleaned up his messes to leave quickly. Now we know two people that Ghost is scared of: Haven and A.R. Why, I don't know, but if A.R had gotten so close to him, it makes sense why Ghost fled and took his men."

Haven frowned. "Perhaps that's why A.R has been so hellbent on helping us out… because he failed the last time. He never got Ghost. And then Ghost hurt his own family. Makes sense. But again, how did this information lead you to us?"

"Shit, right…" Nikita said. "Well, to be short, we took one of the leads we had and tracked down some of Ghost's men. When we were staking out a warehouse they were in, we heard them talking about how two people had been spotted in Mexico and two others in Russia and how Ghost was going after them. Since you all never called or updated, we assumed you didn't know. After calling Jay and A.R, they said they would take care of it and for us to bail on our mission and get to you all first. I guess they got so busy they never called you two. I know they moved their locations of where they were staying, but that was all Jay had updated me with."

Everette sighed. "Jay did end up calling us. I guess their plan didn't work out too well because, during the call, they were literally on the run. Jay told us to leave but by the time we got it all figured out, Ghost's men raided A.R's house."

Nikita frowned. "And you haven't heard anything from them since?"

"Well, when you're taken, drugged, and brutally beaten, we don't have much time to pick up a phone," grumbled Everette.

Haven winced, reaching out to give his shoulder a squeeze. I could see how much it pained her to know that he went through all that just so she could escape. But I had no idea that Haven would have given herself over to Ghost so quickly. I thought she was smarter than that, but again… love makes you do stupid things.

"What do we do now?" I asked, resting my hand against Nikita's thigh.

It had become a habit between us. Most nights when we weren't on the run, we had gotten food and taken it back to the apartment. We spent the nights curled up on the couch gorging ourselves on London's tasty foods and laughing our hearts out as we got to know one another.

Nikita was pretty fucking cool.

Nikita rested her hand on the top of mine, running her thumb over my knuckles. Haven didn't miss the small gesture, and she dipped her head so her hair would fall to cover a smile I knew she was trying to hide.

Mateo leaned forward. "We get you all back to Miguel so he can figure out a plan. Your best bet is to get the fuck out of Mexico while you can. However you got here, you need to go the same way back to the states where you're in familiar territory. That's the only thing you're going to have the upper hand with."

We nodded at him, thinking over the idea. It was true. If we were back with more of our men and women, and in familiar territory, that would be way easier to deal with whatever Ghost threw at us next.

"Has anyone kept in touch with Reese?" I asked, nearly forgetting the poor men who had to deal with all those snarky women back home.

"I called him not too long ago with A.R's burner phone. Everything is good there. No more attacks since we've been gone and the women have been getting informers still. So nothing had really changed for them. He's kept them up to date with training and the commander is still locked away."

Haven grumbled at the name, spitting curses under her breath.

I cocked a brow. "Care to explain how your hatred for the women has grown even more since we left, little one?"

Haven shook her head, rubbing her arms. "Let's just say everything I did to her back at the manor in my spiraling moments is exactly what she deserved. The woman planned on giving me over to Ghost so they could make me a freaking walking incubator."

Nikita's face scrunched up. "As in… like, a baby incubator?"

Haven threw her arms up as Miguel gave Hailey more directions to take. "Yes! She wanted to strap me down so Ghost could have his wicked way with me in order to produce some heir he thinks will have the MOT curse and can take over after him."

I straightened, anger pumping through my veins like pure poison. "What the fuck? You're serious?"

"Unfortunately," Everette muttered. "She's a real bitch."

I scoffed. "I'll say."

Haven looked down at her hands with a conflicted look. "We also learned a lot about the curse that we didn't know originally, so when we get back I need to brief the MOTs as soon as possible."

That didn't sound good.

***

Eventually, Mateo made us park about a mile down the road from whatever place he was taking us to. We went the rest of the way on foot until we reached a huge house, which I believed was Miguel's.

The minute we had all exited the Jeep, a man came flying out of the house. He was older looking, maybe late thirties to early forties. He reached Haven, shouting at her in Spanish as he waved his arms around frantically.

"Miguel! I don't know Spanish!"

He cursed, shaking his head. "How could you be so reckless! You promised me, Haven! You promised that you would only go into that club for answers and then get the hell out. Then I see Ghost men's carrying your unconscious body to a truck. Do you know how frightened I was for you?!"

She grimaced. "I'm sorry, Miguel, but I knew you would try and stop me. I had to do something to get Everette and Hailey free, regardless of where that ended for me."

He shook his head, his face softening some. "You are still a crazy woman."

She huffed out a laugh. "You haven't even seen the worst of me, Miguel."

He grumbled in Spanish once more before saying, "And I don't want to. I felt like I have aged ten years in the past two days because of you. Come, we need to get you all home. I want you out of my hair."

Haven faked a pout. "Miguel… you won't let me stay with you?"

I held back my chuckle at how easily Haven deflected the seriousness of the situation at hand when Miguel snapped back, "Hell no!"

That got a laugh out of us.

It didn't take long for Miguel to set up the plans, getting A.R's jet ready for us. A.R was still not answering any of our calls and Haven paced at the many voicemails we reached. But Miguel insisted that A.R was one tough man and would get Jay and him back home safely. We just needed to listen to his wishes and get back to the states. Hopefully, they were already heading back there.

As the girls went with Miguel and Mateo to get the cars ready, I made Everette stay back. Once they were out of sight, I turned to him with folded arms.

"Care to explain what the hell happened these past few weeks while we were separated?"

He tried to hold his grin back but couldn't. "I don't know how it happened. We just… got close. It helped when we finally opened up to one another instead of trying to rip one another's heads off, but it just kind of fell into place."

I smiled. "You look happy. It's so damn good to see that," I replied, pulling him in for a hug.

He slapped me on the back before pulling away. "I feel happy, for the most part. It's weird, honestly. I never expected us to get together at all, especially not as quickly as we did. But with Haven, it's like all my worries just wash away. She said something similar, too. It's as if we're free when we're with one another. Like we don't have the weight of the world on our shoulders and it's just us existing."

I snorted. "Look at you being all poetic."

He laughed, giving me a shove. "I'm serious."

I reined in my laughter and nodded. "I know. As I said, I'm happy for you, man. You deserve this. I just hope that it all works out in your favor. I haven't seen Haven look so at peace just by being in someone's presence. But I understand what you mean. When she saw you, the way she visibly relaxed and just… fell into you? That's love, man."

Everette frowned. "You think so?"

I looked at him with a shocked but humorous expression. "Why are you asking me for confirmation?! You should know this."

He rubbed the back of his neck awkwardly. "I don't know what I feel just yet. I know I'm definitely falling in love with her, which I cannot deny, but I just don't want to rush it and get my hopes up only for it to come crashing down. Haven is still working down this path with me and I just want to take baby steps so I don't scare her off."

I nodded. "That's understandable and considerate. But man, I think you're in this for the long run. You didn't see what I saw when she flung herself at you in that car. That woman cares more for you than you think."

Everette shifted on his feet, not knowing what to think about it. It was nearly amusing seeing him so lost in his own mind about all of this. We never discussed things like this, and it was clearly an awkward situation for the man who was known for his broody and hardass persona. Everette didn't like to talk about his feelings, so the fact he was actually talking to me about it just proved how much he cared for Haven.

I once thought that he just had an infatuation with her—wanted something he couldn't have—but I was clearly wrong about it all.

They just needed time.

Granted, I didn't think it would only take almost two weeks before they were tangled up with one another, but I guess the heart truly wants what it wants.

"Guys! Let's go!"

Speak of the devil and she shall appear.

We looked over, seeing Haven waving at us. Shooting knowing looks at one another, Everette gave me a pointed look. "If you tell anyone I told you this shit, I will cut your dick off."

I belted out a laugh as he stalked off.

He'll never change.

And I hope he never does.

CHAPTER THIRTY-TWO

Haven

I never thought I would be so grateful to see that damn school, but as our car rolled up to the familiar place, my heart jolted within my chest.

Home, my body screamed.

I was slightly worried about leaving Miguel when he had been so helpful to us and that could potentially put him at risk, but he had waved me off and told me to get my ass on the jet with a promise that he would be fine. So I said my goodbyes and listened to him.

Now I was peering out of the SUV's window as Everette held my hand. Nikita had yet to bombard me with questions but I knew the minute we were alone, it would be all she asked of me. The details. How it happened.

I was almost sad to lose the little bubble Everette and I had around one another with our time away from the group, but I knew it was going to come out sooner or later.

"Man is it good to be back home," Saul stated, throwing open his door.

I looked over to Hailey who stared up at the school with a nervous look. Leaning closer to her, I whispered, "It's not as bad as you think."

She looked at me, chewing on her bottom lip. "What if they don't like me?"

I waved her off. "No one likes me, it's fine."

She let out a shocked laugh. "Thanks, that's *so* helpful."

I shot her a wink. "You'll be fine. They'll love you. Well, maybe not Anastasia, but no one likes her either. Sam, on the other hand, will adore you."

She blew out a breath and nodded, following Everette and me out of the car. When the doors to the car shut, the doors of the school opened. Red hair waved around as the tiny figure shot out of the doors and plowed toward us. I grunted as Sam ran into me, nearly tackling me to the ground.

"Hey, Sam." I giggled and rubbed her back, but my brows rose in surprise. "You've been training. Look at that muscle growth, girl!"

She pulled back, grinning up at me. "I put Reese on his ass three times this morning. And the best part? Anastasia couldn't even get me pinned *once*."

I let out a howl of laughter, giving her a high-five. "That's what I liked to hear. I'm glad someone kept up my reputation around here while I was gone."

She grinned ear to ear. "Always."

She looked beside me at Hailey who stood there looking so out of place. I motioned to her. "Sam this is Hailey. Hailey this is my good friend, Sam."

Hailey offered her a small smile. "It's nice to meet you."

Sam gave her a curious once over. "Are you one of the women Haven went to go save?"

Hailey's cheeks flushed, probably thinking about how our first encounter had really gone. "Yeah. Something like that."

Sam beamed once again. “Well, welcome! It’s actually a nice place here, and I think you’re really going to love it. You would have croaked if you had seen our old living conditions,” Sam said, dramatically shivering and it pulled a laugh from us. She hooked her arm through Hailey’s. “Come on, I’ll introduce you to everyone!”

Hailey cast me a glance over her shoulder that screamed ‘help me’ but I just giggled to myself and let Sam lead her in. If there was one person that could warm Hailey up to everyone, it was her.

Everette walked up beside me, slinging his arm over my shoulder. “At least we saved one of them.”

I nodded, trying to push away that small feeling of defeat. “One is better than none.”

Saul had already vanished into the school, so Everette began to pull me towards it. My heart was beating frantically within my chest as Everette laced our fingers together. It was a bold move, showing up to the school hand in hand after all the women knew what I had gone through prior to leaving.

Making a hard choice, I pulled my hand from him as we walked in and Everette shot me a confused look, hurt flashing across his face. I ignored the ache in my chest at the sight of it and brushed past him before I averted my eyes.

Reese was the first I saw, a happy grin on his face when he moved away from Saul and the others and welcomed me back home with a hug. “It’s good to see you in one piece,” he mumbled.

I gave him a squeeze and moved away so he could greet Everette. “It’s good to see you, man. Thanks for keeping the place from burning to the ground,” Everette joked.

Reese shrugged at him. “It was easy. The women were great with helping out when needed, so we stayed afloat while you were all gone. But man, do you look like shit.”

Everette rolled his eyes. “If only you knew the shit we had to go through.”

Reese looked over at Hailey who was talking to some of the women with Sam. "So only one, huh?"

I tried to remain neutral as I stared across the room at her. "Yes. But we just have to hope that we can take Ghost down and get the others. Our time there was cut short due to some… unforeseeable circumstances."

Reese nodded, giving my arm a small squeeze. "We'll get him, Haven."

I managed a small smile, feeling the exhaustion of our trip finally catching up to me. A yawn broke past my lips. "I think I'm going to head to bed and get some rest. Tomorrow morning, make sure everyone is up bright and early because we have a lot we need to discuss."

Reese gave me a small salute and I turned, catching Everette's stare as I brushed past him. As I walked away, I could hear Reese ask about A.R and Jay. One could only hope they made it back to us like they planned and we didn't have to send a search party to Russia. God knows I've had enough traveling these past weeks to last me a lifetime.

It was safe to say I missed the smell of New York, the busy streets, and the feeling of just being home where I felt somewhat safe. At least here, I knew where I was and could navigate just as easily. I never want to feel like I did in Mexico on the run with no idea where to go. If Miguel hadn't shown up, I have no idea where I would be right now.

No idea if Everette and Hailey would even be alive.

As I neared the stairs that led to my room, I halted, casting my eyes down the hallway to the doors that led to the basement where the commander was.

I had to see her. I had to ask her if she truly was going to sell my body to Ghost.

My feet led me downstairs to her cell, my hands shaking with every step I took, and when I finally reached where she was chained up, the MIR next to her cell shot up.

"You're back."

I nodded at him. "We are. Could I have a moment alone with her?"

"Of course, I'll be outside if you need me." He replied before handing me the keys to the cell.

I waited for a minute, trying to gather and prepare myself for what she could say.

Then I put the key into the lock and opened it. At the sound of the creaking steel, she looked over from her crouched position in the corner, her eyes widening at the sight of me.

"It's been a minute," I mumbled, closing the door behind me.

She looked just as fragile and broken as I left her. Pale skinned. Bloodied form.

I did that.

"What do you want?" she croaked out. "If you're here to catch up on ripping me apart, just know The Men in Red didn't let up on the torture you promised me all those weeks ago."

Ignoring her comment, I pulled up a chair, letting it scrape against the floor as I neared her, and then I sat down before crossing my legs. "Is it true?"

She straightened, giving me a confused look. "Is what true?"

"Is it true that you were going to sell my body to Ghost to play into his sick fantasy about some heir?"

She gulped and lowered her eyes to the floor. "Haven…"

"Is it true?!" I yelled, causing her to flinch.

"Yes."

I let out a humorless laugh and shook my head. "You truly are the devil in disguise."

"Haven I never meant for it to go so far but I owed him—"

I jumped to my feet. "So you think you had the right to pay some fucking debt with my *body*?!"

She whimpered, tucking herself farther into the corner as if I would lash out any minute.

I took a close look at her, my fingers itching to end her life once and for all. I didn't need her anymore. She proved she knew nothing else and was completely useless to me now. But if I killed her, that was letting her off easy.

She didn't deserve easy.

I crouched in front of her, grabbing her chin roughly. "Listen and listen closely. I'm not going to kill you. No, I'm going to make your life hell just as you did for countless years to me and the other women in this organization. You're going to pay for each and every little thing you committed. Do you hear me? Because I refuse to stoop down to your level. I will *never* be like you. I'm not going to take the cowardly way out of this. I'm not going to hate myself and blame myself for something *you* created! I'm going to show these women what a true commander looks like. I'm going to give them everything they dreamed of that you lied about ever providing. And you're going to watch as I surpass you. You're going to watch as I become everything you dreamed of, and you're going to do it from this very cell."

I pushed her away and stood to my feet.

I was done blaming myself.

I was done feeling broken.

It was time to move on and stop Ghost—stop all this shit for good.

So I left her sobbing form and walked out, locking up behind me. I let out a breath of air, feeling as if a weight had lifted from my shoulders.

I can do this.

I had to.

***

Closing the door to my bedroom with a sigh, I yawned once more. I needed to shower, but sleep kept calling to me desperately.

Ignoring the aching of my body and droopy eyes, I headed towards the bathroom that connected to my room. But just as I reached to open the bathroom door, my bedroom door opened and Everette sauntered through with a grim look.

I frowned. "What is it?"

He paced in front of me, only making my nerves grow worse. "Are you embarrassed to be seen with me or something?"

It felt as if someone twisted a knife within my gut. "Everette," I heaved out a deep breath, "No. Not at all."

"Then why did you pull away when we walked into the school?"

I knew this was coming, but I hoped he would have saved this conversation for tomorrow. Instead, I motioned him to my bed and sat at the edge of it, patting the spot next to me. Reluctantly, he sat down and folded his arms.

"I pulled away because I was scared of what people might think of *me*. People knew about Knox and me and the hard time I had trying to cope with losing everyone. I didn't want them thinking I was using you or anything like that. They don't understand the connection we've formed recently—don't understand the bond we've created. This is new to me. You have to understand that I want nothing more than to be with you, but it's just going to take time to let others outside of our small friend group see what we've built."

Everette visibly relaxed, taking my hands into his own. "I'm sorry, I didn't even think about that. I just panicked and thought you were having second thoughts or something."

I shook my head. "Never."

His hand dropped one of my own and cupped my cheek. "Whatever you need, we'll do it. I promise. No more getting panicked."

I let out a small laugh, loving this side of him. To be honest, I expected a heated argument because of our past selves, but Everette was proving me wrong with every step we took further into whatever was happening between the two of us. "Get used to having me around, asshole."

He chuckled. "I guess I can manage, *brat*."

I leaned into him, letting him press his lips into my own. As always, everything felt as if it vanished around us and I got lost within him. We fell back onto the bed, Everette moving to hover over me as he worked his mouth against mine.

I moaned, pulling him closer and loving the feel of him brushing up against my body. Desire swirled within my core, and I had to stop that train of thought before this progressed. I was tired and dirty and in desperate need of a shower.

But like Everette could read my mind, he pulled back and rested his forehead against my own. "As much as I'd love to continue this. I feel as if I am going to pass out at any moment."

I snickered, looping my arms around his neck. "Same. And I stink. I need a bath."

He nodded. "You do."

I gasped, smacking him on the shoulder only for him to pin my arms above my head with a goofy grin. "I'm kidding. But let's get a shower."

I cocked a brow. "Let's?"

He smirked. "You didn't think I was letting you get away that easily, did you? After our last shower together, I think I may have to require you to be in all of mine from here on out."

I shoved him away with a laugh rumbling within my chest. "You're ridiculous."

When I stood, he did as well before wrapping his arms around my waist and pressing a kiss to the base of my neck. "Only for you."

I turned to press one last kiss on his lips. "Better be. Now, if I let you in on this shower, what's in store?"

He let out an exaggerated sigh. "I thought you were tired. I'll never get you sated, will I?"

Rolling my eyes at his cocky look, I said, "I *am* tired, but I might be persuaded."

"I don't know…" he trailed off as if he was in deep thought, faking a yawn. "I'm pretty beat."

When my hand trailed down his chest, his eyes heating under my touch, I gave him a doe-eyed like. "Too tired for me?"

In a flash, he picked me up and began to carry me to the bathroom as I let out a yelp. "Never too tired for you, Red. I guess I could eat. Didn't get any dinner." My jaw dropped as he kicked the bathroom door shut with his foot, a booming laugh escaping him when he caught the look on my face. "Let's just start with actually showering, yeah?"

Ignoring my heated cheeks, I nodded. "I think that's in our best interest after all."

We stripped, trying our best to ignore each other's naked bodies as we got in and began to wash off. We barely made it through the shower without falling asleep standing up, so unfortunately for my overly excited friend downstairs, we called it a night before anything happened and knocked out the minute our heads hit the pillows.

***

"What the fuck!" a voice yelled, waking me from my slumber.

I blinked, my eyes stinging from the sun peering through my windows as I tried to look around. I was tangled in Everette's arms, only wearing one of his shirts and some underwear. He was snoring beside me, unaware of whoever was yelling.

Jay loomed over me, her jaw nearly touching the floor.

I shot up, startling Everette awake. "Jay?!"

Flying out of bed, I tackled her into a hug. She laughed, picking up my small form and doing a twirl. "I'm so damn glad you all are okay!"

When she placed me on my feet, I looked her over and saw she didn't even have one scratch on her. "Same! I was worried."

She smiled. "A.R made sure that we got back okay. You know… he's not as bad as I thought."

Everette groaned, falling back into bed. "How did you get in here? I thought I locked the door."

She shot him her middle finger. "Nice to see you, too, Everette."

He returned the gesture, causing a laugh to escape me. Finally, Jay looked back at me and then cut her eyes to the gorgeous man gracing my bed. "So what the hell is up with that? I thought you hated each other."

Everette snorted, his forearm resting over his eyes. "Shit happened."

She scoffed. "Clearly. So what? Did you two bang or something?"

I let out a gurgled sound, covering my face. "Jay! No."

"Well, you clearly have fooled around." When Everette and I stayed silent, she snickered again. "I knew it. It was a matter of time, honestly. The sexual tension between the two of you was starting to give headaches."

I shook my head at the blunt woman, trying not to strangle her with my bare hands. "It wasn't just some fooling around. There's a lot you don't know."

She paused, narrowing her eyes. "Wait so like… you two actually have feelings for one another?"

I deadpanned at her. "Are you being serious right now? Do you know me? Would I just lay in bed with anyone dressed like this?"

She waved her hand back and forth. "Well, there was that boy Caleb."

I cursed, shoving her towards the door. "Get out!"

She laughed, her head falling back. "Wait! Wait!"

I paused, glaring at her. "What?"

She grinned. "You should see what we brought back with us."

I glanced back at Everette who looked just as confused before I put my attention back on her. "What do you mean?"

She lifted her chin, a proud look crossing her features as she finally went serious. "We saved all of Ghost's women in Russia. We got them back. They're back where they belong."

CHAPTER THIRTY-THREE

Everette

Following Haven down the steps was like trying to follow The Flash himself. She nearly ran downstairs in nothing but my shirt and her cheeky thong until Jay and I both stopped her, making her throw on some pants. Then she was gone. I understood her relief and anticipation to see what Jay was talking about, though.

I felt as if a small weight was lifted off my shoulders. We saved some of them. We didn't fail entirely, and I will take that win any day.

"Where?" Haven rushed out as she flew around the corner, darting into the main area by the staircases.

A.R stood there talking to a few women, and when he turned to see Haven, a smile spread across his face. "Hello, cousin."

There was a group of ten girls all standing behind him with frightened looks. I had to grab Haven's hand, a small warning for her to slow down and not scare them even more, and she gave me a small nod, understanding what I was trying to relay within the small gesture.

"Hello…" she nearly whispered. "It's nice to meet you all. I'm Haven, one of the MOTs here."

They remained silent, looking her over as if she was some laboratory experiment. I knew it would take some time for them to get used to being here, but since their whole demeanor had shifted from trying to literally bite Jay and A.R's heads off to coming with them willingly, I was apprehensive.

I nudged my head to the study room not far from us. "A.R, can we talk? Without an audience?"

He nodded, turning to the women to tell them that Reese would show them around. Reese walked up, flashing them a million-dollar smile, and motioned for them to follow him. I waved at another MIR to go with him, still not knowing if we can trust these women fully.

Haven was still in shock, I think, just by being able to see the women standing before her. I took her hand again and began to drag her with me to where A.R was walking off to.

Once we were alone, he spun to face us with folded arms. "What's up?"

I threw my hands up. "What's up?! Where have you been? How did you get them here?"

He sighed. "After Jay called you all, we were able to get free with the help of those women. Let's just say they didn't take lightly to Ghost putting a tracking device within their bodies and I think that opened up their eyes to see that we truly weren't the bad guys here. Once we were free and in the clear, we made a pit stop on the way home to get their tracking devices removed carefully."

I huffed. "More of your contacts?"

He shrugged. "Maybe."

Haven ran a hand over her face. "And they're not going to like… attack us or anything are they? I can't deal with any more craziness right now and I just know that it's waiting right around the corner for us. I just need to breathe for a few days."

A.R shook his head. "No, Jay talked with a lot of them and they actually opened up to her about their time spent with Ghost. They had no idea that we were truly there to help them and get them back where they belong. Ghost practically brainwashed them. They feared if they stepped out of line in the slightest that he would kill them. He's done it before, according to some of the women."

I cursed, disgust raining over me. "I can't wait to kill that man."

A.R sighed. "It's going to take everything we got in us."

Haven tilted her head to the side a bit. "Did you know that Ghost is scared of you?"

A.R grinned at the question. "I did. Anytime I got remotely close to him when I was on the hunt per your father's request, he found out and fled. He couldn't even face me. Coward," he spit, his face tight. "I can't lie when I say I'm glad I finally got a good look at him. He should be scared."

At the thought of Haven's father, I hiked up a brow. "Any news on her parents? Did you find anything out?"

"No. To be honest, I was focused more on finding the women. If we can weaken Ghost by getting his most prized assets, then it gives us the upper hand. Ghost wouldn't let them be far out of his reach, which means if he was in the states when we weren't… I bet they're still here somewhere. I already planned to start scouting when we got back. I just need some rest and it's the first thing on my list."

I dragged my eyes to get a good look at Haven, seeing that she barely was showing any emotion. But I had started to figure out the small things about her and it was one of her looks she had when she was starting to accept defeat.

"Hey," I murmured. "We'll find them."

She blinked a few times and then took in a deep breath. "I was so focused on the women that I didn't even think to look for clues on them. What kind of daughter does that make me?"

"Haven, you spent years alone with no parents. You're still getting used to having to think about them again. We were busy and it's not like we had much downtime to sit around and think when we were trying to find the lost MOTs," I reminded her, trying my best to ease the weight off her shoulders.

She scoffed. "No child would forget about their missing parents, Everette. I never stopped thinking about them, that's the thing. I spent years apart from my mother and I still yearned for her every day. I never stopped wondering who my father was. I just don't know how to balance all the negative things going on in my life right now."

A.R reached over and gave her shoulder a squeeze. "One day at a time, that's how. We will figure this out, I promise."

Haven chewed on the inside of her cheek. "What if they're dead? I mean, he thought I died. Why would he keep them alive if he couldn't use them against me anymore?"

I pulled her to my side with a sigh. "You can't think like that. We won't stop searching until we know for sure."

Haven didn't get a chance to reply as Sam suddenly walked into the room, calling her name. Our heads turned, taking in the small woman. "We have something to show you," she said, picking at her nails nervously.

Haven gave her a confused look but followed her nonetheless. Catching A.R's curious gaze, we didn't think twice before going after them.

Sam walked us to the back doors of the school and when she opened them, most of the MOTs stood outside with sad smiles. Haven stilled, her eyes sliding over the crowd before her. "What's going on?"

Sam looped their arms together and I watched as Jay and Nikita gave Haven small smiles from the front as they neared. Just as Haven reached the group, it parted, and before her stood a small tombstone.

I could hear Haven's sharp intake of breath from where I stood and I wanted nothing more than to run to her and give her the comfort she needed. Instead, I remained rooted in my spot because this was something she needed to do on her own.

"Knox…" she whispered, letting Sam's arm drop as she slowly stumbled towards the small grave. "Y-you found his body?"

Sam shook her head. "No, but we couldn't just let him be forgotten with all that he sacrificed. For you… for us. So we made him this."

Haven dropped to her knees in front of the stone, her shaky hand reaching out to trace over his name. "Gone, but never forgotten," she read, her voice quivering.

My heart clenched at the sudden sob that broke through her lips, her head dropping while her palm remained flat against the stone. My mind said to go to her, but before I could even move, the women behind her circled in, all grouping together in one big hug.

I don't cry. Ever. Yet just the sight of the women that Haven thought once hated her all joining together to comfort her through such a hard time brought tears to my eyes. They all held onto one another as she sobbed, Nikita and Jay letting their own silent tears fall and I had to take a step back.

I turned, wiping my eyes before heading back to the house.

This was something she needed to get out and she didn't need the guy that came after Knox to stand by watching.

***

I was lying in bed when my door opened. I peered up from my book when Haven filled the doorway, a small smile gracing her lips. "Hey," she said, her voice raspy from, no doubt, the crying that had commenced earlier.

I set my book down on the nightstand next to me and opened my arms to her without a second thought. She sped over to the bed, practically crawling over me and wrapped her arms around me.

"I'm sorry you had to see me like that," she croaked, and my heart clenched again.

"Don't be, Red. You needed that. That was very kind of them."

She nodded, sniffling as her hold on me tightened. "It's so weird to think that he's truly gone. A small part of me used to think that if I kept looking for his body and never found one that there was a possibility that he was out there somewhere. But seeing that grave was like someone gutted me because I know he'll never walk back through those doors."

I ran my hand through her hair, gently nodding my head. "I understand. After my wife died, I didn't want to believe it. Some days I was so out of it that when I woke, I would reach for her as if she was there. It broke me day after day until I finally accepted she was never coming back—would never be in that bed again."

"What was her name?"

I swallowed hard, not having spoken it in years. "Her name was Ella."

"She had a beautiful name."

I smiled up towards the ceiling because for the first time, speaking her name didn't feel as if I had a boulder sitting on my chest. "It was. Just like her."

Haven was silent for a moment before she lifted her head. "We need to get out tonight. We can't mope around here all day or I am going to lose my mind. I am in desperate need of something to take my mind off all this."

I sat up. "What do you have in mind?"

She gave me a sheepish look. "I was talking with Jay and Nikita and may have told them about your club."

I groaned, falling back into the bed. "Please no."

"Please, Everette. We want to see it!"

I pondered on the idea. It probably was for the best if I did go in tonight. I hadn't been there in a while and Reese could only do so much for it while I was away. When I caught the excited look on her face, I knew I was a goner.

"Fine. But no one gets to act like fools tonight. We still have threats all around us."

She let out an excited squeal, flying out of bed. "Then you need to get a grip on Saul because when he heard us talking about it, he mentioned karaoke."

I didn't have time to take back my statement because she was already slamming my bathroom door shut behind her. I cursed, rubbing my eyes. Saul was going to make this one hell of a night if he had anything to do with it.

Grumbling to myself, I got up and walked to the bathroom door, cracking it slightly and hearing the shower running. "If I head to the club to get things ready, can you all manage to get there without burning the whole block down on the way?"

"No promises!" she sang.

I cursed again, shutting the bathroom door a little harder than intended.

God, if you hear me… please let Saul act right.

CHAPTER THIRTY-FOUR

Haven

I touched up my lipstick in the mirror, loving the matte feel it gave to my lips. I hardly ever wore makeup, but when I did, I couldn't lie when I said I felt like a million bucks. And don't even get me started on the dress that Nikita had let me borrow. It was a black bodycon dress, something that showcased the curves I rarely showed, and hugged me in all the right places.

So perhaps my goal of the night was to drive Everette mad, but could anyone blame me? That man was driving me crazy with every touch, longing look, and smile that he cast my way. Tonight, I wanted to forget. I wanted to live in the moment before the whole shit show, called my life, took a nasty turn. And I wanted to enjoy that with him and my friends.

My hair was straightened, the normal waves were no longer in sight, and my eyes were smoked out. It was strange to see myself so glammed up. I hadn't even gotten this dressed up for the club night that Everette forced me into.

I think he would like it, though.

"Okay, hot momma!" Jay's voice drifted into my bathroom.

I laughed, looking over my shoulder at her and Nikita who had waltzed through the doorway. They looked just as amazing. Jay's hair was pulled up into a high ponytail, the ends curled slightly, and she wore an emerald green dress that hugged her curves amazingly. Nikita left her hair down but had makeup on for the first time in years, I believed. She wore a red halter dress that complimented her nicely, and I almost wanted to ask her if that was for a certain man downstairs, but I refrained because… *no*.

This was for us.

Well, partially.

"You two look beautiful," I said, capping my lipstick.

Jay popped her hip out, dramatically flipping her ponytail over her shoulder. "Oh, I know."

Nikita snickered, giving Jay a playful shove. "Come on already. Let's go. I am so about to slay that dancefloor. I haven't felt this excited about something in years!"

The three of us laughed, slinging our arms around one another as we headed downstairs. It was like the night we always used to dream of was finally happening, and despite the threatening circumstances surrounding us, we were *free*.

Free from the manor.

Free from Commander Addison.

Just… free entirely.

"How are the new women holding up?" I asked as we walked into the foyer to wait on Saul.

"They're doing okay," Jay mumbled. "They just need a lot of rest. Reese agreed to keep an eye on them while we're gone so I don't worry myself sick about it."

I nodded, reaching over to tuck a strand of hair behind Nikita's ear that had fallen in front of her face. I took one last final look at us, not being able to stop the smile that crawled onto my face. "I love you guys so fucking much, you know that right?"

Nikita pouted her bottom lip out, looking as if she was about to burst into tears right there. "Don't say shit like that. Do you know how many times it took me to get this winged eyeliner looking right?"

I giggled, letting Jay pull us into one big hug. Jay towered over us, so she was able to rest her chin on the top of my head as Nikita rested her head against my shoulder. "I know we've been through some tough things these past few weeks, and we may have drifted apart for some time, but I will never stop loving either of you. I will never stop *fighting* for you. Understand?"

I squeezed Jay in response, her words warming me like no other. "I don't deserve you guys."

Nikita smacked me on the side of the head, causing me to yelp. "Don't say that."

I playfully rolled my eyes and we only pulled apart when we heard a booming voice.

"Okay, ladies! I see you!" Saul drew out, letting out a long whistle not shortly after.

I grinned, taking in his appearance. Long gone was his MIR uniform and in its place was a white button-down and black jeans. His hair was styled perfectly, not one curl out of place. When he reached us, I could smell the expensive cologne lacing his body.

He looked really damn good.

Smelled even better.

"Are you all ready to party fucking hardy?"

I snorted at his comment, shaking my head. "You are something else. You know that Everette is going to be watching you like a hawk, right?"

He waved me off. "Everette is easy to convince to get hammered so just ignore him. Tonight is about letting loose and having fun, which is what we will all be partaking in. First, drinks. Second is the dance floor. Third? You guessed it, karaoke night." He did little finger guns, causing us three women to lose it in laughter.

Nikita reined herself in, her smile widening as she said, "Honestly? After hearing about your last karaoke night? I'm glad to be participating in this one."

Saul grinned devilishly. "Don't say I didn't warn you."

I almost gagged just remembering the way I felt the next morning. That was something I wasn't looking forward to if our night ended up just like the last one did.

Jay motioned to the door. "Well, then let's get this show on the road!"

Saul held up his hand. "Hold on there, cowgirl, we have one more person we're waiting on."

I made a confused face, wondering who else would be joining us, but when A.R rounded the corner, my brows nearly shot to the ceiling.

"Oh hell no," Jay groaned. "I've dealt with you for too long. Go back to your room. Away, peasant! Away, I say!"

A.R smirked as he sauntered up to us. He was in his suit, which wasn't shocking, but I was curious to see what a relaxed A.R would look like. "I'm game. Let's see if this hitman can keep up."

He shot me a teasing smile. "Oh, I think I can." I didn't miss how his eyes left mine and trailed down Jay's form.

Oh.

"Let's go before Everette shits his pants. He's blown up my phone twenty times already asking what's taking so long and if we're okay," Saul grumbled, shooing us out of the door.

I giggled at Everette's tendencies but couldn't mash down that giddy feeling of his protectiveness. I'm sure if Saul hadn't replied, he would have marched down here himself.

"Who called an uber?" Jay asked, walking down the sidewalk.

Saul replies, "No one. We're walking."

Jay looked as if he killed her cat. "In these heels? Hell no. I'm calling an Uber. We'll meet you all there."

A.R winced. "I don't like you three going to the club alone."

"Then get in the car when it shows up, duh."

A.R grumbled something under his breath. "It's quicker to walk."

She motioned to the road in front of us. "Be my guest then."

Their bickering would mostly last all night. I only knew because that was the same way Everette and I used to be and I couldn't help but wonder where this little… *friendship* would take them.

"Uber is five minutes out, now get to stepping." She motioned.

Saul rolled his eyes. "You text me every minute. I need to get there so Everette can at least think we're on the way. He's going to kill us."

I smiled, giving them a little sarcastic wave as they started to walk down the street. Jay shifted on her feet, putting weight on one foot and then the other. "I shouldn't have worn these heels."

I huffed out a laugh at her. "Then go change while you can."

"Hell no. Do you see how good these make my legs look?"

Nikita shook her head looking amused. "I can't with you."

Not too long after Saul and A.R's departure, the Uber pulled up. Jay walked around the back of the car to check the license plate and then gave us the okay to get in. We piled into the back, and a girl looked over her shoulder with a grin.

"You girls look hot!" said the driver.

Jay glowed at the compliment. But before she could say her normal catchphrase, Nikita and I both said, "She knows."

The Uber driver laughed and started driving. "So Nocturnal, huh?"

I raised a brow. "The what now?"

"The club you're going to? It's what you put in as the address."

I looked at Nikita and Jay confused. "Nocturnal?"

Jay shook her head. "Really, Haven? You're bumping bellies with the man and you don't even know the name of his own club?"

"You're dating Everette Knight?!" the driver screeched.

My mouth opened and closed like a fish out of water. "Well… kind of? No. Well…"

"They're screwing," Nikita leaned forward, informing the driver.

I gasped. "We are not!"

"Well, Hailey said y'all were pretty loud that one night in Mexico."

My face was on fire.

"You seriously haven't screwed that man's brains out?" Jay asked. "I thought you were only saying that to get me out of your room earlier."

I fanned my face, looking away to not indulge in the conversation any further. After a minute, I said, "How do you know Everette Knight?"

"Girls, the club you're going to is one of the biggest in New York. Everette is the well-known club owner and quite the man to look at."

Don't I know.

"So Everette made this club seem like it was nothing fancy and yet he's literally known for it? Nice," I grumbled.

Jay snickered. "I'm so shocked that you didn't search everything about him. I did. I've known for weeks he had a club."

I stared agape. "Am I the only one that didn't know?!"

"Yes," the girls said in unison.

"Great. Just great." I threw my hands up, letting out a huff.

When the car slowed down, it stopped in front of a huge building, lights flooding out of it. There was a line of people standing and waiting to get in and my jaw dropped at how packed the line was. People were literally elbowing one another it was so cramped.

"How the hell do we get in?"

Jay groaned, covering her face. "I literally wonder how you're so smart yet so stupid at the same time. He's our *friend*, Haven. We walk up to the front and go in."

I stuck my tongue out at her as we opened the door and the driver told us to have fun. It was a little nerve-wracking to walk up straight to the bouncers, but when I realized that two of them were in The Men in Red, I wanted to smirk.

People yelled at us as we did so, telling us to get to the back of the line, but they instantly shut up once the men raised the velvet rope and let us through without any questions asked.

"Okay, I just felt so cool," Nikita squealed.

I didn't get a chance to reply because when we walked in and my eyes locked on my surroundings, my jaw dropped. It was a darker club with red color schemes, obviously Everette's small way of secretly tying in The Men in Red, and girls danced above us on platforms as music boomed around us.

I had never been to a club before—well, taking the one in Mexico out of the equation. And I definitely would never have dreamed of getting into a club like this.

Everyone was throwing back shots or drinks, their bodies grinding into one another as they lost themselves within the beat of the music. Jay looked as if her wicked side was about to explode from her body as she took in everything. Nikita, on the other hand, looked like she had no idea what to do.

Same, sister.

I craned my neck up, seeing a glass window pane stretching across what looked like an upstairs. The downstairs was already big enough, so I was curious as to what the upstairs contained. I pointed to it and yelled over the music, "What do you think that is?"

Jay looked in the direction. "I would think it is the VIP lounge! That's probably where the boys are. Let's go."

I was baffled as she grabbed our hands and started leading us towards the steps across the room that led there. I understood that Everette owned this place, but what I couldn't grasp my head around is that it was apparently okay to just waltz up in here as if we owned it. Jay didn't care, clearly.

Two men I didn't realize stopped us, holding their arms out. "Whoa there, are you on the list?"

Jay replied to him, telling him that even if we were on there, she didn't care and to let us through, but my eyes were fixed on the glass pane on the far side of the room where someone stood, looking out.

Everette.

He had a glass in one hand and his other hand stuck in his pocket as he surveyed the crowd. My heart sped up at his appearance. He was wearing all black again, his hair in a sexy mess on the top of his head. When his head turned slightly, looking down to see us girls standing there while Jay argued with the two men in front of us, a sly smirk covered his face.

Let us up, I mouthed pointing to the men.

He broke out into a full-on shit-eating grin and shook his head. I scoffed, nudging Jay to stop her bickering. The girls looked up to see him standing behind the glass. Suddenly, A.R and Saul appeared beside him and gave us a little wave of their fingers as if saying 'toodles'.

"You just had to have an Uber!" I growled.

Jay clicked her tongue. "I sure as hell did because what this ass is about to do on the dance floor will have them letting us upstairs in no time," she huffed, grabbing our hands again. "If they won't let us up, then we'll make them come down."

Oh, I liked the idea of that.

I liked it a lot.

The slowed-down version of "Maneater" started playing at the perfect time as she strutted to the middle of the dancefloor and I could feel their eyes digging into us. Jay spun around once we reached the middle and grinned. "Let's show them what they're missing out on, ladies."

"Hell yeah," Nikita snickered.

Feeling bold, I grabbed Nikita's hand and spun her around to let her dance back on me. She threw her head back in laughter, grinding herself against me. I laid my hands on her hips as Jay pulled a random guy to her, grinning over at us like she just won the fucking lottery.

I spun Nikita around as another song started and we began dancing as if this was our last night on earth. The men still watched us from above, but they had yet to take their eyes off us for a mere second. We jumped to the beat, totally forgetting the seductive stunt we were supposed to pull off. Jay, on the other hand, was still flirting it up with Mr. Tall dark and handsome.

When two guys approached Nikita and me, she looked like a deer caught in headlights. I giggled, urging her forward a bit. And when a blonde-haired guy stepped up to me, that was all it took for Everette to vanish from his post above us.

"What's your name?" the man asked, leaning down next to my ear to hear better.

"Kate," I lied, tilting my head to the side with a sly smile so I could get a better look at him.

"I'm Brandon!" he shouted over the music as he pulled back.

"It's nice to meet you!"

His smile faded as he locked eyes with whoever walked up behind me. I had to stop a cocky smirk from crawling on my face as an arm wrapped around my waist. Everette stared the man down with one single look that had him scrambling away.

"Well played, Red," Everette spoke next to my ear. "I'll get you back for that one later. Now show me what you got."

I yelped as he pulled me to his front, my back pressed tightly against him with his hands gripping my waist. Regaining my composure, I moved my hips letting them rub up against his front, causing his grip on me to tighten as he pushed himself closer to me, if that was even possible, and I could feel how aroused he already was.

Bingo.

A.R wasn't hiding his feelings for Jay as he jerked her away from the guy she had been dancing on and pulled her flush against him. I could tell she was cursing him left and right, but he was just smiling down at her amused.

I had to know what happened between them while they were gone.

Saul was near us, his eyes locked on Nikita looking like a sad puppy as she danced with some other guy. I don't know why, but the look on his face made me frown. So maybe I wasn't reading too much into him and Nikita. Something was happening there.

Yep, that's bonding over trauma for you. God, did we all couple together while being gone? Was that all it took? Two weeks being away from our normal lives to open our eyes up to those around us?

I stepped forward, a plan hatching within my mind, but Everette pulled me back against him. "Where do you think you're going, Red? I'm not done with you."

I turned around, locking my eyes on his face. A content sigh left me when I saw the nose ring back in its rightful place. I think that was becoming my favorite look on him.

"Saul looks like a hurt puppy dog. I have to work my wing woman magic."

Everette snickered. "Didn't you do that already by pushing her towards that guy she's dancing with?"

"It was the wrong move, now that I am officially assessing the situation at hand."

He sighed. "You get her. I'll get Saul."

I grinned up at him, quickly rising to my toes to place a soft kiss against his lips. "This is why you're my favorite."

He narrowed his eyes. "That's a lie, but I'll take it."

Giggling, I took off after Nikita. She didn't get the chance to stop me as I grabbed her arm and dragged her away from the man she was clearly hitting it off with. *She'll thank me later.*

"What are you doing?" she asked as I pulled her to the bar.

The bartender raised his chin, signaling me to tell him what I wanted. "Two vodka Redbulls please!"

He nodded, going off to make our drinks as I leaned against the side of the bar. I gave Nikita an innocent smile as she glared me down. "Haven, explain!"

I leaned closer to her so I could hear her better. "Tell me you don't feel something for Saul and I'll let you run back to that man."

She paused, looking at me if this was a trick question. "Why are you saying this?"

"Because he looked like someone killed his puppy at the sight of you with another man. I know I'm not going insane. You two got closer over your trip, yes?"

She sighed, nodding. "Yeah. I swear I didn't mean for it to happen, but I just feel like he understands me so well."

I shook my head. "Why would I judge? I literally was laying on the shower floor rolling around with Everette just days ago."

Her jaw dropped. "You're lying!"

I shook my head, thanking the bartender as he slid us our drinks. "Tab open?"

I looked back at Everette and pointed to him. "Put it on his tab."

He frowned. "Um, what?"

"Put it on his tab!"

"Yeah! She's screwing him." Nikita nodded her head excitedly.

I elbowed her in the gut, causing her to glare at me, rubbing her side gently. "They're kind of screwing!" she yelled back, correcting herself.

I swear I was going to murder either her or Jay tonight. It was going to happen.

I saw Everette wave him off and the bartender nodded and walked away. Sipping my drink happily, I led Nikita back over to where Everette and Saul stood. Everette looked at me as if saying 'what now' and my mind went blank.

Nikita recovered for me, pointing to the upstairs. "I want to see the VIP lounge!"

Saul held his hand out. "Come on, Kit Kat."

She took it excitedly and let him lead her towards it. Okay, so I'm a terrible wing woman, but at least I got them together somewhat.

Everette leaned in closer to me with a heated look in his eyes. “Care to check out my office?”

The corner of my lips tugged up. “That sounds lovely.”

CHAPTER THIRTY-FIVE

Haven

I didn't have the chance to scope out Everette's office because the minute we entered, he quite literally jumped my bones. The door shook the room as he slammed it shut and jerked me to him before he smashed his lips on mine.

I moaned into his mouth, melting into his arms from the mere touch of him. Everette scooped me up by the back of my thighs and carried me over to his desk and around it, planting my ass firmly on it. He moved back, breaking the kiss with harsh breaths as he calmly took a seat in his chair, taking me in.

I gulped, finally taking the time to look him over in this new aspect of his life that I had yet to see. He *looked* like some big, fancy owner of a well-known club. His elbow rested on the arm of the chair as his pointer finger pressed against his lips. And here, right now, was a side of him that I wanted to see more of.

"What are you doing?" I whispered, my palms flattening against the desk as I leaned back.

"Admiring," he murmured. "Admiring you before I have you screaming my name for everyone downstairs to hear."

My thighs instinctively pressed together when a throbbing desire swirled deep within my core. His eyes followed the movement, causing his free hand to grip the other arm of the chair tightly, the sound of the leather making a slight crinkling noise.

He started to lean forward, but my leg shot up and I dug my stiletto into the center of my chest. "Not so fast, champ. You were so quick to make me wait downstairs."

His jaw ticked.

I slowly slid forward, easily giving him a view of what he desired so badly and hopped off the desk. My hand pushed his chest back so he would relax fully against the chair. As teasingly as I could, I slung one leg over him at a time, slowly settling myself until I was straddling him. I lazily rested my arms on his shoulders and grinned.

I let him place his hands on my hips, feeling his arousal brushing up against my core as he shifted slightly, clearly hating the torture session I was giving him.

I cocked a brow. "What? Not used to not being in control?"

His eyes darkened. "Baby, I can show you real control if you'd like. You're just radiating *brat* energy."

Fuck.

He had us up in a flash, planting me back on the desk. He grabbed my thighs and ripped them open to push himself between them. "If you want control, love, take it. Don't sit back and tease."

I gasped as he pulled me flush against the bulge in his pants, his finger trailing up the valley of my breasts until he gently wrapped his hand around my throat and brought me close to his lips. "Kiss me."

I refused to back down, staring him down with a heated glare.

At the roll of his hips into my own, I moaned, my head falling back and my body betraying me with one simple movement from him.

"Kiss me, Haven," he ordered.

I stared at him with a sultry smile on my face. "No." Then wrapping my arms around his neck, I brought his lips to mine to nip at his bottom lip.

Two could play that game.

But it only caused him to let out a husky chuckle and it was clear he was enjoying this way too much. Instead of bringing his lips to mine like I yearned for, he pressed them to the base of my neck, forcefully turning my head to give him better access. When his tongue swept over a spot that he nipped at, mocking my teasing move from earlier, my mouth fell open.

I was going to break.

Screw brat energy at this point. I was nearly panting like a fucking dog in heat underneath him.

His hands trailed up my thighs, one thumb circling my inner thigh too close to my core. I writhed, his nose trailing up the side of my neck until he stopped next to my ear. "Just give in, babe, and I'll give you what your body is screaming for."

My legs betrayed me and relaxed on pure demand—wanting him just as desperately as I wanted him.

Everette took this as his opening, his hand sliding underneath my dress to rub against the lace fabric covering me. I let out a choked sound, grabbing onto his shoulders.

Be strong, Haven, be fucking strong.

Feeling the need to level the playing field, my hand sought him out, palming him through his jeans. He groaned, his forehead dropping against my shoulder but didn't give up on his tortuous circling rhythm underneath my dress.

I groaned when he moved the fabric aside, touching my bare core. He wasted no time when he found me ready for him before sliding a finger in. I writhed once more.

Fuck this.

Grabbing the back of his neck, I pulled his head back and placed his lips on mine. He let out a sigh of content, working his mouth against me in ways that I craved.

I undid the button of his jeans, ready to slip my hand underneath his waistband, but his hands stopped mine. "Not yet."

I stared up at him confused until I realized that he was already shaking with a hunger that wouldn't last long. I let out a husky chuckle before saying, "Someone can't keep it together."

"With you, Haven McKinley, I nearly come undone with one touch from you."

Only a grown-ass man would live up to that.

But before he could kiss me again, there was a pounding on the door. "Stop fucking one another and get out here! It's karaoke time, bitches!"

Everette cursed at Saul's voice, leaning towards me once more. "Ignore him."

I planned on doing just that, but Saul pounded on the door once more. "I have a key and I am not afraid to use it!"

"Cockblock!" Everette yelled.

Saul's laughter echoed from behind the door. "Come on out, love birds. I won't ask again."

I sighed. "I actually hate him."

Everette muttered something under his breath in response before saying, "We'll be continuing this later, Red."

I shot him a wink as I slipped off his desk and fixed my dress. "I'm counting on it."

He waved me off. "I'll be down in a minute."

With that, I giggled as I left his office so he could rectify the problem at hand.

The minute I reached downstairs, I stared ahead at the stage only to find Saul and Nikita standing there as they talked to someone. I shook my head, walking to the front of it. Perks of having the owner be your best friend, I guess.

When they saw me, their eyes lit up. "Come on up, little one!"

I shook my head, trying to ignore the eyes that were staring us down. I shook my hand across my throat, telling them to cut it out as they kept calling my name. Eventually, Saul had the crowd chanting my name before Nikita pulled me up.

I'm not drunk enough for this.

"It's almost Halloween!" Saul yelled into a microphone and the crowd whooped in excitement. I almost wondered how much he did this but thought against it. There was no telling with this man.

"In honor of my favorite holiday happening in two nights' time, I figured a throwback is in order."

Nikita grimaced at Saul and handed me a shot I didn't know she had gotten. "You're going to need this," she whispered.

I didn't think twice before I threw it back. Looking at the other one in her hand, I grabbed it and tossed it back, too. She stared at me with humor dancing in her eyes. Secretly, I knew she was thriving at this moment.

When a song broke out, I covered my face in embarrassment. There were so many meanings in the song that I knew Saul fully intended on using to his advantage and I couldn't help but grin at him as he shot me a wink. Before I realized it, Jay was running up on the stage, her hair a mess.

I chuckled at the blonde as she gave me a sheepish smile, knowing damn well that I knew she had just been off with, most likely, A.R doing God knows what.

"Ghostbusters" flooded the club and despite the childish throwback, the crowd sang along like it was any other hyped-up song.

Nikita and Saul were yelling their hearts out as Jay and I laughed at the two of them, clearly loving it too much for our own good. We cheered them on, pumping our fists as they really got into it.

Saul went still, cutting his eyes at me as he said, "I ain't afraid of no ghost."

I snickered, chanting the lyrics with the crowd.

If Ghost himself saw us right now, obviously mocking him, he would lose it.

I looked over, seeing Everette and A.R standing at the edge of the stage with folded arms. Gone was Everette's serious heated expression from just moments ago and in its place was a goofy smile.

He was *laughing*.

Full-on laughing.

And God, was it a beautiful sight.

When the song ended, it prompted us to take more shots before I ran over to the DJ, giving him another song. When the familiar tune picked up, my friends burst out laughing. It was either the alcohol making it funnier than it was, or we were just purely that entertaining because the crowd of people went right along with it.

"International Harvester" began to play and I grabbed a mic with Saul. How he knew the song, I had no idea. I stumbled upon it one day many years ago and for some reason, it was too damn catchy.

Jay nearly fell over as Saul began stomping his foot before belting, "I'm the son of a third generation farmer…"

I brought the mic to my lips, cackling as I sang, "Been married ten years to the farmer's daughter!" I bobbed my head as Saul held his mic out to me. "I'm a God fearin' hard workin' combine driver."

He moved it back to his lips. "Hoggin' up the road on my p-p-p-p-plower…"

"Chug a lug a luggin' five miles an hour," I laughed out.

At the same time, we nearly screamed with the crowd. "On my International Harvester!"

I looked over, seeing Everette staring at us in pure horror. Jay was in a fit of tears next to him, barely able to catch her breath from laughing so hard as Everette nudged her, telling her to change the song, but she shoved him away and pumped her fist in the air.

I don't think I've ever smiled this much in one day.

CHAPTER THIRTY-SIX

Haven

I let out an obnoxious burp, slumping in the booth of the small diner we had all come to. A.R was busy outside with Jay as she threw up her guts and Nikita and Saul were still on their karaoke high. Everette, on the other hand, could not keep his hands off me in the slightest and I had a feeling I knew where our night would lead us.

He sat next to me in the booth, ordering God knows what for all of us. We were in desperate need of some greasy food or tomorrow we would all feel like shit. Everette had pulled us off the stage at the club after our fourth song of the night, grumbling something about the club's reputation, and made us put karaoke night to a halt.

But not a halt to the drinks. We kept throwing them back, even getting Everette to join in, and when Jay had threatened to dance on the bar, Everette decided it was time for us to head back home. Well, until we convinced him to stop for food.

"Did you get the cheese fries?" I asked him, drunkenly leaning forward to look at the things he was pointing out to the waitress.

Everette let out a deep sigh. "Yes. And your burger. And your cheese sticks. And your coke." I sighed happily, leaning into him. He finally relaxed and huffed out a laugh at me, tossing his arm around my shoulder. "You're not going to eat all of it, though."

I scoffed. "Yes, I will."

"It's so weird seeing you two like this," Saul said, finally looking up from his phone.

Nikita's eyes drooped as she rested her head on his shoulder. "I think it's cute," she yawned, finally losing some of her buzz from earlier.

A.R suddenly appeared beside our booth. "I'm going to take Jay home. She isn't feeling too well."

Everette nodded. "Okay. You two be safe. We'll be home shortly."

Just as A.R gave him a small salute, our waitress came up with our drinks and followed up shortly after with our food. My stomach grumbled with hunger and my mouth watered at the sight of all of the unhealthy items. "Please don't scarf all of this down and then puke on my shoes later," Everette mused, sliding the plates over to me.

I grabbed the burger, just as Nikita got her own, and we both moaned at the greasy bite of meat we took. "This is the best burger I have ever had," I spoke dramatically, my eyes nearly rolling into the back of my head like I was on a food high.

Everette shook his head at us, popping a fry into his mouth. Saul had been somewhat quiet after we got here and I couldn't figure out why. My alcohol-laced mind told me to shoot forward and ask, but as if Everette knew me like the back of his hand, he pushed me back into my seat, gently shaking his head no.

I shrugged, digging back into my food. I only managed to get down a few fries and half my burger, giving Everette a sheepish look. He rolled his eyes and took my cheese sticks so I wouldn't let them go to waste.

“So what’s the plan after we leave here?” Nikita asked, ketchup on the side of her mouth from her burger. Saul snickered, taking a napkin to wipe her mouth. I smiled at the sight of them, desperately hoping something truly comes out of that pair.

They are both too good of people.

“Sleep,” Everette mused. “You all need lots of sleep and some water.”

I looked up at him curiously. “How are you not plastered?”

“I can handle my alcohol.”

I made a sound, not believing him. “You didn’t the last time.”

“That would be because Saul made us play those stupid drinking games. At least being at my own club, I can control what’s being shoved my way and how you all act.”

Saul took a sip of his water, waving Everette off. “Don’t act like it wasn’t fun.”

“Maybe if we were back in college. Sure.”

I covered my mouth from Everette’s view as I whispered, “He’s old.”

Nikita mirrored me saying, “And grumpy tonight. Maybe you should get him laid.”

I gasped, chucking a cheese-covered fry at her. She screeched, pulling the fry from her hair after shooting me a deadly glare. Everette knocked his knuckles against the table. “Yep, we’re done here. Saul, can you get Nikita home safe?”

I perked up at this. “Why aren’t we going home together?”

Everette tossed some money onto the table, giving me a small smile. “I want you to myself tonight.”

“I won’t argue with that!” Nikita chirped, shooing Saul out of the table and snatching her basket of fries up. “Go!”

I looked over at Everette with a raised brow. “Where are we going?”

He stood up, holding his hand out. “My house.”

Oh.

I grinned as I took his hand and let him lead me out of the diner. Excitement bubbled up inside me as he flagged down the nearest taxi.

Everette was letting me stay the night with him at his real house. Was I dreaming?

That's a big move, wasn't it?

As we got situated in the back of the taxi, Everette turned to face me. "Are you sobered up?"

I shook my hand back and forth. "Definitely still buzzed, but the food helped a lot."

His eyes darkened a little as he faced forward again. "Good."

I couldn't help but press my legs together, knowing that look on his face. This was really about to happen. There would be no one to interrupt us. No one to stop something that we've been wanting to happen for weeks now. I let out a shaky breath, directing my attention out the window as the streets of New York passed by us.

I was practically itching to reach out and touch him, just wanting his hands on me again. But the further we got from the outside of the heart of the city, my nerves grew. This wasn't where his house was.

I eyed him, something feeling off. "Everette? This isn't where your house was. At least, the one you took me to the last time."

The corner of his lips tugged up. "I know."

Suddenly, my body tensed. I've been here before. I've been in this exact situation where I think I knew someone and then it all went to shit.

"Everette?" my voice raised. "Where are we going?"

He looked at me with a confused expression as if he didn't understand my sudden alarm. It took him a minute before his features morphed and he was quick to grab my hands with a worried look. "Haven, baby, I promise it's nothing bad. Shit, I wasn't even thinking. You can trust me, okay? Always. You'll see soon."

I let out a breath of relief. "You can't pull shit like that with me," I muttered, my heart still beating furiously within my chest.

He squeezed my hand. "I'm sorry. I wasn't even thinking. I know your trust in people has been broken a lot but do know that I would never put you in harm's way. I told you I was taking you to my house and that's where we're going."

My eyes narrowed. "You have two houses?"

"Kind of. Well, not in a few weeks I won't."

"What do you mean?"

He opened his mouth to reply but stopped as the taxi slowed down. I craned my neck to see a beautiful house, protected by a long, gated driveway, next to us. Everette thanked the driver and got out. I was still in shock at the huge house in front of me and I didn't notice Everette pulling my door open to help me out.

When the driver sped off, I stared awestruck. "You got a new house?"

"I was notified the day we got back that the paperwork went through. My old house was… full of memories. And although they will always be a part of me, I was ready to start a new part of my life. A new part to make new memories with."

A smile broke out on my face as I stared up at him. "It's beautiful."

"Wait until you see the inside. The day we got back, some of the MIRs moved some of my things over for me. It's everything I used to dream of in a house."

He punched in a code to the gate and it swung open, letting us through. We walked down the driveway hand in hand, and I could feel my heart picking up its pace. I've never been in any sort of relationship like this. This felt too real. Too intimate.

I kind of loved it.

When Everette put the key in the door and pushed it open, I waited for him to flick a light on. When he did, my jaw dropped again. It was a dark wooded color scheme and definitely had masculine vibes to it. I giggled and stepped further into the house and walked out of the foyer to what looked like the living room.

It wasn't fully done yet, but I let myself admire the homey feel of it. Everette wrapped his arms around my waist from behind and rested his chin on my shoulder. "What do you think? Do you like it?"

I smiled. "I love it. But do *you* like it? It's your home after all."

He let out a soft chuckle. "Well, I did buy it. But I wanted your opinion because… because I'd hoped to see you here more. With me."

My smile faltered some and I had to make myself turn fully to face him. "What are you saying, Everette?"

He removed his arms from my waist and pushed the hair from my face and then gently cupped my cheeks. "I'm saying that I want you here with me. Don't worry, I'm not asking you to move in, but I would love for you to stay here some. It would give us a break from the school and prying eyes. I'm serious when I say that you've consumed me, Haven. I would love nothing more than for you to stay here whenever you liked."

My heart skipped a beat. "You're serious?"

He gave me a goofy grin. "I am."

I let out a shaky breath. "I'd like that. But… what does this mean for us? I mean, there is an *us*, right?"

He belted out a laugh. "I'd sure hope so."

"So… eventually we'll have to tell people we're seeing each other?" I asked.

He nodded. "Eventually, but we'll take it at your pace. But before you start declaring me as your knight in shining armor, I'd like to take you out on a proper date first at least."

It was my turn to laugh. "Deal."

He slowly leaned in, taking his precious time to place his lips on mine. It wasn't like our normal, starved kiss. It was full of passion and admiration as we clung to one another, finally entering a new phase in our lives. And although this was fresh and new, I felt as if I had known this man my whole life.

Is this what true love felt like?

Everette pulled back with a certain gleam in his eyes. "How about we break this place in?"

I bit my lip as he stepped back and took my hand in his. I nodded and he began to pull me towards a set of stairs. With each step we took, his hand behind him gripping mine as he led the way, I started to grow restless.

There was no turning back after this.

We went down a hall until he opened a door, showing me a huge bedroom. I gazed around, taking in the black and gray color scheme.

Totally Everette.

My eyes locked on the huge king-sized bed and I raised a brow. "That better be memory foam."

He snorted. "Only the best, but we'll have to break it in for sure," he teased, nodding his head as he shot me a wink. "Brand spanking new."

I liked the sound of that.

I closed the door behind us, pausing for just a minute to gather myself. But when I turned to face him, he had a conflicted look on his face.

"What is it?" I asked.

"You're sure about this? We can wait."

I knew it right then. I knew it will my full being that I completely and utterly loved Everette Knight.

I walked up to him, wrapping my arms around his neck. "Why wait when we don't know what tomorrow will bring?"

His forehead fell against mine as he let out a shaky breath. Apparently, I wasn't the only nervous one about this whole thing. "You have a point," he mumbled.

"Then why am I still fully clothed?"

That was all it took to make that switch flip inside him. His hands snaked down my body and gripped the ends of my dress. I raised my arms to let him pull it over my head and toss it aside and he groaned, taking a step closer to skim his hands up my hips to grip my waist. "Fucking beautiful."

I moved my hands behind my back to find the clasp of the black, lace bra I was wearing and unclipped it. I dragged it down my arms and let it fall to the floor as he drank in every bit of me. I brushed up against him, letting his hands wander while I unbuttoned the shirt he was wearing.

Slowly, I started to back him up towards the bed. I expected the dominant side of him to come out, refusing to let me take charge, but he remained calm in the moment and looked pleased to just let me do whatever the hell I wanted.

Once all the buttons were done, I pushed it over his shoulders, enjoying the sight of his muscles rippling underneath my touch. Gaining the confidence I needed, I pushed him back and let him fall onto the bed. Everette grinned, scooting back as I crawled onto the bed towards him and finally straddled him.

My hands trailed down his defined abs, my core heating as he shifted slightly to let me know how much he craved me as much as I needed him. A whimper broke past my lips at the friction he created, causing me to lean down and place a kiss on his stomach, feeling him tense beneath me.

His bruising grip was enough to tell me that he was ready to flip me over and have his way with me, but he refrained and let me continue my tortuous kisses up and down his chest. Finally, I rolled my hips to try and get that deep moan out of him that drove me insane.

I succeeded.

I wasted no time smashing my lips on his. One hand found its way into my hair as he moaned into my mouth, his other pulling on my hips and making me roll them again for all the friction I could get. He pulled my mouth from his and forced me to give him access to my neck as he nipped, sucked, and kissed all the right places to have me panting above him. His hands caressed my breasts, teasing the most sensitive part of them to make traitorous whimpers escape me.

"More," I breathed.

This man completed me. I have accepted that and it made me wonder how I hadn't realized before just how much he fit perfectly against me. It was like we were made for one another, our bodies moving in a perfect rhythm to give each other what we wanted. And we took and *took* from each other, only pushing us closer to that finish line.

Everette's mouth latched onto one of my breasts, causing me to throw my head back and slam my eyes shut at the delicious feelings he caused. My hands were clawing down his back, pulling at his hair, pulling his body closer—they were everywhere.

I couldn't get enough.

Everette flipped us, moving his mouth back to mine as his hands began to pull off the teasing lace I had worn just for him. When they were gone, he sat back and ran his tongue over his bottom lip as he took in the sight of me completely naked and panting in front of him.

"Fuck, Haven, I can see just how ready you are for me."

I reached forward to pull him closer to me, but he pushed my hands away and pulled my legs farther apart and descended upon me before I had the chance to process it.

"Fuck!" I cried out, my head falling against the pillows again as his tongue swept over my core, causing my toes to curl in pure pleasure.

"Scream for me, Haven. There's no one here to hear you. Let it out," he ordered, his grip tightening on me before he swept his tongue over me once more.

I was sure I saw stars at the way his tongue worked, his fingers joining them in a teasing, torturous way that had me squirming and writhing beneath his huge figure.

"Everette!" I gasped, trying to stop the upcoming reaction to his tongue that was nearing its peak. "I'm gonna…"

His husky chuckle was what made me come undone, shaking beneath him as he lapped every part of my release up. I was panting as he leaned back with a heated look, digging in his back pocket. He pulled out his wallet and retrieved a condom and tossed it beside us.

As he unbuttoned his jeans, I stared at him with heavy eyes, but not nearly done with this man. My body craved more.

Craved him.

He slid his jeans and boxers off in one go, giving me the perfect sight of his naked body. Everette reached over me and grabbed a pillow. "Raise your hips for me, baby."

I followed the order, letting him place the pillow beneath me, and didn't even have the time to praise him for knowing his ways to please a woman in bed before he crawled back over me, bringing the foil to his mouth before tearing it open.

I finally managed to raise my arms and wrap them around his neck as he rolled it on, aligning himself with me. "Last chance to back out," he teased.

"If you don't shut the hell up and have your wicked ways with me, I might literally murder you in your sleep."

He chuckled. "Don't say I didn't warn you."

Then he entered me in one, single thrust.

I gasped at him filling me, desire building within me again at his groan. "Fuck, you feel amazing, Haven."

I raised my hips, needing him to move. Needing him to let go and give me everything my body was demanding. He obeyed the silent plea and moved his hips slowly, pulling out of me before thrusting back in, and we moaned, our foreheads touching as he finally set a pace between us.

"More," I breathed, hating the pace he had set.

It was too gentle—I knew he was holding back.

Once again, he listened to my plea before he slammed into me harder, our bodies moving together perfectly as I met him thrust for thrust and he smashed his lips to mine. My nails dug into his back as I lost myself within him.

Everette nipped at my bottom lip, his hand moving between us to rub against that one spot that had me mewling. I gasped as he rubbed it, his tongue snaking in to meet my own and making me enter that blissful high for a second time tonight.

As he thrust deeper, hitting a spot no man had ever reached, I had to bury my face in his neck to stop the cry that was wanting to leave my lips. He slowed his pace and said, "Eyes on me."

My mouth fell open when he stopped his thrusting, and I moved my head. "Why are you stopping?"

"Eyes. On. Me. I want to see you."

I locked my eyes on him when he picked his pace back up, angling himself in a way that had me crying his name, my body tensing up.

"Open your eyes, Haven, or I'll stop again."

I cursed, opening my eyes to take in the beautiful blue hues of his eyes. His didn't leave mine as he quickened his rhythm, making the headboard crack against the wall as my body screamed when my climax hit me so hard that I couldn't even make a sound.

We came together, our groans filling the room as our bodies tensed and our foreheads touched, our eyes never leaving one another.

I loved this man.

I truly loved him.

"Fuck," he breathed out while I panted, feeling completely and blissfully spent.

He gave me one last soft kiss before pulling out of me and I felt as if I couldn't move—wouldn't be able to move for the next few days. Everette went to the bathroom for a minute before I heard the water running. He padded back out, a smile on his lips as he scooped me up in his arms.

"Let's get you cleaned up, Red."

I rested my head against his chest, curling into his body and never wanting to leave his arms.

"Everette?"

"Hm?"

"Thank you."

He chuckled. "Thank you?"

"For… for being able to be with me, despite all my flaws." Tears welled up in my eyes as I finally realized that for the first time in my life, I openly admitted such a thing. That I was finally letting myself *love*. "Just… thank you."

His eyes softened as he leaned down to lay a gentle kiss on my lips. "Always, Haven." He placed me in the tub, genuine happiness radiating from him. "Nothing will ever change the way that I see you, which is like a fucking Goddess. You complete me."

I smiled, loving the relief the warm water gave my body. I motioned him forward and let him climb in behind me. As I relaxed against his chest, I said, "Likewise."

My heart felt full and my body felt amazing.

I hoped this never changed.

CHAPTER THIRTY-SEVEN

Everette

Waking up with Haven curled against me completely naked was something I could definitely get used to. She was wrapped around me like she didn't want to ever let go, and my heart warmed just at the sight of her.

I knew I loved this woman.

It was so clear to me now. The way my heart skips a beat when a genuine smile crosses her face. The way my hands clench when I see her remotely frown, fearing something was upsetting her. The way my mind goes crazy when she isn't near me. The way it feels just to be graced with her presence.

I loved her.

And last night? Fuck, it was amazing. Coming undone with her was something I never wanted to stop doing. Just to catch the sight of her mouth parting, her breathing coming out in short, harsh pants as I gave her everything her body desired.

I shifted, cursing myself as I hardened just at the thought of it, but the sudden movement caused Haven to stir.

She yawned, raising her head as she blinked a few times, and I grinned at her dazed state as she looked around, taking everything in. Eventually, her eyes drifted to mine and my grin widened. "Morning, Red."

A goofy smile covered her face as she snuggled into my side. "Good morning."

I rubbed her bare back, feeling her breasts push up against me, and had to fight down my friend that was waiting to happily greet her this morning. "Sleep well?"

Her cheeks were cherry red as she replied, "Yes…"

I scoffed. "Oh, don't get shy on me now, Red." I rolled us over, hovering above her and she let out a soft laugh, wrapping her arms around my neck. "Last night you had a mouth on you that was just *so* demanding."

She moved her hands to cover her face. "Shut *up*."

I moved her hands away, placing a kiss on the tip of her nose. "I'm just teasing."

She suddenly raised her head, trying to give me a quick kiss, but I easily deepened it, pulling that mouth-watering moan from her lips.

When my hands snaked up her hips, she stopped them and pulled away. "As much as I would love to continue this, I am about to piss all over your new bed."

I snorted, moving off her. "Anddd the mood is over."

She giggled at me, grasping the comforter in her fists, and yanked it in one go as she hopped up and ran towards the bathroom. I shook my head at her, adjusting the thin sheet back over me as I relaxed back into bed, my forearm covering my eyes.

If only we could stay in this moment forever.

A few moments later, I grunted as Haven jumped on top of me, nearly knocking the wind out of me. My eyes flew open to stare at her in shock. "A warning would have been nice, you almost kneed the goods."

She rolled her eyes, slinging a leg over my waist as she straddled me. "It wouldn't have been a sneak attack if I would have warned you."

I rested my hands on her hips, the comforter still draped around her shoulders and rubbed my thumbs in gentle circles. "I like you like this."

She tilted her head. "Like what?"

"Carefree." I bit my bottom lip, trailing my eyes over her. "It's a beautiful sight to see."

She moved forward to give me a quick kiss. "I like it, too."

"Mhm," I mumbled, trying to pull her back into me, but she leaned back teasingly. "Aren't you supposed to make me pancakes when I bring you to your knees?"

This cocky, little brat.

I hummed. "If anything, I believe you were the one begging for more, so maybe *you* should make *me* some pancakes."

Haven scoffed. "Oh please, as if you weren't begging even more than me. *Eyes on me, Haven*," she mocked in a deep voice.

I flipped her in one go, attacking her sides as her laughter filled the room. "What was that?"

"Stop! Stop! I take it back!" she laughed out, squirming to get away from my hands.

I stopped my hands, smirking down at her. "Your brat energy is really showing today."

"Don't act as if you don't like it."

I leaned down next to her ear. "I like it a little too much and that should worry you." She let out a shaky breath, starting to pull me closer, but I stopped and sat up. "Anyway, I have some pancakes to make."

She made a frustrated sound. "You're serious?"

I winked. "Dead. Besides," my grin faltered some, "I need to talk to you about something."

At the look on my face, she grew more serious. "About what?"

I patted her thigh. "Let's get dressed and get some food in us and we'll talk."

***

Haven practically scarfed down her breakfast just so I would get on with whatever I had to tell her. She stared at me intensely, as if I was about to drop a bomb in her lap. Well, if you considered that I was somehow now a part of the MOTs, then I guess it could be considered that.

I sighed, setting my fork down. "Do you remember how my wound quickly healed? And shortly after you channeled Katerina?"

She nodded. "Yes? And?"

I swallowed hard. "Well, when we were fighting those people on the boat in Mexico, I had this excruciating pain in my stomach. It caused me to hunch forward as if someone had just thrust a sword through my stomach, but when I looked down… there was nothing there. A second later, a sword cut through the air above my head. Had I not lurched forward, I would have been dead."

Haven paled. "You mean…" Her eyes drifted down to the scar on my shirtless stomach. I stood, letting her see it. "You have the curse?"

I shrugged. "I'm not sure. But Katerina said she… made an exception for me. She literally welcomed me into the MOTs."

Haven stood, walking closer so she could trail her hand over the scar. "How?" she breathed out.

"I don't know. I've been wondering about it ever since it happened and I didn't know how to tell you with everything that had been going on."

Haven removed her hand, looking up at me with worried eyes. "That's how you were able to see my scar. She… inducted you into our curse. But what doesn't make sense is how. How could a soul have that much power?"

I gulped. "I think it was through the blood bond that was done so many years ago through those two people I told you about within our organizations. I think that way, she had some type of connection between us that she was able to play with. Apparently, she trusted me enough to bring me on board I guess. I don't know."

Haven sighed, running a hand through her hair. "We need to read those books." She turned, walking out of the kitchen.

"Where are you going?"

"To get my stuff! We need to get back to the school. I put off reading those books long enough."

I blew out a puff of air and followed after her.

It didn't take us long to get our things before we headed towards the school. The ride there was silent, our blissful bubble from earlier popped. I wanted to curse myself for bringing it up, but I refused to hide things from Haven. She already had enough trust issues to begin with, and I wasn't going to be a person that she ever lost trust in.

When we entered the school, it was silent, everyone probably still sleeping. Haven didn't waste any time before she ran up the steps towards her room where the books were. I heaved out a deep sigh, trying to keep up with her.

"Haven!" I called out as she ran into her room.

"I can't waste any time. God knows when Ghost is going to make his next attack happen and we have to get to the bottom of this."

I covered her hand with my own as she picked one of the books up. "And if these books contain nothing useful? As far as we know, this has never happened before. I'm the exception, remember?"

Her jaw ticked. "I have to try something."

"Why are you so hellbent on figuring this out right at this moment? Let's talk to the others and get their opinions and we all can scavenge through the books to make it quicker."

"Because I can't have this fucking curse ruining you like it has ruined me!" she yelled, making me take a step back from her abrupt reaction.

"Haven, I'm fine."

"But I'm not! God, just when I feel like I'm getting some piece of happiness within my life it just has to be fucking *ruined*. You don't deserve to have this burden on your shoulders. It's not fair!" She threw her arms up, her hands shaking in pure rage.

When her eyes darkened slightly, I kicked into gear and pulled her to me, fighting her until she slouched within my hold. "Deep breaths."

She inhaled and exhaled a few times before croaking out, "It's not fair…"

I rubbed her back, closing my eyes in defeat. "Life isn't fair, Red. We just have to make the best of it. The curse has helped you, yes? What's to say it won't help me?"

"But the life of informers and—"

"When's the last time you had one?" I asked, raising a brow. "This curse knows more than it lets on. It knows when we're in a crisis and it helps however it can, I've picked up on that much. It could have let informers find you during all this, but it hasn't. And until we stop Ghost, I doubt it will. You're the key to this, Red. You're the key to all of it. The last female Holden. The one person who is able to channel Katerina Holden herself. Don't you understand? It's only a curse when you make it out to be that way."

She sniffled, shaking her head. "But you haven't lived the life I have."

My grip on her tightened. "I haven't, but you can't stay in the past. The commander has no more control over you. That life is long gone, baby. I'm here. Jay and Nikita are here. Saul… the others. We're all here and we will take on this new path *together*. Do you hear me? When the time comes for this curse, or whatever you want to call it, to call upon me, I know I'll have you hear with me to teach me every step of the way. You cannot stress the unknown."

She let out a sob, clenching my shirt in her hands. I held her just as tight, closing my eyes again as she got out all her tears. I didn't let go for a second until she was the one pulling back, wiping her eyes.

"I'm just so scared. I can't lose you."

I wiped a stray tear from her cheek. "You won't."

She blew out a breath of air. "We never got to have that meeting with everyone like we planned on. We need to do that. They have to know everything."

I nodded in agreement. "Let's get everyone up then.

It wasn't long until we were knocking on doors, waking people from their peaceful slumber. Once I got Saul up, he was quick to help wake the other sleeping members of the school. Eventually, we all gathered in the study area.

And Haven told them everything. There were gasps, shocked stares, and unshed tears. No one liked hearing that the curse they harbored was something that had built rage within their souls for years and they had no idea how to properly harvest it. And they definitely didn't like hearing that Haven was slowly losing herself to it and would continue to until she found a way to channel it properly.

"So what now?" Sam asked, her eyes wide.

I sighed. "We don't know, but we're going to try our best to figure it out. Starting with everyone getting into groups and reading some books about the truths of this organization."

A.R and Saul walked into the room, dropping piles of books onto the table. "I have read a few of these and learned a lot about your organization, but what is in here is easier for you to read yourself than for me trying to explain it to you all. Grab a book and get to reading," A.R ordered.

The MOTs and even the MIRs obeyed the command as they shot up to grab one. Haven scooted closer to me, chewing on her bottom lip as she watched everyone. I so badly wanted to pull her to my side, but I had to respect her wishes and refrain from doing so until she was ready for everyone to know about us.

Nikita and Jay walked up to us. "We were talking last night before bed and a thought came to us."

"What's that?" I asked.

"If Ghost has one of Haven's swords, it still has a tracker in it, yes? If he's hiding somewhere in the states, we could possibly pinpoint him by looking up the tracker to see where it's at."

Haven frowned. "What's to say he didn't just toss it out?"

Jay shook her head. "The man is obsessed with you, Haven. I have hunted down many men like him in the past and they always keep their trinkets."

I nodded. "It's worth a shot."

Haven looked at me. “Then why wait for him to come for us if we can come for him first? If he’s here, he could have my parents with him. This could be our only advantage.”

“Exactly,” I mumbled, flagging over Saul and A.R to tell them the plan.

The minute Saul heard, he was off to look it up. I pointed to the books before I said, “Well, better get to reading while we wait.”

And so we read.

We each grabbed a book and sat down to start reading. The one I had picked up talked about the beginning of the curse and refreshed me on the ways that Katerina Holden first appeared to Bethany seeking her vengeance.

I knew a lot about The Messengers of Truth, but it was so wild to me to finally get a picture of what it used to be before corrupt commanders shifted the organization into something terrible.

Minutes later, Saul dashed into the room. “He’s in the states! He has the sword.”

We shot up. “Where?”

He gulped. “New York. He’s been right under our noses the whole time.”

Haven looked over at me with a pleading look. “We have to go. We can’t waste any time.”

I hesitated, looking over at the MOTs that were staring at us hesitantly. “But what about the books? We need to understand this better.”

“We can understand it after that man is dead and my parents are back here to help us. Please, Everette! We have to do this.”

I straightened. “Group vote then.”

Haven turned, raising a brow to the women. “I won’t make you do anything you don’t want to, but this is time that is just ticking away. We could potentially stop him before he gets to us first.”

Sam stood abruptly. “I am with you wherever you go, Haven. We’re in this together. Count me as a yes.”

Nikita and Jay stood with hardened faces. "Is that even a question? We're a yes."

Reese spoke up, "I'm with you."

Suddenly, one after the other, each MOT was standing on their feet. All except one. Everyone's eyes trailed over to Anastasia who had a conflicted look on her face. After a minute, she finally stood. "To hell with it. This is for Knox."

Haven gave her a deep nod, the only respect Anastasia would receive from her, and looked back at me. "Looks like we're doing this."

I clapped my hands together. "Let's get a plan in order."

CHAPTER THIRTY-EIGHT

Everette

We ran like shadows through the night. No one made a sound as we darted from rooftop to rooftop. And Haven led us all like the rightfully born leader she was. There was something in the air that charged us, making us run quicker, think quicker, and just overall fight towards the justice each of these women deserved.

We were going in blind and we knew it, but there was a small feeling of unity that fell around us that screamed we were done with being fucked with—that we were done with power-hungry men trying to take from innocent people.

Together we could achieve anything.

We could very well lose anyone tonight, but no one dared to think about it as we scaled down the side of a building, nearing the location that would determine the outcome for the rest of our lives. I couldn't help but watch as Haven's angered expression didn't leave her as she dove throughout the night.

She was ready to release the rage that was burning her soul with each day that passed and I didn't know if that should scare me or not.

Jay and Nikita flanked her as we finally reached the location where Saul's tracker pinged. He looked down at his phone that he brought with him and gave us a slow nod. Our numbers were larger with both of us here, which gave me some peace of mind, but I knew Ghost had just as many people hiding in that building.

We were on the outskirts of New York, which made this night even more nerve-wracking.

Everyone took a minute, looking one another over as we remained silent. Haven slowly placed her hand over her heart, tears welling in her eyes as she looked the MOTs over. They mocked her actions, gently slapping their chests twice.

This was all for her.

She nodded, a stray tear finding its way down her cheek as Hailey and Sam emerged from the crowd. The look on their faces said it all: *give him hell.*

Haven bowed her head at the two women, turning away as she stared at the building yards away. I stayed back, letting Haven have this moment as she slowly raised her hand and signed the familiar signal that I used, too.

Charge.

Everyone took off, unsheathing their swords. Haven's new and deadly swords shone under the moon of the night as I ran up beside her, never letting her go through something alone again.

We were in this together.

And just as we expected, men came rushing out of the building the minute we neared it. War cries left us all as we met them, slinging our weapons through the air. It was a blood fest. Screams of pain and cries of anger surrounded us with each thrust of swords, daggers, and more coming out to join us in this last battle.

Nikita ran past me, a sword taking her normal dagger's place, and she swung it as if she had been wielding the weapon for years. Saul was near her, ripping himself through men left and right.

And Haven… Haven was cutting men down as she pushed herself to those doors.

But just as I thought we were gaining the upper hand, the doors to the building flung open again, and when Ghost's familiar women came flooding out, my heart felt as if it stopped for a brief second.

There had to be at least thirty of them, passing our numbers by a landslide.

"Don't hold back!" Haven ordered. "Kill them all. I don't care what scar is on their face!" She thrust her sword through a man's chest cavity and yanked it back, not seeming like herself. "They had a chance to join the right side and they failed!"

After a minute, I heard a gunshot crack through the air and men started dropping like flies. My head snapped up, looking at a certain laser beaming down from a tall building next to us.

A.R had reached us.

I slid to my knees after one of Ghost's women started charging at me, and my sword sliced her abdomen from the ground up. She let out a choked sound, dropping to the ground beside me as I moved on to my next opponent.

But the harder we worked to get to the building, the more we were pushed back as men kept leaving the house to join Ghost's numbers. I could hear Haven's curse when she realized we weren't gaining any ground.

There couldn't be any more of his men here. There just couldn't. It was as if he was expecting us. But how? He had no idea about the tracker.

That… or he was scared shitless after Haven's escape. Just as the thought crossed my mind, the scar on my abdomen throbbed, causing my eyes to widen as I fought alongside Haven.

"He's scared!" I yelled to her. "He's been scared. He's here. I just know it. We have to get to him before he gets out of there!"

Haven's eyes cut to mine after she yanked her sword back from some woman. "I know." She looked over. "Surround the building!" she ordered.

Some MOTs and MIRs didn't ask twice as they broke out of the shitstorm and took off. As the men and women spread out, I finally got a good look around us.

I saw red and black cloaks littering the ground, causing a sick feeling to wash over me as I stumbled forward.

"No," I breathed, seeing some of my own men lying dead in front of me.

And it only continued to grow worse. Our men and women were weakening by the minute, and I knew if we didn't get to that building soon, we were all doomed.

Forcing the image of my men out of my head, I continued my path, my chest aching with each slash, thrust, and hit I made.

These people willingly gave up their lives for this tonight and if we left here empty-handed, I would never be able to forgive myself.

A scream cut through the air and chilled me to the bone. It was familiar, too familiar. Haven and I craned our necks in the direction, only to see Sam dropping to her knees, holding her bleeding stomach.

"No!" Haven sobbed, running full force towards the small girl.

But right before Haven could reach her, the man that had stabbed her raised his sword to her neck. Haven cried out, not being able to get there quickly enough. Eventually, we were all running towards Sam.

Anger like I'd never felt before blinded me as I went on my rampage to get to her.

But it was too late as he gave that blade a hard jerk, causing my jaw to drop, and the world felt like it went into slow motion.

Haven stilled, her eyes locked on Sam's bleeding figure. Men continued to swarm around us and I had to ignore the gut-wrenching feeling to yell, "Fight, Haven!"

Haven's hands shook as she slowly took in her surroundings and I had to fight to make my way back to her. She was going to get herself killed.

Suddenly, Haven winced, her head jerking slightly. I knew that look. Her scar was telling her something.

"Haven!" I yelled, pushing a man off my sword. "*Haven*!"

She slowly looked up at me as if everything made sense to her. Suddenly, she began to raise her swords. "A sacrifice," she mouthed to me and my heart plummeted.

"No!"

Move, Everette, fucking move!

"*I'm* the sacrifice to release their rage!" she yelled to me.

I halted, panic seeping through me. "Don't you dare!"

I didn't care that men were running around us, the stench of blood coating the air. I was frozen in pure horror as Haven crossed her swords over her neck. "I love you!"

Then she jerked them.

"NO!" I roared, running to her figure that dropped to the ground, her eyes wide as her neck gushed blood.

No, no, no.

Not her.

He can't have her too.

"Haven!" I let out a frustrated cry, nearly making my way to her as I heard Nikita and Jay let out sobbing screams, cutting their way through men like I'd never seen before, their eyes nearly black with rage.

But just as I reached her, it was like I smacked into an invisible barrier. "What the fuck?" I mumbled, slamming my hands against whatever was keeping me from the woman I loved.

My head snapped to the side, seeing that all the MOTs were still raging behind me, cutting and carving up men and women like no other. But when I turned back to face Haven, tears leaking down my face, a breathless gasp left me.

Hundreds of people littered the yard we were in, all surrounding Haven as they peered down at her bleeding form. Suddenly, the crowd parted, and out walked a woman in a black cloak. She was a familiar face that contained the same mark as the others, but just as the last time I had seen her, it was bloody. The first scar. The beginning. One name.

Katerina Holden.

Her hair blew in the wind as she looked around before she lowered herself to her knees. I felt as if I was invisible and so were they as Ghost's men and women breezed past us all like we weren't standing right there in front of them.

Slowly, Katerina placed her hands on Haven's shoulders. "A sacrifice for a sacrifice," Katerina spoke.

One by one, the people surrounding them placed their hands on one another trailing down the lines as if it was a small prayer circle and finally the last two placed their hands on each one of Katerina's shoulders.

"It's been a long time since I filled somebody with my rage." She grinned.

And then the souls that Haven McKinley had avenged over the years vanished into Katerina and suddenly, Katerina vanished into Haven.

A gasp broke through Haven's lips, the cut on her throat clearing up into a mere scar as she flew up, her eyes a dangerous and dark color.

I let out a sound that sounded like something between a gasp and a sob as relief like no other flooded throughout my entire being. Haven slowly leaned down, picking up her swords, and the minute she did… it was like that invisible barrier lifted.

But I could tell that wasn't Haven.

That was a Holden.

And she was about to release hell on earth.

Her body darted forward, effortlessly slaughtering people around her as if it was nothing new to her. She used techniques not even The Men in Red had taught her. But I could see her shaking hands with each battle cry that left her, the MOTs around her joining her in their screams of rage.

And before I knew it, The Messengers of Truth were in a straight line, and with each movement Haven gave, they followed her as if they were in perfect sync with her.

The perfect art of battle.

I looked over at Saul in shock who looked like he couldn't believe what he was seeing. He held his side, limping over to me as the MIRs watched the women before us pushed themselves effortlessly to the building.

Until there wasn't one. Last. Man. Standing.

When it was over, Haven barked an order and the MOTs moved at her command. She shook her head slightly, blinking as if she was trying to compose herself, but was losing herself to the rage with each passing second.

"Haven!" I called out, trying to somewhat get her to come back to me, to push through it, but it was as if my voice meant nothing to her.

Instead, Haven motioned for the women to enter the building, and like obedient soldiers, they marched in, causing me to speed after them as worry started to drown me.

She wasn't thinking.

The building was lit with one faint light, crowded with boxes and shelves, looking as if it once had been an old inventory warehouse.

Just as we began to scope the place out, more men left the shadows of the dark building, letting out their battle cries be known as they ran towards the women, but they didn't make it far. It only took a few swings from Haven and the other's swords before more men were littering the ground, choking on their own blood.

"Spread out," Haven ordered, and it wasn't long until I heard more men's cries of pain as the MOTs took their rage out on them.

Haven was grinning maniacally when I finally reached her and grabbed her hand. "Haven. You're not thinking clearly. Who knows what Ghost has in store for us inside here? This could be a trap."

She jerked away from me as if she had been burned and I watched as her eyes shifted hues like she was trying to battle the curse and overcome her rage to breach the surface. But just as those beautiful hues of green and blue resurfaced, they were gone and Haven shoved me aside before growling out, "Get out of my way."

I looked over at Saul who was in shock. "It's taking her," I said, a pleading tone in my voice as I stared at him not knowing what the hell I was supposed to do.

I can't lose her.

I just can't.

Saul slowly shook his head. "Let her get this done, Everette. You can't stop her."

I felt betrayed as I staggered back, looking over at Haven who was slowly turning her head, surveying her surroundings. Her head ticked again, seeming like she picked up on something none of us were hearing.

And then she took off.

I didn't catch on right away until I caught sight of a group of men running towards the back doors yards away. Haven unsheathed one of her daggers and sent it spiraling through the air, reminding me of the night on the boat, and when it struck one of the men's back, they all halted as the man tumbled to the floor.

Slowly, one man turned around.

"Move and you're next," Haven snarled.

The MOTs trickled into the main area again and began to circle the group. If the suit and tie were any indications, it was clear Ghost resided in the middle of them, looking completely pale and his dark hair out of place.

"Long time no see," Haven snarled.

Ghost held his chin high. "And we finally meet again, Haven McKinley."

"You're not getting away this time. *Surrender.*"

Ghost suddenly snickered and a chill crept down my spine at his sinister look. "Am I?"

And as if that was a cue, a cloaked figure dropped down from above, his sword swinging out as it slashed through the MOTs blocking Ghost's exit. Haven darted forward as Ghost took off, her sword cutting through the air, but the cloaked figure darted before her, his sword clashing against her own to stop her sudden attack.

I gulped when I finally laid my eyes upon his face.

"Impossible," Saul whispered from next to me.

Haven shook her head again as if she couldn't believe what she was seeing. And then she whispered one word that made me feel as if my whole world came crumbling down.

One *name.*

"Knox?"

ACKNOWLEDGEMENTS

Wow. I don't even know where to begin. I am just so blown away by the love of this series that I don't even know what to do with myself. The idea of Haven McKinley started as a short story in one of my college courses and I never dreamed it would go this far. Truly, thank you all from the bottom of my heart for making this possible. I don't know how I'll ever be able to repay the kindness that you have shown me.

As always, thank you to my friends and family for supporting my journey as an author. And a huge shout out to booktok for making The Avenging Series even possible. To be completely honest, I would never have written Scared Scars if it wasn't for your persistent comments on a simple TEASER I had posted about the book. I love you all more than words can explain.

Thank you to my best friend, Bee, who helped me through the tough nights and many tears as I tried to get this book together. I am so glad that we found one another through booktok and I am honored to call someone so freaking amazing my best friend. I cannot wait to see what our future as best friends hold. Thank you for being so real and being there for me to pick me up when I felt as if I couldn't continue this book journey any longer.

Raven, thank you for editing this book and helping me shape it into something amazing. I am so glad that I found an author bestie like you that can sit through my crazy rants and crazy story ideas. Who knows what I would do without you? And thank you to the other people helping me on this book's journey such as Justin Harris (proofreader), Nia (witchlingsart/cover art creator), Maja (cover designer), and Daiana (formatter). This wouldn't be possible without you all.

ABOUT THE AUTHOR

KEYLEE HARGIS is currently in the midst of publishing her first series "The Bond Series" and her second series "The Avenging Series" with Sacred Lies being the second installment. Keylee hails from Bowling Green, Kentucky, and enjoys spending time with her friends and family. When she's not reading or writing, you can catch Keylee filming weddings as a videographer or spending time with her fur baby, Callie. As she furthers her career as a writer, she is excited to see what the future holds.

Lightning Source UK Ltd.
Milton Keynes UK
UKHW041816120223
416649UK00023B/730/J